Firesong

Tabor Heights, Year 1, Book 7

Michelle Levigne

M Zion Ridge Press
Books Off the Beaten Path

www.MtZionRidgePress.com

Mt Zion Ridge Press LLC
295 Gum Springs Rd, NW
Georgetown, TN 37366

https://www.mtzionridgepress.com

Published in the United States of America
Publication Date: May 15, 2025

Editor-In-Chief: Michelle Levigne
Executive Editor: Tamera Lynn Kraft

TABOR HEIGHTS

Welcome to Tabor Heights:
A friendly little town on Ohio's North Coast, where sweet romance is always in
the air.

Here you'll be able to explore the lives of the members of the congregation of
Tabor Christian Church in the space of two years. The stories overlap, and
there's no one right place to start.

Just like any small town, you come in, you meet someone, you hear their story
and get to know them, and they introduce you to their friends, tell you
something about them, and you learn those stories. As you get to know these
new friends, they introduce you to other people, and tell you about other
interesting stories in town.

It's the same way with Tabor Heights. Start with the story that interests you the
most, and then branch out.

Settle back and enjoy your visit.
Welcome!

<u>Year One</u>

THE SECOND TIME AROUND
DETOURS
COMMON GROUNDS
WHITE ROSES
THE FAMILY WAY
FORGIVEN
FIRESONG
BEHIND THE SCENES
THE MISSION
ACCIDENTAL HEARTS
A QUIET PLACE

<u>Year Two</u>

COOKING UP TROUBLE
THE WRATH OF BUBBLES
INVITATION TO A WEDDING
TRUCK STOP ANGEL
A BOX OF PROMISES
WHEELS
THE TEDDY BEAR DANCER

Chapter One

Nine Years Ago
Tabor Heights, Ohio

Dani Paul's life changed on a Wednesday night late in May, when she was eleven years old. Some changes were her choice, and some ambushed her with all the force of a volcanic eruption.

That day began like any ordinary morning; dawdling through breakfast, dropped off at school by her cousin, Tom Gibson, giggling with her sixth-grade friends, and feeling antsy in the late May sunshine. Mrs. Green drove her daughter, Katie, and Dani home to her aunt and uncle's house so the girls could spend the afternoon together, doing homework and baking cookies for that night's girls' club activities at church.

The fourth through sixth-graders met outside that evening at Tabor Christian. Mrs. Olentangy handled announcements and finished by asking for prayer requests and volunteers to pray. The same girls made the same requests, the same girls volunteered to pray, and the same girls sat on the grass and drummed their heels on the ground, impatient to get through the lesson and be free.

Dani wished she could spend the evening with her brother and cousins, practicing their band's music in the barn behind the Gibsons' house. She had an idea for lyrics to go with a melody her brother, Andy, had been working on for three weeks now, and she hoped if it was good enough, the boys would let her join the band.

"All right, girls," Mrs. Olentangy said, when the prayer ended, "how about our missionaries of the month? That's Dani's parents, the Pauls, doing short-term service in Columbia. Does anybody know what they do? Sue-Anne?"

Sue-Anne Ehrenbull stood, struck a pose and pursed her lips. She was the only girl in the group who wore jewelry and makeup. She was also desperately in love with Andy.

Half the girls at Tabor Christian Church were in love with Andy. The other half were in love with the three Gibson brothers. Dani was pretty sure that was because they had a band, good enough to play for the youth group parties four times since they were formed.

"Mr. Paul flies airplanes to take supplies to the missionaries in the jungle," Sue-Anne announced with appropriate hand gestures and widening eyes, as if it was the most amazing thing she had ever heard of.

"*Mom* flies the plane and *Dad* is the mechanic," Dani muttered, just loudly enough for Katie and a few other girls to hear. They giggled and rolled their eyes. Sue-Anne was a favorite with no one.

"That's right." Mrs. Olentangy gave Dani and her friends a reproving little frown. "Everybody remember to pray for them this week."

Then Mrs. Randolph had the lesson, asking the girls to think about what it meant to them, personally, to stay true to God and serve Him. A handful of girls decided that meant sacrifice, making changes in their lives, even giving up something that meant a lot to them.

"Like what?" Sue-Anne challenged. "What does God want us to give up? And why do we have to give up anything, anyway?"

"Like make-up and jewelry and getting new clothes every week," a girl called from the back of the group. Dani didn't turn around fast enough to see who it was, and she didn't recognize the voice. She was pretty sure the speaker was one of the girls who practically never spoke up. There were four or five who only came because their mothers made them.

"Why would God want me to do that?" Sue-Anne whined, her eyes wide with horror.

"To show God and the rest of the world that He matters most." Dani was surprised to hear those words come out of her mouth. True, she had been thinking along those lines for the lyrics she was writing, but she hadn't imagined actually speaking them.

"Very good," Mrs. Randolph said. "But we're not talking drastic sacrifices, girls. We're talking about little things that add up to big things. I'll bet a lot of you stop at Heinke's or some convenience store to get a candy bar, ice cream, or some kind of treat on your way home from school. Think about the benefits of waiting until you get home and eating a piece of fruit instead. Your teeth are better, your health is better, and you can save that fifty cents or a dollar to help someone with a greater need."

"Like going on the trip the senior high kids are doing this summer, to help build an orphanage in Mexico?" Katie asked.

"Exactly." She nodded.

"Did God tell you to leave Hollywood and stop making movies?" Bridget Turner asked from the far side of the group.

"In a way, yes." Mrs. Randolph glanced at Mrs. Olentangy, took a deep breath, and turned back to the girls. "That's an example of how the world tries to trap us, I suppose. I had a very good career in Hollywood, but it wasn't what God wanted me to do with my talent. My heart wasn't right with God, and no matter how famous I became through my movies, it wouldn't have made up for the hole in my soul from disobeying God. You all know what happens when you disobey your parents, don't you?" Her sunny smile returned, a little crooked, when mutters and grumbles and giggles rippled through the group. "Ah ha, I see. Well, when you disobey your parents, you know they still love you, but you're not really comfortable at home, are you? You can't really talk with them, and I bet if something nice happens, it isn't as much fun."

"I had a big fight with Dad just before my birthday party," Nikki James offered with a shrug. "Mum still had the party, but it wasn't as great as I thought it would be."

"Exactly! Part of why I left Hollywood was to get my heart and soul and mind back in alignment with God. To get rid of all the distractions, so I could listen to Him and hear what He was trying to tell me. I'm sure you all have distractions in your lives. Think about what you need to change, in your heart, your mind, your daily life, so you can hear God telling you what He wants you to do and to be."

"But why do we have to give up stuff?" another girl whined, sounding like a Sue-Anne wannabe.

"I gave up Hollywood," Mrs. Randolph said with a shrug. "But if I hadn't, I wouldn't have met my husband. We wouldn't have our family or live here in Tabor Heights or run our theater. I think God gave me far more than I gave up."

Dani thought about that while Mrs. Olentangy coaxed the girls around her to think of things they didn't really need, or that might be distracting them, things they could do or have instead that would be better for them.

"How do you figure out what isn't good for you?" Katie muttered, leaning closer to Dani as some girls shouted out suggestions for their friends and nemeses. Fortunately, most of the reactions were amused, laughter instead of scorn and hurt feelings.

"I don't know. Look at the other girls and figure out what's stupid on them, and don't do it." Dani glared at Sue-Anne. "Don't waste money on makeup and jewelry. And don't chase boys. Most of them are dorks, anyway."

"Not your brother or your cousins."

"That's 'cause they're cool and they're musicians." She grinned. "They'd be more cool if they'd let me be in the band."

"They don't have a name yet, do they?"

"All right!" Mrs. Olentangy said, laughing, and standing up to get everyone's attention. She gestured for the girls to quiet down. "We have a lot to think about until next week. I think this exercise would be far more beneficial to all of us if we'd think about what to clear out of *our* lives, instead of someone else's." She swept her gaze around the group, not letting it rest on any one particular girl. Giggles answered the gentle rebuke. "All right, you're dismissed."

Shouts and laughter cut through the cooling air as the girls leaped to their feet and snatched up Bibles and notebooks. Dani turned to look at the parking lot just as Andy pulled in from the street. He was seventeen, driving a battered old rust-bucket of a pickup truck that was his pride and joy; completely paid for, and costing more in repairs than he had paid for the truck in the first place.

His normally smiling face was visibly strained, even from ten yards away. Dani wondered what bothered him. Andy shoved the passenger door open for her and just sat there, waiting. Normally, he shouted for her to hurry so he could get back to rehearsal.

"Dani!" Sue-Anne scurried up behind her.

"What do you want?" she asked without looking. A shiver ran up her back as she watched Andy. There was something wrong.

"Will you tell your brother I think he's cute?" the other girl whispered, agony on her painted face.

"Tell him yourself." Dani didn't have to look to see the terror that wrinkled her nemesis' face. It was becoming a bad habit, no longer funny.

"I can't!" Sue-Anne backed away. "He's so cute..."

"He's just my brother." She turned sharply on one heel and glared at the other girl. "Besides, if you can't talk to him, what makes you think he wants to talk to you?"

Sue-Anne just stared with fearful longing at Andy, with his angular face, his black curls cropped short, and dark gray eyes. He wore the usual 'uniform' of the band: white t-shirt, faded jeans, battered brown work boots. Tears made Sue-Anne's mascara run, badly enough to trickle around her mouth in a drippy Fu-Manchu moustache. Dani snorted in disgust, turned, and loped across the grass to Andy and his truck.

Definitely giving up makeup, jewelry, and party clothes. Maybe I should give up boys, too. She rolled her eyes in disgust at that thought. *Even if there were any worth chasing, I wouldn't waste my time.*

"Problem?" Andy asked and nodded toward Sue-Anne.

"The usual. Let's get out of here, Tonto." She grinned at him and slapped the hood of the truck for emphasis as she stepped around the open door to climb in.

Andy didn't smile like he usually did. Dani's stomach twisted, and a cold feeling ran up from her gut.

"Dani, is it still okay?" Katie hurried to join them.

"Huh? Oh, sorry. Katie's dad had to work late again and Kurt's being a jerk, as usual, and can't pick her up either. Can we give her a ride home, so she doesn't have to wait until her mom gets out of the worship team meeting?" Dani thought Katie's cousin was only about two degrees less of a jerk than Sue-Anne. Just because he was going to spend the summer doing an internship with the Allen Michaels Evangelistic Association, he thought he was a super-saint and had better things to do than drive his only cousin around. He was living with the Greens while his parents were overseas.

Kurt Green was the best reason in the world for Dani to swear off boys and dating and the whole stupid romance game, even before she became old enough to date.

"Sure." Andy tried to smile and gestured at the front seat of the truck. "Anything for my sister's best friend."

He took them to the Dairy Freeze first and treated them to cones, which just reinforced Dani's sense that something was wrong. He should have been fidgeting, aching to get back to rehearsal. Instead of talking about the chance to sing at a music festival in Columbus that summer, he asked about school and summer plans and other neutral topics. Dani kept quiet and let her best friend and brother carry the conversation. She listened to the engine rumble and wondered why the ordinary evening felt so very wrong.

"Do you mind if we don't go straight home?" Andy asked, after they had dropped off Katie and got back on Sackley Road.

Dani shook her head. If Andy didn't care about getting back to band practice, why should she worry? Except that, she did worry. Andy and their cousins lived for their music.

They went into the Metroparks and parked at the waterfowl refuge. In the winter, when the water lilies and other floating plants died out, they came up here to ice skate. Now, ducks and geese floated among the patches of green. There were no other cars. Dani only glanced at the lake as evening visibly slid a shadowy blanket across the landscape, and turned to really concentrate on her brother now.

Andy tried to smile, shrugged, then reached for the door handle. He got out and Dani followed him to the observation deck. They leaned against the split log railing and gazed out over the water, the silence broken only by the rumble of cars trundling past in both directions on the Metroparks road. Dani heard an engine roar as a car approached the spot where the road made a sharp turn and the asphalt jogging path ran along the gravel berm. Tires squealed around the turn at probably twenty miles over the posted speed limit. The passing car caught gravel from the berm, spitting it out behind as it roared away.

"One of these days," Andy growled, "somebody is going to go right over the path. Then there'll really be trouble. They ought to put up a guard rail or something."

"Trees'd stop a car, wouldn't they?"

"Probably." He glanced at the water again and gripped the railing so hard his knuckles went white. "Ever wonder what it's like when you get to Heaven?" he asked without looking at her.

"Huh?"

"Wrong start." He flashed a crooked grin. "Okay... remember that last letter from Mom and Dad, about the weather problems they were—"

"What happened?" She clutched at his arm.

Tears filled Andy's eyes. Dani relived every nightmare she had for the past two months, about their parents' plane going down in flames.

"They're—they crashed—and they—" She couldn't force the words out and begged Andy with her gaze to tell her she was wrong.

"Dead," he whispered, his voice cracking.

She burst out in gulping sobs and Andy wrapped his arms around her. They held each other in the gathering darkness, alone with only ducks and geese and swans for company.

"It'll be okay," Andy whispered when her sobs finally slowed and softened. "I promise. We'll stay with Uncle George and Aunt Betty and I'll take care of you, Dani. We'll always be together."

The hurt made his voice ragged. Dani felt his arms tremble, and suddenly she knew Andy needed her as much as she needed him. She took deep breaths, fighting her tears, and squashed down the trembling deep inside, fighting for calm. Andy needed her.

"You were wrong, before," she said, gulping down the last of her sobs.

"About what?"

"Katie isn't my best friend—you are."

Andy shivered and wrapped his arms even tighter around her. Then it was finally time for the details, the dry facts of the crash, the arrangements their aunt and uncle were making for the funeral and bringing the bodies home and all the disgusting, boring, adult details Dani hoped she never had to deal with.

They drove for a long time, past full darkness, silent in the truck, not even the radio playing. Andy loved the Eagle, a new radio station that played Contemporary Christian music, and he usually had it on from the moment he started the engine. If he didn't reach for the radio button, Dani did it for him. Tonight, neither one turned on the music that usually had them singing along at the top of their lungs. Even at ten at night.

Andy took back roads through the rural section of Tabor Heights, weaving back and forth between Cuyahoga and Lorain counties, crossing and re-crossing the same railroad tracks. Just traveling, no destination. Their headlights and the lit windows from houses set far back from the road provided the only illumination for miles in any direction. The moon looked huge, hanging low and bright and almost full.

They had passed through the tears into the numb stage where it was enough just to be together. Dani leaned against Andy and he drove with one hand, his other arm around her shoulders.

"You know," he murmured, breaking the silence after what felt like hours of just humming down the dark roads, "when I die, that's the way I want to go."

"They crashed! Nobody found them for three days! They would have been okay if—" Dani pressed both hands over her mouth and squeezed her eyes tight shut against more tears.

Andy pulled over to the side and slid to a stop, the tires grumbling against the gravel. He wrapped both arms around her and rested his chin on the top of her head.

"Yeah, stupid way to say it, huh?" A broken laugh escaped him. "You're the one who's good with words. What I meant was, when I die, I hope I'm busy working for God."

"Why did God make them die?"

"I don't know."

"We need them." Her voice wavered and she swallowed hard to fight more tears. "Right here. Right now. It's not fair."

"I know."

"They were working for God. He didn't have any right to take them away from us."

"Hey, idiot—you're talking about God, remember?" Andy shook her. Incredulous laughter crackled in his voice. "Since when do we tell Him what He can do?"

"But—"

"I'm only going to say this once, okay? I'm older than you and that just might make me smarter—even if I am a guy." He paused, obviously expecting her to take advantage of the opening, but Dani clung tighter to him and waited. "Whatever happens," Andy continued, his voice dropping to a whisper, "God knows best. Just because we don't understand, doesn't mean there isn't a good reason."

"Do you really believe that?"

She needed to hear the certainty in his voice, needed to know there was something strong and sure and reliable. Dani looked out through tear-blurred eyes at the darkness beyond the windshield, and it felt like they were the only two living creatures in the entire world. She felt very small, very cold, very alone. Small enough to be stepped on or swept away without anyone or anything caring. She was only eleven. A teenage brother and a rust-bucket truck weren't much protection. Especially when God seemed so far away.

"I know it's the truth. It's just going to take a little while to get down to my heart."

"You and me forever?" she whispered, drawing back so she could see his face. "Promise?"

"Forever. Promise. We'll look out for each other, always." Andy held out his hand, palm up.

Dani's hand shook a little as she lay her palm flat against his. She grinned crookedly as they went through their own secret handshake, rubbing palms together, then hooking their pinkie fingers and pressing their thumbs together, hard enough to ache. When they finished, Dani sat back and wiped away her tears with a fist. Andy winked at her. She lightly punched his shoulder.

"I gotta look out for you right now."

"Don't get any delusions of grandeur, shorty."

"Aren't you supposed to be rehearsing?"

Andy checked his watch and groaned. Dani leaned across him and turned the key in the ignition.

Their aunt and uncle's farm wasn't that far away, despite their wandering. Even driving without any real purpose, Andy had kept them heading toward what was now their only home. Dani honestly liked living with the Gibsons when her parents went on short-term mission trips, but right now, she wanted to be a little kid and shed the practical side that always made her parents so proud. She wanted to curl up into the comfort of someone else's support. Her parents' support.

When they reached the farm, light spilled out through the gaps in the siding of the old barn that had been converted into a garage and practice studio for the still-nameless band.

"I don't know why you guys even bother," Dani said, as the truck slid to a stop in the gravel drive. "You don't have any decent equipment and you all need singing lessons."

"Hmm. Maybe." Andy gave her a crooked grin, barely lit by the moonlight. "At least we aren't lip-synching anymore and playing tennis rackets. We have real instruments now." He winced when he turned the key and the engine chugged a few seconds after it was supposed to stop.

"That's an improvement? At least people could listen when you sang with the records."

"Watch it, shorty. I have a loaded squirt gun in the glove compartment."

"Yeah?" She thumped the panel of the glove compartment with her fist and the stubborn old lock refused to cooperate. Dani groaned. Andy laughed and slid out of the truck and hurried into the barn.

Dani waited until the sounds of instruments tuning up filtered out to her. She picked up her books from under the seat and trundled off to the barn.

Inside, the makeshift practice studio was already warm from a dozen bright lights. Tom did a few practice riffs on his battered electric guitar. Jim put his saxophone down and picked up his trumpet to check the valves that always seemed to stick at the wrong moment. Jason knelt in front of the amplifier that had been threatening to start a fire for the last three weeks. Andy sat at the keyboard, flexing his fingers and looking over the sheet music he had been notating and changing whenever he could find a spare moment. He ran his fingers along the keys, and even though Dani could see the red power light was on, nothing came out.

"How come this isn't working?" Andy demanded.

Jason got up and walked over to the jury-rigged breaker box. He nudged a few cables, then nodded to Andy, who tried the keyboard again. A rippling chord emerged from the speaker extending from the keyboard. Andy grinned, nodded his thanks and went through his warm-up. Dani stayed in the shadows. She made herself comfortable on a stack of empty crates.

When practice ground to a halt two hours later, she was in that half-doze that let her see and hear yet wouldn't let her move. Dani lay curled up on her side, hair in her eyes, her arm flung across a book.

The four boys gathered around Andy's keyboard, hammering out a few questionable transitions. Tom nodded, finally satisfied. He yawned, his mouth opening so wide Dani thought the barn cat could jump into it.

"Okay, sounds pretty good. Guess it's time to turn in."

"Come on," Jim protested, "we can still go on for another couple hours. We can't let it die now, just when we're getting it good." He gave Andy a guilty look when his older brother glared at him.

"Hey, it's okay guys." Andy looked too tired, with dark smears under his eyes, to be upset at the verbal misstep. As he bent to unplug the spider's web of electrical cords, his gaze landed on Dani. She would have laughed at his chagrin, but she couldn't seem to do anything. "Oh, great."

"So?" Jason said with a shrug. "She's the one who's in trouble with Mom, not you."

"I promised I'd take care of her. Especially now..."

"She shouldn't have been here anyway." Jim scowled.

"Dani and me, we're a package deal from now on, understand?" Andy headed across the packed dirt floor toward her. "You and me forever, shorty," he whispered, as he picked her up and carried her out of the barn, to the house, to put her into her own bed.

~~~~~

Between health regulations and diplomatic requirements and other delays, the Pauls' remains weren't processed and returned to Tabor Heights for a month. It felt like ripping a half-healed scar open to finally hold the funeral and bury the small box with the intermixed ashes.

Dani sat by herself on the side steps of the house the day of the funeral. She wore her Sunday clothes, but she was barefoot. Her sandals sat on the steps next to her. She hunched down on the steps, knees drawn up to her chest, arms wrapped around her legs. She watched the people talking softly outside, heard her parents' names in every conversation. Everybody had come back to the Gibson farm to eat and to talk after the
~~~~~

funeral. Most of her friends had come to the funeral, but their parents had taken them home already. Dani felt like she was invisible.

A herd of young men came around the corner; Andy and their cousins and nearly all their friends who had their own transportation. They nodded to her as they trooped up the steps into the house. Andy paused and reached down to tousle her hair.

"You don't have to stay out here."

"I know." She considered going inside and hiding in her room with a book and that bag of mini chocolate bars Katie had given her last night. She had proven herself Dani's best friend once again, saying with a hug and chocolate what hundreds of adults hadn't been able to say yet.

"This isn't really for Mom and Dad. All this fuss is for the people left behind."

"Aren't we the ones left behind?" Dani flushed and ducked her head, hating the quaver in her voice.

Silence for a few seconds. She expected Andy to continue up the steps into the house. Instead, he reached down and grabbed her hand and dragged her to her feet. Dani let him lead her to the barn. She finally dared to look at his face and melted inside, letting go some of the aching hardness that wrapped around her. Andy wasn't angry with her. Suddenly, that was the most important thing in the world.

In the barn, Andy turned on the single spotlight over his keyboard. He gave Dani a shove toward the makeshift piano bench in front of it, then scurried around, plugging in cables.

"You've been bugging me to teach you to play. Why not now?"

Chapter Two

Dani could only grin and nod. She scooted over to make room for him on the bench and he settled down next to her. Andy nodded at the keyboard. Dani tried to place her hands as she had seen him do it and tapped the keyboard. A wavering chord undulated through the air.

"That's pretty good for a first try. You haven't been sneaking music books into the house to read under the covers, have you?" His words earned a groan from her. "Nah, didn't think so. Want to help me with something? I have this tune going around in my head, but I can't seem to find any words. Want to help me find them?"

"Write a song with you? Can I?" For the first time, she thought of the lyrics she had tried to write, the day they learned of their parents' death. Dani couldn't remember where she had put that paper. It felt like a hundred years ago.

"Won't know until we try." The melody that rolled out from under his fingers stayed in a minor key, despite the pulsing tones that gave it energy. Dani closed her eyes and tried to hear the words inside the notes.

"You know what I dream about?" Andy whispered as the music filtered through the dusty, shadowy barn. "Playing and preaching for a living. Make music and be a missionary all at the same time. You'll probably be married before that happens."

"It'll happen though, someday, won't it?" She bit back the urge to tell him that she had decided she was never going to get married.

"If that's what God wants us to do, we'll do it."

"I don't know if I want to trust God for anything anymore," Dani said in a very small voice.

The music stopped with the thud of Andy's hands on the keyboard. "You're kind of young to be so cynical."

"I feel really old right now."

"Yeah," he sighed. "I know. But it'll be all right, Dani. You and me forever, remember?"

The Present
Tuesday, March 26
Quarry Hall

"You know, I remember coming here on a field trip when I was in junior high, I think it was." Kurt Green looked through the French doors, out over the wet lawn and the sprawling theme gardens behind the Great Hall. "It's kind of hard to wrap my mind around..." He turned back to face Nikki James and Joan Archer, who had just finished giving him a tour of the mansion. "Sisters. I mean, yeah, seeing the two of you together, it's obvious."

"So obvious, nobody saw it for the four years I was living in Tabor, maneuvering to run into Nikki as often as I could." Joan settled down on a hassock. Her companion dog, Ulysses, settled down next to her.

"There is none so blind as she who will not see," Nikki offered. She stepped over next to him and glanced out at the wet afternoon. "I'm going to miss this place."

"Thirty miles away."

"What are you talking about?" Kurt wondered if he had missed part of the conversation.

"We're sending Nikki back to Tabor. First to check out the Mission, see if we'll be partnering with Tabor Christian." Joan tipped her head to one side. "Do you have any idea what we're talking about?"

"Yeah, the Mission is in the old Eloise Elementary. The church bought it a few years ago, to use as an outreach center. Daycare, senior center, food pantry, lots of other ideas."

"That's it," Nikki said. "Lots of ideas, not enough funding. It was all Anne's idea."

"Her friend, Lisa Montgomery," Joan corrected. "Lisa is an artist, she works at the Mission, and she's also doing the cover art for Firesong's new CD. They're doing a fundraiser concert for the Mission, and it all came together into a brainstorm, which she passed on to Anne. And we lost you, didn't we?"

"Considering I'm here just to arrange for Arc to be headquarters for all the pre-crusade meetings of the local pastors. Did you say Firesong?" Kurt sat down on the couch facing Joan.

"They're a band that basically operates out of Tabor Christian," Nikki said, moving over to join him on the couch, with her companion dog, Gray, settling down immediately at her feet.

"I know who they are." Kurt shook his head, grinning, feeling a little blindsided. "My cousin, Katie, is engaged to one of the guys in the band."

"That's right—Katie Green." Nikki laughed. "We were in school together. So Katie and Andy finally got together. I wonder if Dani arranged it."

"Dani is the drummer?" Joan said.

"Dani is Andy's sister, and the other three guys in the band are their cousins." Nikki scooted off the couch and darted into the next room.

"I take it this is turning into old home week," Joan said.

"Yeah, and nobody warned me when I walked through the door this morning." Kurt chuckled and settled back, stretching out his legs. He flinched when Gray let out a rumbling woof, and shifted his legs a good foot away from the dog.

Joan snickered. "He won't bite you."

"You say."

"Our dogs are trained not to take food from anyone but their assigned persons."

"Thanks very much." Kurt made a face at her, which just made Joan laugh louder. He decided he was saved when Nikki ran back into the room. She tossed a CD to him before settling down on the couch again. "Firesong, huh? How come Katie hasn't sent me any CDs?"

"Don't ask me, ask her. Just how much contact do you have with people back home?" Nikki said. Kurt decided it was wiser not to answer and stayed silent.

The truth was that he got most of his news about his relatives in Tabor through the grapevine, meaning his parents told him what news they picked up in letters and phone calls. Kurt had only made contact via email and phone in the last few weeks when he learned he was being sent to Northeast Ohio as part of the crusade preparation team. Allen Michaels was holding a week-long crusade at the Cuyahoga County Fairgrounds in August.

Kurt turned the CD over and felt a jolt at the image that filled the back. He recognized everybody. Dozens of memories rolled through his mind. He remembered taking an inflatable kayak down the Rocky River with the three Gibson brothers, in the middle of a torrential downpour. He remembered playing basketball in the church parking lot with Andy. He remembered Sunday school picnics and being deathly bored in youth group meetings. Most of all, as he stared at Dani Paul with her big, dark eyes and waist-length waterfall of dark hair, he remembered tormenting her with water balloons and reading her diary out loud. He stole it when she had a sleepover with Katie while he was living with his relatives.

If Dani had just ignored him or expressed the usual scorn that Katie and other girls threw his way when he had been an arrogant snot, he would have forgotten about her and left her alone after a few sallies. Dani, however, got his attention because she was disgusted with him, personally. It took him until he passed through his rebellious, backsliding phase before he realized why.

She expected better of him. She had decided he was supposed to be a better person, and she wouldn't cut him any slack, even if he was acting like any normal, hormone-rattled, ego-centric teen boy.

Kurt hadn't forgotten Dani Paul, even if he hadn't consciously thought about her in years.

He wondered if she ever thought about him.

Ironic, that even after he learned about Katie becoming engaged to Andy Paul, Kurt hadn't made the connection—Katie's fiance was the big brother to Katie's best friend. It had taken the group photo of Firesong to finally bring everything together.

"I assume, since you have the CD, you listen to them. Any good?" he said, finally breaking the silence.

"They're great. I'm pumped about finally being able to catch one of their concerts." Despite that, Nikki didn't look thrilled about going back to Tabor Heights.

He understood her trepidation. He had been a self-righteous jerk, as Dani had told him quite often, when he had lived in Tabor Heights. He hoped everyone he had irritated and fought with had grown up and were willing to give him the benefit of the doubt that he had done the same. Otherwise, he was going to spend valuable time mending fences that he should be using to prepare for the Allen Michaels crusade.

Nikki had run away from home when she was barely seventeen. As the foster-daughter of a prominent family in Tabor Heights, the Butler-Williams University community, and Tabor Christian Church, she had a lot of visibility. That meant a lot of people knew her flaws and sins. Kurt admired her courage in returning home. Only a fool would blithely waltz into town and expect everything to be forgiven and forgotten, just because she had turned her life around. Even the best Christians had a hard time forgetting and forgiving.

"So, they're that good, huh?" Kurt said, after flipping the case open and reading the liner notes, the titles of the songs. He smiled, noting that Dani had written the lyrics for more than half the songs. She always had a way with words. He remembered quite clearly, now, how she could rip his hide with eloquence and humor. Even while his face burned and his blood pressure rose, he had to laugh at her wit.

"They're great, and they're about to land a manager ... and we should really get back to business," Nikki added, glancing at Joan, who just smirked again.

"What she wants to ask, is if you know the agent's name and reputation," her sister said. "Sophie ran a check on him, and he has a solid reputation. Someone who's tough and pushes his groups and won't let anybody pull any tricks on them."

"But?" Kurt prompted, getting that dropping sensation when Nikki squirmed, and Joan's smirk faded. "You said solid, not good. There's a difference."

"Well, he's not a Christian. That's a big problem. Firesong started out doing youth rallies and singing for camp programs and Bible School, things like that." Nikki shrugged. "I know how easy it is to get sidetracked and pulled away from your first love. I don't want Dani and the guys to fall into that trap."

"What's the agent's name?" he asked, feeling a little flattered that they wanted his input.

"Troy Danziger. Know him?"

"Oh, yeah." Kurt nodded slowly. "It's all accurate. Tough, protective of his people. And definitely not a Christian. But if Firesong holds true to their goals, they shouldn't have any trouble with him."

"Shouldn't, being the operative word?" Joan said.

"Danziger got that good because he won't take no from anyone. The only problem is if his vision for Firesong conflicts with their vision." He shrugged. "I guess I'm going to have to check with Katie and Andy a little more closely. Good thing I'm coming into town for a few months. Umm, when's that concert at the Mission?"

"Next Friday," Nikki said.

"Good. I'll be in town, so I'll see you there."

~~~~~

By the time he finished with his preliminary chores for the crusade advance team that night, Kurt had listened to the Firesong CD three times on his car's CD player. Neither Nikki nor Katie had been exaggerating when they said Firesong was good, solid, talented, and ready to take off with their career.

Kurt settled into his hotel room, down Sackley Road a few miles from Tabor Heights, and started his report for his supervisor, Ned Vandewitt. He honestly looked forward to moving into his furnished apartment in a few more days. Even though he liked being on the road for the Allen Michaels organization, there were times he got tired of living out of a suitcase. He had maybe three weeks of work, making contacts and scouting locations and services and suppliers before the rest of the team showed up.

He propped up the CD case next to his computer and slipped the disk into the drive, so he could listen again while he worked on his report. One song in particular had caught his attention. It would make a good reflection and invitation song in the youth mini-crusade that would take place during the major crusade events. Music had been one of his many ministry areas with the organization, and he kept his hand in, helping various musical groups and their managers, even helping behind the scenes of music festivals. People respected his input and judgment when it came to the Contemporary Christian music scene. He thought Katie would be pleased if he recommended that the crusade use Firesong's song. It would give the band exposure, if nothing else. A snort and a grin escaped him as he thought about seeing Firesong on the stage of the
~~~~~

crusade.

Why not?

He mentioned getting the CD and listening to it in his report, quoted the lyrics to the song, and added the connection to the band, just in case Ned saw a conflict of interest. It was always better to look for potential problem spots and areas where other people could lodge complaints, rather than just assuming people would be understanding and then being blindsided by accusations at the worst possible moment.

Kurt was still smiling when he washed up and climbed into bed, just short of 11 p.m., and turned off the light.

Friday, April 4
The Mission
Tabor Heights

At the Mission, the former elementary school's gym was jammed to the walls with audience spilling out both doors. The air inside was already fifteen degrees warmer than the April night outside and getting thick, but no one at tonight's fundraising concert seemed to care. They clapped and cheered, welcoming another favorite song as the opening guitar chords slammed out from the stage and bounced off the ceiling joists. Firesong was in rare form, only into their fourth number of the evening.

Dani and Jim shared the microphone, already sweating and giving everything in their lungs and hearts. Dani's long, straight hair swung in time with the music, where it wasn't plastered to her glistening face and neck. It wasn't late enough in the concert for her to pry off her sneakers, but the cousins had already peeled out of their royal blue Tabor Heights High School letterman sweaters, and dark spots stained their white T-shirts.

Andy, at the electric keyboard, jumped to his feet and nudged aside his padded stool with his knee. He watched Dani, his fingers flying up and down the keys. Tom strained the speakers with a crash of chords on his electric base and Jim ripped into the ceiling with a near-impossible shriek from his tenor saxophone, battling with Jason on drums.

The cousins were all cookies from the same cutter: tall and lean, dark-haired and vibrating with single-minded passion for their music.

Standing in the back of the jam-packed gym, Kurt nodded approval. Katie hadn't exaggerated either Firesong's popularity or their talent. It felt like a century since his family had moved from Tabor Heights to full-time mission work. His memories of the Gibson and Paul cousins had returned since that talk at Quarry Hall a little more than a week ago. His memories of Dani had multiplied in number, and he was pleased that he remembered many occasions when they hadn't been tormenting or sniping at each other. According to Katie, Dani was the driving force behind the band, and Kurt hoped she had some good memories of him. If they got to talk tonight, he didn't want her to punch him, like she had threatened the last time they saw each other, nearly nine years ago.

"Whatever she's doing, it's just right," he murmured.

A figure moving past him caught his attention long enough to spare two seconds from the music. Kurt barely glanced at the shadowy figure walking down the side of the gym and heading for the doorway out into the hall.

A chill slithered up his back, sparked by subconscious recognition. Kurt turned his head to watch the man move out into the lighted hallway. That too-long nose, receding hairline and sharp chin were familiar enough to prompt Kurt to follow.

Troy Danziger. So, Nikki had been right about the man negotiating to become Firesong's manager. Unfortunately. Kurt had prayed several times that no matter how good Firesong was, Danziger would decide they were too God-oriented to be worth his time and effort. He certainly wouldn't waste his time checking out a band playing a charity event unless he thought there was something to protect, career-wise.

Kurt nearly shouted a 'Thank You, Lord!' as the man turned right into the main body of the school instead of left, heading backstage.

Danziger was a mover-and-shaker in the music industry. Long before Kurt had met the man face-to-face, he had heard enough from other friends in Christian music to want to avoid him permanently. Danziger was good at what he did, able to juggle four full-time bands, always willing to help talented newcomers get a leg up in the industry and prod a group wavering in its commitment to choose the high road to success.

Kurt headed for backstage. Katie claimed Firesong put their ministry first, but the allure of fame had corrupted older and wiser heads and hearts. Besides, he had to protect Firesong. They were practically family, with Katie marrying Andy soon. Kurt vowed he would do whatever it took to guard the backstage door and keep Danziger from undermining the band's commitment and ministry.

The only problem was that his focus was supposed to be that crusade in August. How was he going to keep tabs on Firesong's activities, the progress in their career, their negotiations with Danziger, and not fall down in his many and varied duties?

"Okay, Lord, I'm hoping You sent me here for a reason, and You'll make a way for me to get all the jobs done," he muttered as he walked down the short access hallway to the backstage entrance.

Kurt grimly smiled and nodded his dark head. Now he had more reason than ever to be glad he had come to town for the summer. Before tonight, it had been enough to sit still for a few months, and maybe regain some friendships that had dropped by the wayside.

He came around the corner and stopped short. A big, white-haired, broad-shouldered man with a bushy moustache came through the back door from the old playground. Could that be Pastor Wally? The elderly minister should have retired years ago, but he ran the Mission now. Kurt hadn't really expected him to show up tonight. He was glad to see Pastor Wally still active, and paused as a flood of memories of Sunday school picnics and youth group outings filled his mind.

A muscular, dark-haired young man in a wheelchair shot out of the doorway from backstage, popped a wheelie, and executed a three-sixty turn without a single squeak. He saluted Pastor Wally, who chuckled and slid past him through the door backstage.

That had to be Tommy, brother to the Mission's assistant director, Claire Donnelly. Katie had told Kurt all about them. Kurt nodded to Tommy as he approached the doorway.

"Red alert," Tommy said in a good robotic voice. "You are passing into the danger zone. Security clearance required."

"I'm Katie's cousin," Kurt said, holding up both hands and grinning. He had been warned about Tommy, who could never say a serious word to save his life.

"Password accepted." He winked at Kurt, flipped his chair up in another wheelie, and spun across the hall.

Kurt grinned and saluted and stepped through to backstage. He paused in the darkness to let his eyes adjust.

A tall, slender woman with shoulder-length red-gold hair leaned against the railing at the top of the short flight of steps. She nodded in time with the pounding music. That had to be Claire. Katie stood a few steps behind her. Laughter gleamed in her gray-green eyes and her wheat-colored curls bobbed in time with the music. Kurt wondered about those shadows in her cheeks, hoping all the work involved in the upcoming wedding wasn't too stressful.

"Hey!" Tommy shouted behind Kurt. "Can they turn up the volume? I can't hear out in the hall!"

"In a few months, he'll be able to wheel up onto the stage," Katie had to shout.

On the stage, Andy turned just enough to give his fiancée a grin, then crossed his eyes at her and stuck out his tongue before turning back to the stage. Katie and Claire burst out laughing. Kurt grinned along with them. He had liked Andy even back when they were teens and getting stupid with hormones. He was glad Katie had chosen him. The concert was a good excuse to come look around and catch up with everybody without making a big fuss about moving back to town.

Firesong's concert tonight might be to raise money for renovations to the Mission, but it wouldn't hurt their reputation, either. Tabor Christian Church had bought the building from the school district six years ago. Only half the rooms were filled because of the need for renovations and equipment and supplies. Handicapped accessibility was first on the list. Senior citizens could contribute to the community if facilities would accommodate them. The Mission's staff envisioned serving both ends of the age spectrum—daycare and nursery, and a senior center—and then reaching out to everybody in between.

Kurt said a quick, silent prayer that Nikki's assessment and report on the Mission would lead to the Arc Foundation coming alongside Tabor Christian to support all the outreach into the community that was so desperately needed. Nikki was somewhere out in the audience. Kurt had seen her talking and laughing with some girls he vaguely remembered, so he hadn't approached her. He hoped her presence here tonight, with friends, meant her return home was coming along without any problems.

"How's it going?" Pastor Wally boomed, reaching the top of the steps to the backstage area. He smiled genially, as if he didn't hear a single nerve-jangling burst coming from the band. He could have been at one of his beloved cultural festivals, nibbling on pierogi and listening to accordion music. Kurt remembered that about the man and grinned. He had truly missed all these small-town details.

"Fine. We might have to spend half the money on hearing aids, but I think this was the best idea yet," Claire said. She started down the stairs as Pastor Wally stepped back.

"Kurt! You made it!" Katie slid down the steps past her and flung her arms around the newcomer. "Claire, Pastor Wally, this is my cousin, Kurt Green. He works for Allen Michaels, did I tell you that?"

"Several times," Tommy said, *sotto voce*, out in the hall.

"You—behave yourself!" Claire stuck her tongue out at her brother.

"I always behave. You just never tell me *how* I should behave," he returned, then popped another wheelie and managed to squeal both tires as he fled down the hall.

"One of these days I'm going to take out his center bolt and put him up on blocks," she muttered. When Kurt's mouth dropped open, she burst out laughing. "My little brother's a professional comedian. It's a matter of survival to keep a sharp tongue."

"I can imagine." Kurt managed to muffle his laughter. He nodded toward the stage. "They sound even better than that CD you never bothered to send me, favorite cousin of mine." He pretended shock when Katie stuck her tongue out at him. "Nikki was kind enough to loan me one of hers. Hard to believe this is the band that lip-synched with the Imperials and Petra and Dallas Holm, and played tennis rackets when we were kids."

"Oh, they've improved a little," Katie said, muffling a chuckle. She gestured for him to get closer.

Kurt took the steps two at a time and crossed the backstage area to take her previous spot in the wings. He stood perfectly still, ignoring the single drop of sweat that trickled down from his thatch of dark curls and along the long slope of his nose. He barely blinked as he watched Firesong finish their song and smoothly transition to Geoff Moore's *A Friend Like You*. He smiled as Dani and Andy sang to each other, hamming it up for the audience and trading banter with their cousins between verses.

The audience laughed as brother and sister bounced up and down, deliberately off the beat and out of synch with each other. A local band playing for old friends, there were in-jokes between the members of Firesong that the people in this college town of Tabor Heights understood. Kurt felt a pang as some references passed over his head. What had he missed, leaving his childhood friends behind? Lately, he had started to wonder if he had chosen the right path.

"She's changed a lot, hasn't she?" Katie asked, sidling up next to her cousin.

"Hard to believe that's the tomboy with the skinned knees and baseball cap who was always getting you into trouble."

"I got her into just as much trouble. We were practically sisters when we were kids, and we're going to *be* sisters now. That makes her almost your cousin. So be nice." She slapped his shoulder and grinned, teasing.

"Oh, I will."

Kurt stayed there as if planted in the scarred old wood backstage while Firesong finished their number. His gaze stayed trained on Dani more than half the time, no matter where she went on the stage.

Chapter Three

"Okay," Tom said, taking the microphone. "Now, everybody knows why we're here tonight. How many of you folks out there attended this place when it was still Eloise Elementary?" He shaded his eyes against the two rented spots shining in his face. "That many, huh? How many of you were allowed to graduate?"

Laughter rippled through the audience.

"Who's that he keeps looking at?" Kurt whispered, as Tom listed the goals of the Mission and the present needs.

He pointed at a silvery blonde who looked like she belonged in high school, sitting at the front corner of the audience. Every other sentence, Tom looked over to her.

"Oh, that's Stephanie." Katie pretended shock when he gave her a blank look. "Stephanie Avalone? You never went to camp on Kelly's Island with the rest of us, did you? Her grandfather ran the place. Now her parents have taken over."

"Oh. Yeah. Wow, everybody really grew up... nice, didn't they?" His gaze wandered back to Dani, who noticed Tom's wandering attention and pointed it out to the others.

"Nice enough to get married."

"What?" Kurt winced when his voice grew just loud enough to be heard on the stage.

Everyone but Tom turned to look into the wings. Katie waggled her fingers at them. Andy winked.

"When are they getting married?" Kurt demanded in a harsh whisper.

"Already are. Just about a month ago."

"Next you'll be telling me Dani is married, too." His voice cracked the same moment his heart skipped sideways in his chest.

"Not a chance in the world. Dani's going to spend the rest of her life on the road, singing and preaching. She says God called her to ministry, not to marriage." Katie tipped her head to one side and studied her cousin, who towered over her. "But I bet God's a whole lot more willing to change His mind than Dani is." She giggled when Kurt's face burned.

The opening bars of Mendelssohn's *Wedding March* jangled through the tiny gymnasium, breaking into Tom's remarks. He stuttered to a stop and turned to glare at Andy, who snagged his microphone.

"Hey," Andy sing-songed, "did you guys hear Tom got married just a few weeks ago?"

Mixed cheers and clapping and unintelligible comments rang out from the audience. Tom went red. Kurt saw Stephanie slouch down in her folding chair, but she was laughing. Dani leaned toward Jim to say something. Her cousin laughed.

"What's going on over there?" her brother demanded. "No secrets on stage."

Dani staggered back a few steps, laughing. Jim shook his head and reached for the microphone.

"We were talking about Islam while we were setting up this afternoon. Yes, folks, we do talk about something besides music. Anyway, we were talking about Arab culture. Did you know that it's considered normal there for girls to marry their cousins?"

"That means guys have to marry their cousins too, right?" Jason said with that dumbstruck tone Kurt remembered from Sunday school, when they ran substitute teachers ragged.

The audience reacted sooner than the teachers ever had, with groans and laughter.

Dani yanked the microphone from Jim. "I'm just glad I wasn't born in the Middle East. Then I'd have to marry one of these guys." She shuddered and made a gagging motion, index finger pointing down her open throat.

Girls in the audience shrieked laughter. Several called out something Kurt couldn't hear. The band and at least half the audience responded with laughter. Dani cupped one hand around her ear, pretending not to hear. The audience didn't quiet, but the girls tried again, louder.

"You want me to adopt you?" Dani stumbled backwards in mock horror. "Is there a psychiatrist in the house?"

Louder laughter and cheering answered her. With her hand over the microphone, she conferred with Tom, who grinned evilly. He gestured for Jim and Jason.

"Hey," Andy said, playing the opening chords of Beethoven's *Fifth*. "No family conferences without me."

"Oh, no secrets," Dani said, as her three cousins picked up their instruments. "We figured, since you started all this talk about marriage, we might as well finish it." She turned back to the audience, who quieted in anticipation. Tom plucked gentle, tripping notes on his guitar. "Does everybody know Andy's engaged, too? Yep," she said, in response to a few shouted responses that Kurt couldn't make out at all. "D-day is just about a month away. Which is great, until you figure what a cheapskate my big brother is."

That got another slammed chord from Andy, whose shoulders shook, visibly fighting laughter. Kurt glanced at his cousin. Katie shuddered with laughter and steadied herself on the nearby wall.

"I mean, it's his bride-to-be's *birthday* in the same week. That means he can combine birthday and anniversary presents all in one!" Dani waited for the audience to finish responding to that salvo. "But, hey, I'm really happy about this. He's marrying my absolutely best friend in the whole world. And in all seriousness folks, this one is for Andy and Katie—who is hiding somewhere back there." She stepped back and craned her neck as if she could penetrate the shadows.

Kurt held perfectly still, wondering what he would do or say if Dani recognized him. Would she say anything?

"They're really hot tonight," a sharp, slightly nasal voice said from behind Kurt, at the level of his elbow.

He turned and saw the last person he wanted to encounter tonight emerge from the dark well of the stairs.

"Hi, Mr. Danziger." Katie smiled, and Kurt sensed discomfort beneath his cousin's politeness.

He held perfectly still and prayed Danziger didn't recognize him. After all, it had been three years since the man had berated him at a mid-sized music festival, infuriated when Kurt talked an up-and-coming trio into spending their summer traveling with an Allen Michaels team instead of signing on with Danziger. He had already promised their singing talents to several small music festivals, before he had their signatures on the management contract. That problem had been cleared up after some minor negotiations. The last thing Kurt needed was to get into a shouting match with the man who was on the verge of being Firesong's manager. Kurt prayed Firesong hadn't signed anything yet. He thought of Dani under Danziger's money-grubbing influence and felt his stomach twist into knots.

"Have you been able to hear the show?" Katie continued.

"Wouldn't miss it. Great as always." He smiled thinly and turned his hungry, small eyes on the band on the stage.

Dani slid into the opening stanza of Pat Terry's *That's the Way It's Got to Be*, an oldie-but-goodie for wedding songs. The audience cheered approval.

"Mr. Danziger has signed up with the band to be their manager," Katie said. "Isn't that great?" Her voice cracked only slightly, and anyone who didn't know her would have been fooled. Kurt was glad Katie didn't like the man. He wondered what was wrong with Firesong, that they hadn't listened when Katie voiced her concerns after he contacted her, to pass on his information.

"Great," Kurt said, though he thought it was anything but. He wavered between regretting concentrating on crusade work instead of diving into a matter that was none of his concern, and shooting off an angry prayer, asking God why He hadn't intervened in some way. Unless

Kurt was supposed to intervene, and he had misinterpreted God's prompting? "Blast Point wouldn't be where they are without your guidance at the start of their career." He held out his hand. He wished more young bands held to their mission focus like Blast Point had. Rumor was that Danziger hadn't even offered to renew their contract after the trial year of their relationship had ended. Kurt could only pray for the same for Firesong.

"That was a little longer ago than I like to admit," Danziger said with a tight chuckle. His hand felt cold and damp when he shook Kurt's hand.

"Oh—sorry—this is my cousin, Kurt Green," Katie said. "Allen Michaels is doing a crusade at the fairgrounds at the end of the summer, and Kurt is part of the advance team. Isn't that great?"

"Green?" Danziger narrowed his too-small eyes and looked Kurt up and down. "If you're the same guy I'm thinking of... you talked Mercy Ship into going on the road, didn't you? Kind of a far cry from working for a preacher, ain't it?"

"I like to keep a lot of irons in the fire." It was all Kurt could do not to wipe his hand on the seat of his pants.

"Yeah, well, keep your irons to yourself." Danziger turned and trotted down the stairs without another word.

"Well." Katie moved to the edge of the steps and watched him vanish. Tommy, Claire and Pastor Wally talked in the hallway, warding off the heat with cans of pop. "What was all that?"

"How long ago did they sign?" he asked, lowering his voice.

"Two weeks, maybe. I didn't find out until today. I was out of town with Mom, chaperoning that high school field trip to Taylor University, and... well, there were a lot of things going on, and we didn't talk about the band when I did see Andy."

"Yeah, and you're supposed to all the time?" He shook his head, offering her a teasing grin. "Just tell them to be careful. He'll sign them to a label that'll choose their music before they can even turn around."

"Oh, don't worry." Katie slipped her arm through his and led him back to the wings to watch the band. "They had Pastor Glenn and Andy's Uncle George and Xander over at the legal clinic all look through the contract and revise it to suit them. They figured it was a good test, that Mr. Danziger would only accept their changes if God wanted him to be their manager."

"Changes. Danziger *accepted* changes to a contract he wrote." He felt a little breathless. Maybe God had heard his desperate prayers before he even prayed them. "What kind of changes, exactly?"

"They made sure the band has the right to say no to anything Danziger wants to set up for them, and they can agree to gigs like this without his approval. Mission and service come first, rather than money."

"Yeah?" Some ice left his stomach. Kurt knew he grinned stupidly, but he couldn't help it.

"Like Dani says, put God first and He'll take care of things like new equipment and groceries." She nodded at the band as they swung into a bouncy tune. "Relax and enjoy the evening, will you?"

Kurt nodded and shifted his arm so he could wrap it around her shoulders and let her lean against him. Seen this close, Katie did look thinner than usual, but what did he know? He was lucky if he got to see his father's side of the family once a year. He turned his attention back to listening to Firesong and watching Dani Paul. He wished he could forget about Danziger, since the problem seemed to be averted. He would much rather spend the evening watching Dani and comparing the feisty little girl she had been with the slim, fiery, impassioned musician and performer she had become.

~~~~~

The audience had vanished into the night. The tiny crackerbox gym felt like a cavern in the half-light. The volunteer crew had finished picking up the dropped papers, pop cans and candy wrappers, put away the folding chairs, swept, and vanished. The door out to the playground and parking lot, in the hall outside the gym, stood propped open with a microphone stand. Free of the last stragglers among their many friends and fans, who had all wanted to talk afterward, the members of Firesong wearily packed up their mismatched equipment and made trips to the pickup trucks parked outside.

Dani stood by the stairs backstage, staring with drooping eyes at the empty stage, coiling cables while her brother and cousins packed their instruments and took them out, then came back for the equipment. Why, she wondered, did it always take longer to tear down after a concert than it did to put everything together? Logic said it was easier to take apart than to construct. Was it just her weariness, or her reluctance to go home, back to her ordinary college-and-job life?

The only flat note in the whole exhausting, exhilarating evening had been that Lisa Montgomery hadn't shown up. As the cover artist for the band's homemade recordings, she had a place backstage. Between marriage problems and getting sick early in her pregnancy, Lisa was smart to stay home tonight. Still, Dani missed her. She made a mental note to call her friend in the morning. They really did have to get together soon and finalize the cover art for their upcoming CD.

"Did you see that big, deluxe tour bus at the Convo Center last week?" Jim asked, breaking the comfortable, weary silence. "Someday, we're going to be big time like that and play for thirty, forty bucks a ticket. We're going to have a bus with bunks and a bathroom — "

"Who empties the tanks?" Jason asked with a grin.
~~~~~

"We'll hire somebody to do it."

"Well," Andy said, coming back from outside, "I wouldn't worry about it, if I were you."

"I'm not worried. I just think we're good enough to be big time, y'know?"

"You are," Danziger said, sauntering around the corner. "We better get to work on that professional CD. Those demos you've been passing around at the fairs and charity gigs are fine if that's all you want to do, fairs and charity gigs. You're ready for the big time, boys and girls. You need a CD from a major label."

"What do we need to do to get an appointment and studio time?" Dani said, glancing up from the final coil of electrical cord as she looped it up and bound it tight.

"You leave that to me." He bared his teeth in a hungry grimace that made her think of sharks. "That's what I do best."

"Which label?" Andy asked.

"I'm working on it. Hey, hey, don't you kids trust me?" Danziger stepped back, blinking rapidly as if shocked. Weary grins went around the group.

"If we ever get to the big time," Andy said, when their new manager had left the gym to find Pastor Wally, "we'll be on the road three-quarters of the year, instead of weekends. Did you ever think of that? We won't have regular jobs to fall back on. Who'd hire somebody who can only be there a few days a week?"

"We won't need other jobs!" Jim said.

"Well, speaking as one newlywed to an about-to-be," Tom said with a crooked grin, "it's nice not to be away too much."

"Oh. Yeah." Jason and Jim exchanged chagrined looks, while Tom and Andy grinned at each other.

There was quiet for a few more moments. Jason finished balling up the last of the duct tape used to hold their cords flat to the stage. He frowned, rubbed at his eyes, then looked around at the rest of the band.

"Um... isn't it more important to serve God? I mean, shouldn't we put what we want into second place?" he asked, as hesitant as Dani had ever heard her cousin.

"How can anybody get into a spiritual discussion this late at night?" she returned with a shaky grin.

Such thoughts had bothered her since Danziger approached them at a mid-winter praise festival. Firesong had always claimed all her passion and energy, ever since she could remember. Back when she had hung on her brother and cousins' shirttails and stayed in the shadows of the Gibsons' barn while they practiced. And later as she worked her way up from sound technician, keeping their much-repaired amps and speakers from short-circuiting each other and blowing up, to writing lyrics, to a full-fledged member of the band. She checked out information on the Internet and made phone calls. She wrote songs and arranged for studio time at Butler-Williams University, to record their homemade CDs. She discovered Lisa Montgomery to do artwork for them, right in their own backyard, and managed the band's checking account.

Firesong was her life, but was it enough? What exactly did God want them to do with the talent He had given them?

"What she said." Stephanie appeared around the corner with Katie in tow. "Can we go home? This place gives me the creeps when it's empty like this."

"I'll protect you." Tom swaggered over to his wife, waggling his eyebrows and twirling an imaginary moustache like a cartoon villain.

"I think that's our cue to get out of here," Dani said, amid groans and laughter from the others. She tossed the cables into their crate, heaved the crate up to her shoulder and walked out to Andy's truck.

When she came back a few moments later, she nearly tripped over the threshold. Kurt Green had showed up. Pastor Wally stood like a benevolent mountain, grinning as if something wonderful had happened.

Katie had said Kurt was moving back to town temporarily, to set up the crusade later that summer, and he might show up tonight, but Dani had forgotten. Until now.

Kurt's hair was clipped short, instead of the rebellious, tangled mane it had been the last time she saw him. His eyes were still as big and deep and dark. He still looked like he spent time in tanning beds with that wheat-colored skin, and from the smooth lines under his polo shirt and the muscles in his bared arms, he worked out. According to Katie, Kurt lived from a suitcase. Somehow, he managed to stay in shape.

She supposed that was one of the benefits of having his spiritual priorities straight. Kurt focused on God's business, and God took care of the rest. Dani envied him. Maybe while he was in town they could talk and he could give her some pointers.

Why did the thought of spending time with Kurt Green make her feel jittery? He had to have grown up in the years since he had lived with the Greens, while his parents were on the mission field. He couldn't still be the arrogant, self-righteous jerk, making rulings on what pleased God and what didn't, and getting offended when others didn't live up to his standards. Just because he was an MK and got left behind in the U.S. while his parents went overseas, that didn't make him instantly holy.

That was years ago, she scolded herself. *There's no way he could have gotten so high up with Allen Michaels if he never learned humility.*

A moment later, she laughed at herself, blaming the late hour and the dregs of the evening's excitement. How could she go from admiring and envying his full-time ministry and spiritual maturity to loathing the adolescent jerk he had been? She knew she had grown up a lot, too. She hadn't been the nicest person to spend time with when it came to church matters, either. God had changed her. How else could she have made friends with Sue-Anne Ehrenbull after all the clashes and loathing they had indulged in all through elementary and middle school? She had been a bridesmaid when Sue-Anne got married last year. That was a lot of growth.

All in all, it might be nice getting to know Kurt, learning how much he had grown up, too. It was a given that she would run into him a lot in the next few months, with the crusade coming up, him living in Tabor Heights again, and Katie and Andy's wedding in another month.

Dani stayed silent in the doorway while the others talked, getting used to the image of Kurt Green, all grown up. He had always been a little quiet; a little too watchful. She could never decide if he was being a snob, or just more sensitive and alert than the other boys his age. He had always been one of those boys in church the girls watched from doorways and giggled and whispered about behind their bulletins in the church service. He had never gone through that ugly adolescent stage, with bad skin and uncoordinated limbs and breaking voice.

Dani wondered what she had looked like in his eyes, dancing around on the stage, teasing her cousins, throwing everything she had into the music.

"Ouch," Andy said, as the shared reminiscences between Kurt and the others slowed. "If you're here, that means the wedding is really soon, huh?" He grinned when Katie scowled and punched his arm.

"And Saturday is even sooner," Dani said, deciding this was a good time to join the conversation. "Come on, guys. Some of you have to go to work in the morning."

"Yeah," Jim muttered, just loud enough to be heard. "Our favorite thing to do is work on Saturday."

"Just think about that new microphone you want."

"Still looking out for everybody, Dani?" Kurt asked with a smile that made everything jerk to a stop inside her. She couldn't identify just what it was about his smile that hit her that way. It wasn't any different from the smiles he gave the rest of the band. Was it her?

"Somebody has to," Katie said. "And she's right. Everybody go home and go to bed."

"Yes, mother," Andy whined. He ducked and danced out of her way when she came after him, waving a fist and giggling.

"Can I give you a ride home?" Kurt asked Katie, but his gaze strayed to Dani as she and the rest picked up their scattered coats and shoes.

"Thanks," Katie said. "I'm riding with Andy."

"You drove from your apartment?" Dani asked, and her face warmed. Why had she said that? It was none of her business. Maybe the couple of blocks from the Parkview Towers, across the Triangle and up two streets to the Mission did seem like a long walk to someone who hadn't lived in Tabor Heights for eight or nine years. Especially when he anticipated walking back after dark.

"I was getting some groceries and ran late," Kurt said with a shrug and a grin. "Can I give you a ride?" he added. "Give these two lovebirds some privacy?"

"What privacy?" Andy looped an arm around Katie's waist. "Dani has to drive, because I'm not wearing my contacts."

"You better start wearing your contacts, or bring your glasses," Dani retorted. "I can't be your taxi service after you move into your own apartment next week."

After a few more comments about the concert and how much money they thought had been raised for the Mission, Kurt made his farewells and headed for the front door with Pastor Wally.

"You know, I wanted to be part of a crusade team when I was your age," the big man boomed as they vanished down the hall. "How is it, traveling from coast to coast every year?"

"That'd be the life," Jason murmured, blocking out Kurt's response. "Setting up for crusades and seeing the world."

"Yeah, I bet it would," Danziger said, coming out of the shadows of the stage doorway where he had most likely watched the little reunion. Something glittered dark in his eyes. "Take a word of warning from me, boys and girls. That there is a dangerous man. He's ruined the careers of lotsa hot young bands."

"Kurt wouldn't hurt anybody," Katie protested.

"Didn't say he did it on purpose. He's just so tight focused on what he's got to do, he can't see the big picture. Keep that in mind, kids. I'm your manager. I know what you gotta do to get where you want to be." Then his signature smile returned. "You done good tonight. Made me proud. You keep up this energy when you're getting *paid*, there's no limit. Remember that." He saluted them, two fingers tipped off his eyebrow. Then he strolled out the back door into the chilly April darkness.

"Doesn't he ever let up?" Stephanie murmured.

"Aw, come on," Tom said, "your dad is the same way. Always working, planning, protecting people. Hasn't he said the same thing to us a few dozen times, about planning ahead and not letting other folks sidetrack us?"

"Well, yes, but from Daddy it doesn't sound so..." She shook her head. "I don't know. Mercenary?"

"Kurt said to warn you. Mr. Danziger knows the music industry, but he doesn't know the ministry side of Christian music, like all of you do," Katie said, frowning as if her head hurt. "Kurt said he's talked other Christian bands into turning secular."

"Won't happen to us," Tom said. "Not never."

"Not ever," Dani corrected absently. They were beyond tired, because no one teased her about being a frustrated English teacher.

"I know," Katie said. "You were smart and got those contract revisions, so Kurt's not too worried. He says Mr. Danziger will be good for Firesong, as long as you stay on track."

"No chance of anything else," Jim said, shaking his head. He nodded toward the door. "Can we get going? Saturday is a little closer than I want to admit."

Chapter Four

Despite the cousins' weariness and Kurt's warning, the night had been too much of an exuberant success for them to feel down for long. They had raised nearly $1,600 for the Mission, just in ticket sales. People had dropped donations in big garbage cans sitting inside all the doorways on their way out of the building. Those now sat inside Pastor Wally's office, waiting to be counted in the morning.

For a while, the Mission was free of worries about little things like the electric bill, children's craft supplies, or tea for the seniors, and a few necessary modifications and repairs.

That worry might be resolved permanently if the Arc Foundation sponsored the Mission, working alongside Tabor Christian Church. Nikki James had come back to town as Arc's representative, to work in the Mission and analyze the needs, the possibilities, the community's response to and interaction with it. Still, having the Arc Foundation's support didn't negate or diminish Firesong's contribution.

And now that she thought about it, Dani felt a little guilty, too. During the years since Nikki ran away with a man nobody knew much of anything about, Dani had looked down on her former friend. All right, she could admit it now — she had stood in judgment on her. How could Nikki have broken the vows of purity they had made during their "True Love Waits" class in church? True, she had been a wreck when Rich Thomas, her steady boyfriend for nearly two years, had broken her heart, and that made her vulnerable when Brock Pierson showed up in town. Rich's betrayal and Nikki's foolishness, running away at sixteen-nearly-seventeen with Brock, had simply reinforced Dani's promise to herself never to get involved with a guy. Turning her back on the ministry God had given her through Firesong certainly wasn't worth the risks, the pain, the brainless choices she had seen other girls make over the years for the sake of a boy.

But Nikki was back, mature and repentant and far stronger in her faith than she had been before. Dani supposed this was one of those times where God brought a lot of good for many people out of tragedy and heartache and even rebellion and sin. Sort of like with Joseph, being sold as a slave by his own brothers, and rising up to be Prime Minister of Egypt, to save both Egypt and his family during the famine.

"You're kinda cool like that, God. But You know something?" she whispered, so softly she almost couldn't hear herself speak. "I hope You never have to do something so drastic in my life to get my attention and knock me back on track. I'm happy being used for small things, thanks very much."

Dani smiled to herself, humming softly with the radio for the next ten minutes as she drove home. Andy had fallen asleep less than five minutes after they dropped Katie off at her house. They were always that way after a concert; Andy nearly comatose as soon as he sat down, and Dani flying on the residue of energy for hours.

The only drop in her smooth flight of exhilaration and satisfaction was when Kurt Green's lean, golden face returned to her mind's eye. Dani tried to concentrate on a song she had been writing, but instead of the words appearing on the screen of her imagination, she kept seeing Kurt. Smiling at her. That expectant little quirk to his smile. Had he asked her a question? Was she supposed to understand what he wanted?

Why did it bother her that he was around after all these years? Once the Allen Michaels crusade had finished at the fairgrounds, he would be gone again, putting together yet another crusade. That was his job, his ministry.

It had to be due to the late hour that such a thought made Dani feel tired and old.

~~~~~

Kurt groaned when he stepped through the door of his one-bedroom apartment and saw the light flashing on his answering machine. When he had called crusade headquarters that afternoon, there had been no messages for him. What did they need him to do that couldn't wait until Monday? He dropped down on the couch and reached to tap the button on the machine sitting on the end table. He prayed it wasn't an emergency. He wanted to go to bed.

"Kurt? Pick up the phone," a sweet, alto voice called. "I know you can hear me. It's very juvenile to refuse to answer your own phone."

Hallelujah, Belinda Kain finally realized he was avoiding her, hiding behind his answering machine and refusing to answer when she called his cell. Was it only his tired imagination, or was there a whine in that once-delightful voice?

"Why do you insist on staying in Tabor Heights? Uncle Ned says you can stay at headquarters and get off the advance team if you'd only ask. Anyway, I want to coordinate schedules with you, so I can visit. I don't like not seeing you for weeks at a time. Call me, sweetheart. Ciao."

"I'll never call you sweetheart," Kurt muttered, swung his legs up onto the couch, and covered his eyes with his arm.

Belinda was niece to one of Allen Michaels' top men. She had worked summers for the crusade team, starting in high school, leading the singing
~~~~~

for the teen meetings. Kurt had worked with her in the crusade ensemble for nearly five years. Belinda hated living on the road. One weekend a month was the limit of her tolerance.

When she made that clear, Kurt had backed away from their deepening relationship. Belinda wanted marriage, three children, a two-car garage, and a husband who came home for dinner by five and stayed home to cut the grass on the weekends. The whole idea of giving up the road for Belinda had made Kurt panic. When the panic passed, he felt resentment, anger, and a sense that he had escaped a trap.

Worse was his sense of being deceived. Belinda never told him how much she hated traveling and the hectic schedule of crusade work until they started sharing their ideas of marriage and family. Belinda knew how he felt about his ministry, so why did she think he would give up everything that made him feel fulfilled and worthy of his Savior, to marry her?

She refused to listen when he told her he had no intention of leaving the crusade advance team. She pursued him, even when he told her their relationship was over.

Fortunately, Ned Vandewitt supported Kurt and helped him avoid his niece.

Should he call Belinda and leave a message when he knew she wouldn't be there? Tell her he had no time to visit with her? Or just ignore her and never call back? How much neglect would it take before she dug her matrimonial claws into someone else?

"The problem is, I think the poor girl really is in love with you," Vandewitt had said, just before sending Kurt off to Ohio two weeks ago. "She believes love conquers all, and her love will convince you to choose her idea of happiness."

"Maybe I should tell her if she loves me, she'll commit to living on the road," Kurt had muttered, staring at the cluttered top of Vandewitt's desk.

"She'll take that as a proposal, and *still* not give up her plans. Stay away from the girl until she gets angry enough to dump you."

"Well, I believe miracles still happen."

The two had chuckled together and Vandewitt let it drop until Kurt was heading out the door.

"Don't let Belinda and her schemes put you off marriage. Somewhere out there is the perfect wife and partner for you, prepared by God's hand."

Kurt wouldn't admit to his good friend that the Belinda problem had made him vow never to marry. He didn't dislike the *concept* of marriage, just the idea that a woman who claimed to be a devoted Christian would expect him to put her dreams ahead of his service to God.

He remembered sharing similar gripes with a friend who worked in another branch of Allen Michaels Evangelistic, now assigned to setting up the first boot camp for the organization. Eve Miller had grown up working for AMEA since middle school, starting out as a Vacation Bible School worker and rising through the ranks to her current position. She had proved her worth early on so that AMEA had paid for most of her college education. She had been engaged in college to a young man with a promising music ministry. Their short romance fell apart when she realized her fiance and his mother expected her to abandon her years of ministry, training, and commitment to AMEA to become an invisible, never-work-outside-the-home minister's wife.

Kurt and Eve had laughed over that little detail, because both of them had encountered many ministers' wives in the intervening years, starting with Jenny Michaels, who were involved in much more than raising children, leading sewing circles, and cooking for visiting ministers. That kind of thinking was outdated, yet too many seminaries still impressed that mindset on their pastoral students. Eve was happy as she was now, single and able to move wherever AMEA asked her to go. She hadn't completely negated the chance for marriage and a family, but it was far in the future.

Relationships focused on marriage as the end-all and be-all, both she and Kurt had agreed, were nothing but trouble at this current point in their life journeys.

Lying on his rented couch now, Kurt snorted bitter laughter. What had Katie said tonight about Dani? She believed herself called to ministry, not to marriage? Maybe Dani had escaped a boyfriend who demanded she give up her music and stay home on Friday nights to entertain him.

"We're a matched pair, aren't we?" Kurt whispered.

A shiver ran through him, wiping the weary heaviness from his bones. Slowly, he lowered his arm from his eyes and sat up.

Three times before, Kurt had felt that shiver in response to a remark he or someone else had made. Each time, his life had been changed. Whether it was the prompting of the Holy Spirit or simply his own subconscious at work, Kurt didn't know or care.

Him and Dani Paul?

He grinned at the blank wall across the room from the couch. Katie had blatantly played matchmaker tonight, hadn't she? His cousin certainly knew Dani better than he did. Even if he could put her motives down to the starry-eyed happiness of every bride-to-be, Kurt still wondered.

Dani *would* be the perfect marriage and ministry partner.

The phone rang before Kurt could start a list of all the reasons why that was a silly idea. He reached for the phone, yanked it out of its cradle and answered before it occurred to him this might be Belinda again.

"Yeah, Kurt? Wade Klinghoffer," a raspy voice growled.

"Wade? Hey, brother, you sound like death warmed over." Kurt forced a chuckle.

"Thanks. That's an improvement. Need a favor from you. Are you free, weekend after next?"

"I think so. What's up?"

"Need you for some babysitting. And I mean, *baby*. How these arrogant snots can call themselves Christians..." Wade's voice faded, broken by the foghorn honk of blowing his nose. "Sorry. Got sideswiped and ended up trapped in my car up to my pits in swamp water for three hours before they cut me out. I don't know what's worse, my broken leg or this killer cold."

"Whatever you need, I'll clear my schedule." Kurt's mind finally slipped into gear. "Talking about that new group you just signed? The White Knights?"

"Unfortunately. Their music is sweet and hot. Too bad they have the maturity of kindergartners. I'll be out of this cast in two weeks, tops, but I have therapy before the doc'll let me drive again. They're doing a youth leaders conference in two weeks. I need someone there I can trust. Keep them out of trouble, do bed checks in the middle of the night. Maybe beat some sense and compassion into them. Know what I mean?"

"I sure do." Kurt thought about Firesong, how they had taken time to talk to all their fans that evening and make them feel important and appreciated. The gym had held maybe three hundred people; much easier to handle than the thousand or so the White Knights reportedly drew at each concert. Still, Kurt knew Firesong would handle the adulation with Christian maturity. He wished Wade had found them before Danziger.

"Let me get some paper, then tell me what you need me to do," he said, and reached for his briefcase sitting on the floor.

Monday, April 7

"Come here often?"

Fortunately, Dani turned around before she shot back with her elbow to connect with the male form looming up behind her. It was a natural reaction, after putting in a full day working at the Mission, with Rich Thomas breathing down her neck every time she left the classroom. She surrounded herself with children whenever possible, while avoiding the classroom where Rich's daughter, Aurora, spent her days. She hoped one of the first changes Nikki made at the Mission was to either fire Rich from his position as custodian, or make him wear a bell around his neck. Or maybe issue pepper spray for all the single, female workers. The problem with complaining about Rich was that he never said or did anything that could be specifically pointed to as threatening. He worked at the Mission, he was the janitor, hence he was everywhere.

If that slime-dog had followed her from the Mission to Heinke's Grocery, she could lodge a legitimate complaint with Pastor Wally.

The problem was that Dani didn't want Rich to get into too much trouble. He had a daughter to support, after all. Then again, he had been an absolute jerk, romancing Nikki when they were in high school, giving her a pledge ring when he went off to college, and then jumping into every bed he could as soon as he got half a state away from Tabor Christian Church. That was how he ended up being a single father. Her broken heart had been the main reason Nikki had fallen for Brock Pierson.

Now that Dani thought of it, maybe she wouldn't have to say anything to Nikki to get her to fire Rich. There was no way Nikki could have any good feelings where Rich Thomas was concerned.

Then she finished turning, prepared to defend herself with a plastic shopping basket to the mid-section.

The man grinning at Dani and the basket she held out in front of her was definitely not Rich.

"What?" she finally said.

"You must be as tired as I feel." Kurt gestured with his half-filled basket. At a glance, it looked like he was taking advantage of the prepared meals-for-one that Heinke's Grocery offered in the deli area. "Busy day? What do you do, anyway, in between concerts?"

"College. And Jill-of-all-trades at the Mission," she added after a moment's hesitation.

"Doing what?"

Somehow, they ended up heading down the outside aisle of the store, moving from the bakery to the produce section.

"Anything and everything. Fixing office equipment, filling in on the playground, helping the nurse, replacing light bulbs, helping in the kitchen."

"Sounds like you spend all your time making life easier for everybody else, so they can get their work done." Kurt snagged a box of chocolate-frosted chocolate donuts as they rounded the corner.

"Maybe. Sounds like that's what you're doing, too." Her face warmed when he frowned a little, visibly puzzled. "Katie was talking about all the things you do for Allen Michaels."

"Oh, yeah. Guess maybe she's proud of me. Finally." He grinned.

"Katie was proud of you even when you—" She decided now was a good time to stop, before she inserted both feet in her mouth and had to finish her shopping by bumping along on her bottom.

"Uh huh." He chuckled. "I can guess what you're nice enough not to say."

"You've grown up."

"Yeah, so have you," he said, his voice softening.

That was the last thing Dani wanted to hear. Not the words, but the thoughtful tone.

His cell phone rang. He shrugged, his grin going crooked, and shifted his basket to his other hand so he could pull the phone out of his pocket. One glance at his display, and he went all serious.

"Excuse me." He turned his back to her and flipped the phone open. "Yeah, Ned?"

Dani had a chance to get out of there with her dignity intact. She stepped around Kurt so she caught his gaze, waved, and headed down the nearest aisle as fast as she could without looking like she ran away. Who cared if it was the pet supply aisle? It led to the front of the store and the registers. She needed to get out of there as fast as she could... as soon as she got those half-dozen items Aunt Betty had asked for on her way home. Groaning, Dani hurried to the end of the aisle and planned her route so she could get everything without running into Kurt again. Would it be cheating to pray he stayed on the phone for a long time?

Definitely, this was a sign from God that being interested in guys, beyond good pals or co-workers, was a bad idea. Look what one surge of her hormones had done to fry at least a quarter of her brain cells.

Thursday, April 10

"So... what's with you and Rich?" Dani said, as she helped Nikki inventory the closet off the gym that held furniture and tools dating seemingly from the Civil War.

"Nothing, I hope." Nikki straightened up from digging through a box that looked like it held nothing but scraps of wood and dust. She slapped her hands together and stepped away from the cloud she generated. "I went out with him last Thursday, but..."

"It's complicated?" She wondered if she should have registered her complaints about Rich a long time ago, even if she did sound like a back seat kid, complaining that "He's looking at me!"

The entire Rich Thomas problem might have been fixed, and Nikki wouldn't have to deal with that ghost from her past on a daily basis. If he was trying to resume a relationship with her, was that a good thing? Rich had been practically invisible around the Mission for the last three days, keeping busy with work instead of loitering in the halls.

Meaning he was straightening out because Nikki was in town. Was that a good thing, or bad?

"Major complicated," Nikki said. "Then there's the whole baby problem."

"Aurora's adorable, but yeah, I can see how you wouldn't want to get stuck with someone else's responsibility."

"Huh?" Nikki went pale, then a moment later went red. Then the glisten of tears touched her eyes.

"Hey!" Dani caught hold of her hands and led her over to a splintery bench splattered with enough different colors to have survived a paintball war. "What's wrong?"

"Nobody knows, do they?" She wiped at her eyes with her clean wrists and leaned back against the wall for a few moments. "Arc does a fantastic job, keeping things quiet. I was terrified of the gossip when I came home, but..." She sighed.

"Knows what?" Dani sat down next to Nikki and dug in her pockets. No tissues.

"You heard about the big mess, when I was trying to come home?"

"Yeah, you broke up with Brock and left him, and then his boss kidnapped you to use you as a shield for some deals he was trying to make."

"Brock was working for the DEA, getting evidence to use against Ringo. It turns out all the witnessing Mum and Daddy did when he was here did have some effect. Delayed, but..." Nikki closed her eyes and wrapped her arms tight around herself. "I was pregnant, and Brock ordered me to abort, so I left."

"Good for you," Dani whispered.

"He knew I wouldn't abort. He did it to make me leave, before I got hurt. But Ringo decided a pregnant woman and then a new mother would be the perfect decoy. Nobody would suspect what he was up to and ... There was a fight and Brock nearly got killed and an accident and... I was seven months along. My baby lived for a little while." Her eyes snapped open and she gasped, fighting a sob. "I named her Mercy Grace. She's buried at Quarry Hall, in the willow garden."

"Okay. Makes sense."

"It does? Because I haven't been able to stop thinking about Mercy since I saw Aurora. And it scares me, every time she wraps her arms around me. Which doesn't make any sense."

"I'm taking psychology classes right now. It's classic transference—" Dani stopped to think. "At least, I think that's the term. But it means you're afraid you're substituting Aurora for your baby." She licked her lips, trying to frame what she wanted to say next, then deciding it wouldn't sound any better no matter how she said it. "And you're afraid maybe you're drawn to Rich because he offers an instant family?"

"I hope not." A gasping laugh escaped Nikki. She rubbed at her eyes with her wrists. "Does that sound like sour grapes?"

"Sounds like common sense. Rich is a creep. He was always good at hiding it, up until he got away from the people who kept him in line. Now that he's shown his true colors, he figures, why make the effort any longer?"

"And the last thing I need in my life is a man complicating it and distracting me. I have so much work to do." She levered herself up from the bench, moving as if she ached.

"Yeah, but it's good work." Dani followed her back to the boxes they had been digging through. "And I made that decision a long time ago."

"What decision?"

"Stay away from romance and dating and all that gook. It just sidetracks you. There are better things in life to worry about."

"Uh huh. Then how come you're maid of honor for Katie and your brother?"

"That's different."

"Uh huh." Nikki glanced up, smirking just a little. Her eyes still looked reddened.

"They're family. Katie's always been like a sister to me, and..." She let out a sighing scream of frustration and gestured as if she would hit her.

Grinning, they settled back to work for another twenty minutes in silence, broken only by the sound of discards landing in the ashbin set outside the closet door.

"Is Katie feeling all right? She looked kind of tired, dark around her eyes, when I ran into her at the concert," Nikki said after they hauled a sawhorse with a broken leg out into the hall.

"Lots to do to get ready for the wedding, I guess."

"Yeah, probably." She snorted and grinned as they headed back into the closet for the other sawhorse. "I just about screamed when Kurt walked into Quarry Hall a couple weeks ago, and we realized we knew each other. I was shocked he remembered me at all."

"Kurt wasn't that much of an oblivious, arrogant jerk."

"Hmm, maybe. But it sure seemed like he didn't know I was alive. If all the girls our age weren't in love with Kurt, they were in love with Andy." Nikki shook her head. "We were such stupid kids when we were that age."

"True. But at least I got smart and decided not to let guys mess up my mind and my life at an extremely early age." Dani felt that dropping sensation in her chest when Nikki's smile faded by half. "Oh, sorry. That was a stupid thing to say. I wasn't criticizing you. I mean, honestly, you had such rotten deals, first Rich and then Brock and then..." She wrapped an arm around Nikki's shoulders. "We're good just like we are. God has given us work to do, and we don't need anybody but Him, right?"

"Right." Nikki managed a tight smile, and a sharp, decisive nod. "And we definitely don't need this old sewing machine." She brushed her hand across the cover of the big cabinet machine with the treadle mechanism sticking out from the bottom. Her hand dislodged thick curdles of dust and revealed wood grain that had opened up and splintered into dust over the years. "Why is that stored in here? I know they never taught Home Ec when this was a school!"

By the time they struggled to tug and shove and pivot the behemoth, battered antique out of the storage closet, they were dusty and sweaty and laughing, and Dani was glad to put the conversation behind them.

Chapter Five

Saturday, April 12

"What do you think?" Lisa Montgomery sat back from the table at the back of the church social hall and watched the milling women storming the refreshment tables at Katie's bridal shower. She smiled, her eyes going misty, and rested both hands over her waist, where she hadn't even started showing her pregnancy yet.

Dani didn't know if she envied her friend her coming baby, now that things seemed to be looking better between her and Todd. She suspected Lisa would be one of those women who would look barely pregnant a week before she gave birth, and probably go through her pregnancy without a flicker of discomfort.

On the other hand, what Lisa had gone through recently made Dani leery of marriage, too. Lisa's father-in-law had tormented her from day one because as an artist, she didn't fit his narrow-minded image of what a "good Christian wife" should be.

Todd had finally awakened to his father's cruelty, and he and Lisa were mending their marriage. There was a great deal to be said about the power of love, even bruised and battered. And the power of prayer. Dani had been praying hard for Lisa for weeks now.

"It's great." She looked down at the sketchbook lying open on the table between them. "Of course, I'm biased. You're my favorite artist. And no, I have no idea what Mr. Danziger thinks of your artwork for the CD. That man tells you everything he thinks you need to hear, but not what you *want* to hear." She sighed, feeling again that tickle of discomfort.

His shark-like attitude made him a good manager and promoter, but was it a Christian attitude? Why couldn't Kurt have passed on that warning about Danziger through Katie about three weeks earlier? Katie mentioned Kurt was filling in for a friend of his who managed Christian bands, who had been in an accident. Why couldn't Kurt have asked his friend to look at Firesong, before Danziger even approached them?

The horse is out. Too late to shut the barn door, Dani told herself. The entire band would just have to pray three times harder about their careers and choices for the next year, until this contract expired. And she would personally kick Kurt Green from Cleveland to Nashville, if he didn't step up and help them find a better, more God-oriented manager to take

Danziger's place. After all, if her brother was marrying Kurt's cousin, that kinda-sorta made them tenuous relatives, right? Family helped family.

You're going nuts, with everything going on, Dani scolded herself and turned her mind back to the conversation.

"Tell me about it. Reminds me of the people I dealt with before I got my agent." Lisa brushed her fingers over the country church with the tall white steeple, wrapped in rose vines and ivy, for the wedding program. "Will the lovebirds approve?"

"They'd approve a skull and crossbones right now. I'm glad the wedding is only a month away. They'd starve and die from lack of sleep if their families weren't looking out for them."

The two friends chuckled and glanced around to make sure no one had heard. Andy and Katie sat enthroned on a raised platform at the front of the pale green fellowship hall/gymnasium, under streamers of ivy and trailing flowers hanging from the disguised basketball hoop. On one side of them sat a table full of beautifully wrapped presents. On the other side was a table of unwrapped presents, haphazardly stacked. As maid of honor, Dani had recorded the names of the gift-givers for more than an hour, so the couple could send thank-you notes to the right people.

The sight of all those presents waiting to be unwrapped made Dani's hand ache. She was glad they had stopped to eat. She seriously doubted Andy and Katie knew they had stopped, the way those two leaned close together, whispering and smiling and holding hands.

Not even a rehearsal with a lot of clashing chords could drag her older brother away from his fiancé right now, and that was saying a lot. Dani envied Andy and Katie, but she would never do anything to thwart their happiness. She simply wished she could know what they felt.

"What's wrong?" Lisa whispered. "It's finally hitting you that you're losing your brother?"

"Losing him, nothing!" She shook her head and leaned back in her chair, too. "I'm gaining a bathroom. No, gained. He moved into their new place yesterday. Besides, Katie is my best friend. I'll see her more often than ever once they get married. I just wish sometimes..." Dani saw the wistfulness in Lisa's eyes. "So, how are things going with you and Todd?"

"Better. We have counseling scheduled with Pastor Glenn and Dr. Harris every week. Todd couldn't have cared less when I was decorating our apartment. Now, he's practically taking over my plans for the baby's room. He insisted on doing all the work, when we switched places. So, I'm living in the dream house and he has my apartment over Rick's. I used to think he didn't know the difference between baby blue and Little Boy Blue." Lisa shuddered, and for a moment, old pain gleamed harshly in her eyes. Then she forced a smile. "Todd loves me. He's agreed that we won't live together again until Pastor Glenn and Dr. Harris and I are all convinced he's mended his ways."

"The old Todd would just laugh and say he goofed up a little and get mad if you didn't let him come home."

"The old Todd would never admit he was wrong." Lisa shook her head. "Todd *is* changing. It's like he was living in this tiny box and now he sees there's a whole world out there that doesn't care one way or the other about him." She rested her chin in her fist, elbow on the table. "It's very freeing. When you realize the world doesn't depend on you to keep going, it takes a lot of stress off."

"Stressed isn't how I would have described that husband of yours." Dani stopped before she dredged up more pain.

She sighed. Everybody was in love except her. She wished she didn't feel so alone and left behind. Seeing her friends falling in love, getting married and having babies, Dani felt incomplete and hated it. Like nightmares where she went to the first day of college without a schedule and found herself standing at the front of a full lecture hall, suddenly a teacher, without any notes, half-naked, and trying to figure out what class it was supposed to be. There was something she was supposed to do, something she was supposed to know, but what?

Don't be stupid, she scolded herself. *With a career and a ministry, who has time for goo-goo eyes?*

Her gaze drifted back to Andy and Katie, leaning so close together their noses and foreheads touched.

Andy's going to be miserable once Firesong takes off. So much time on the road. Katie even said Kurt will never leave the road, and she knows he'd love to be a father.

Now, why in the world did she think of Kurt? Other than the fact that he had shown up nearly everywhere Dani had been for the last week, at the Mission, the grocery store, church, the Greens' house. It seemed like he was more interested in what was going on in Tabor Heights, all the changes that had taken place since he had left, than in the crusade he was supposed to be setting up.

The conflict facing both Andy and Kurt told Dani she was right. If someone so full of charisma and good looks couldn't find someone to share his life on the road, then no one serious about a music ministry should think about marriage. Ever.

Still, despite the vow she had made and the certainty she was right, she couldn't stop wishing...

Just a few dates, a few kisses, a chance to giggle with friends over the vagaries of boyfriends. Dani had never been on a date, and that hadn't bothered her until now. Her life had focused on learning the intricacies of writing music and anything else that would make her valuable to Firesong.

Dani regretted some of the things she had never been able to do, but she had no regrets for the things she *had* done, and that was far more important.

Katie stumbled as she exited the fellowship hall. Dani leaped to her feet and followed, alarmed by the sudden exit and the lines of strain and discomfort she saw around Katie's eyes and mouth. She glanced back as she went through the door. Andy was right behind her.

"I've got her," she told him, as Katie vanished through the swinging bathroom door. "You're not having second thoughts, are you?" she asked, entering the pine-scented yellow bathroom.

"Lost your receipt and can't take the present back?" Katie rasped. Her back arched. She made gagging noises and barely got to the row of sinks.

Nothing came up, and in a few moments, the dry heaving stopped. Katie fumbled for the faucet. Dani turned the handle and waited until her friend cupped some water to her mouth and then spat it out. She touched her forehead. No fever or sweats.

"Not the flu, is it?" she murmured.

Katie shook her head. She leaned into the wall, pressing her forehead against the cool tiles. "Stupid headaches, but they get so bad they drop into my stomach and I get dizzy and... it's just stress. Got to be."

"Hey, I've felt a lot worse, living with Andy and those other slobs," Dani offered. "Occupational hazard just being related to them. But you get used to it, and then you get immune."

Katie managed a grimace. A moment later, she shuddered and her legs buckled. She slapped at the wall, trying to brace herself. Dani caught her and led her over to the creaky, threadbare couch tucked into the corner, between the mirror and napkin dispenser.

"Are you eating all right?"

"Sure, I had a..." Katie frowned. She swallowed hard, took a couple of deep breaths, and managed to open her eyes. "I skipped breakfast. Too busy, I guess."

"Low blood sugar and nerves. Classic combination. I nearly passed out on stage a few times, doing the same thing."

"That's got to be it." She let out a little yelp at a soft tapping on the bathroom door.

Dani made sure her friend was steady before she went to the door. Andy begged her with hisses for some good news. It was a toss-up between laughing at him for being silly, yelling at him for turning Katie into a ball of nerves, or hitting him out of pure jealousy. When would anyone feel so tied into her? Andy was her brother. They were pals, sworn to take care of each other forever, but he didn't love her like he loved Katie.

"Make yourself useful and get your fiancé a decent meal." Dani bit her lip against laughing when Andy's face transformed from pathetic worry to relief.

The sooner this wedding is over and things settle down to normal again, the better for all of us.

Food and some breathing space was all Katie needed. After half an hour of quiet and more than punch and ibuprofin in her stomach, she was back to normal. She had a sparkle in her eyes and blush roses in her cheeks as she and Andy threw themselves into opening the rest of the presents. She nearly screamed as she held up the confection of white and silver lace the bridesmaids bought for her. She dropped it back in the box before anyone else realized how skimpy and sheer the negligee was. Anyone else but Andy.

"Do I hug you or strangle you?" he asked under cover of handing the box to Dani to put on the gift table, short-circuiting the requisite inspection by the guests.

"Wait until you survive the bachelor party," Dani retorted. "I've overheard the guys planning things that can't be repeated in church."

"Oh, no!" Andy hid his face in his hands, but he was laughing, so Dani didn't worry.

Besides, she owed him at least a little hint. After living with their Gibson cousins for ten years, Andy could guess the bachelor party he would get. Nothing filthy, but embarrassing and exhausting.

~~~~~

Dani bent to pick up another stack of boxes to take from the fellowship hall out to Andy's truck. The shower was over and she could only breathe a sigh of relief as she thought about it. The wedding would be much easier to handle, because she wasn't choreographing everything.

"So, how did it go?" Kurt asked, coming up behind her.

"Don't do that!" She nearly dropped the boxes.

Kurt leaped forward to catch and help re-balance them in her arms. There was a box with a set of frying pans on the bottom, three boxes with towels, one with cooking utensils, and on the very top a box filled with tissue paper and airy spun glass napkin rings. Someone hadn't bothered reading the registry of practical items Katie and Andy had requested.

"Sorry." He grinned and didn't look repentant. Just like she remembered from when they were children. "Need some help? Aunt Kathy's sure there won't be enough room in Andy's truck."

"Yeah, well, some people aren't very practical. I mean, I said to just give them money." She shrugged, nearly losing the napkin rings. Kurt came to her rescue again. "Lead the way!"

They made uncounted trips out to the cars and truck waiting in the parking lot, aided by other members of the bridal party. Andy and Katie directed and packed up their gifts, deciding what went to Andy's new apartment now and what went to Katie's house until after the wedding.
~~~~~

Kurt didn't say much, but every time Dani turned around, she found him watching her. That little tilt to the head, the slight upturn to one corner of his mouth, the sparkle in his eyes — what was he thinking?

"Okay, what's up?" she demanded, when they came back into the fellowship hall and were alone for the moment.

"Up?" Kurt shrugged and jammed his hands into his jeans pockets. "Nothing. Yet."

"Uh oh." She grinned as she realized she felt very comfortable around him. It was easy to fall into the same teasing pattern she had with her cousins and Katie.

"Hope not." He stepped up to the main table, half-emptied, and held out his arms for her to fill. "I was just wondering where I could take you, if you'd go out with me."

"Go out with you?" For a few seconds, the words made no sense.

"Yeah, you know, maid of honor and the bride's cousin? It's the law, gotta spend some time together."

"You're crazy. Which makes sense, considering your family." Dani was glad to finish loading his arms and turned away to pick up a stack of thin boxes and put them into a huge wicker laundry basket she seriously wanted to borrow from Katie.

"Does that mean you won't go out with me?" Kurt didn't sound at all discouraged, and she rather liked that.

"Your job keeps you on the road, and I'm busy with the band or keeping up with college or working. Our schedules would never coincide," she explained as they headed down the hall.

"Yeah, but what does that have to do with going out for pizza and a movie?"

"Ask Katie all the things I have to do in the next few days. Rehearsals or fittings. Homework, college classes, and we're leaving Thursday night for a three-day gig." They reached the parking lot. Andy's truck was gone, taking a load to his apartment. Dani was relieved. She didn't want witnesses when she turned down her very first date. "This is a date, isn't it?"

"Only if you accept. Which I guess you're not." Kurt managed to shrug without dropping his boxes.

"You're being awfully reasonable about this. Should I be insulted?" She slid her boxes into the back seat of his car and turned to help him put his own load in the front seat.

"Nope. I figure I'll corner you at the wedding and maybe get a yes then. You think?"

"Maybe. You've got a full load. You should take it over to your aunt's before everybody leaves, so they'll help you unload." Dani prayed she wasn't blushing. That gleam in his eyes made her feel all fluttery inside, worse than stage fright.

"Sure." He nodded, that curve to one side of his mouth more pronounced. "What are you going to do until I get back?"

Dani felt her face warm. She turned away and brushed her hair out of her face when the wind caught it.

"Keep packing, of course. Maid of honor's duty, y'know?"

~~~~~

Dani made a stop at Homespun Printing on her way home. She pushed the speed limit down the quiet residential streets of Tabor Heights because she was late. The Randolphs knew she was coming with artwork for the wedding program, and they would stay open past their usual closing time for her. She hated making them do that. They had already done so much to give Firesong a boost when they were just starting out. Posters printed in exchange for help with music during productions at Homespun Theater, and other trade-offs that Dani was sure cost the Randolphs far more than they would admit.

Max was on duty at the front desk, frowning over a stack of papers as Dani hurtled through the front door. She grinned at the younger girl and raked one hand through her tangled dark hair.

"Have fun at the shower?" she asked, giving her a wide-eyed look of innocence, which Dani didn't believe for a moment. Max Randolph had two actors for parents, and even if she preferred building sets and writing scripts, she was a good actress.

"Traitor," Dani growled, and slapped the folder of artwork down on the desk. Then she grinned and stretched her arms to the ceiling. "It's over!"

"Yeah, I know the feeling. Honestly, Mom and I would have been there, but we had to go to that meeting of the Triennial committee."

"Lucky you." She opened the folder. "What do you think?"

"Lisa does great work." Max nodded, her gaze flicking over the delicate artwork. "She knows exactly what we can do and what we can't without help, and that makes our job a whole lot easier. Dad's talking about upgrading some of the equipment, but... "

Dani nodded. She knew what it was like. Homespun Theater and Homespun Printing ran on the narrow edge of things, just like Firesong did. At least Firesong didn't have to worry about feeding, housing and clothing a family, and payroll for a cast of actors and technicians. New, high-tech equipment and special effects were a dream for both the band and the Randolph family.

"So, how's Lisa doing, anyway?" Max asked, as she got up to put the folder in a box on the shelf behind the counter marked "Green-Paul wedding."

"She smiles a little more every time I see her. I think that jerk Todd is
~~~~~

finally turning into a human being."

"Come on, Dani." She grinned. "He couldn't be that bad, or Lisa never would have married him."

"Yeah, he was Prince Charming until he got what he wanted, then he turned into his father. I swear, I will never get married until I know what a guy's entire family is like. If anyone is a jerk, I'm out of there!" She took a step back and blinked, wondering where that had come from.

"I know." Max seemed not to have noticed. "Despite what people say, you do marry the entire family. Look what Dad got when he married Mom!" She grinned and jabbed a thumb at herself. "At least he only got me. Mom's family hasn't talked to her since she left for Hollywood."

"Did you ever think about... you know, finding someone like your folks did?" Dani wondered, was it just the epidemic of marriage and babies spawning such thoughts?

"Sometimes. But I realized a long time ago I was called to be single."

"What about Tony?"

"Tony is my best friend. My writing partner. The last thing I want to do is mess it up with romance goo." Max wrinkled up her nose and shuddered dramatically.

"You *write* that romance goo."

"That's how I know it's goo."

Sunday, April 13

"I think I've got a chance now. Does that sound crazy?" Drew Leone said. His voice crackled over the phone as he laughed. "Yeah, I'm crazy. And if I had told you about me and Eve before you transferred me down here—"

"I would have warned her you were coming, or I wouldn't have let you go down," Kurt said. He closed his eyes, and tipped back his kitchenette chair, so he balanced on the back two legs and rested his head against the wall. The phone had been ringing when he came back from a long, relaxing Easter Sunday at his relatives' house. The last person he expected to be calling him today was Drew Leone, who in a previous life, under another name, had been the college fiancé of Eve Miller. Threats from a false prophet of a minister had forced him and his mother to change their names. Maybe it had been part of God's plan to bring Drew through the fire and put him into ministry alongside Eve. Kurt wasn't sure even now, after the story Drew had related to him. When he discovered last fall who Drew was, his history with Eve, it had been too late to stop him from being transferred to the boot camp being built in Coshocton under her leadership. Kurt had tried to do some damage control, but he had feared his friendship with Drew had been damaged beyond repair. Today's phone call, however, made him believe in miracles again.

"Maybe it was meant to be. I'm ready to believe God has been maneuvering things," Drew said. "I ran into her this afternoon at the camp and she was crying and... I had to talk to somebody who knows her."

"Not just knows her. She's referred to me as the big brother she never had, remember?"

"Yeah, and I thought you were going to hand my head to me, when you came into the office last fall." He chuckled roughly. "Man, what a mess I made of our lives. Right from the start. Bottom line, I was jealous. She knew where she was going with her life. I was still jumping around, trying to figure out what I was supposed to do. And then there was Mom, pushing me into ministry."

"You've got a good ministry now," Kurt offered.

He remembered the two mini crusades they had worked on together, winter youth festivals. He had been impressed with Drew's musical knowledge and skills, and his dedication both to ministry and to Allen Michaels Evangelistic. He only knew a little bit about his past, how he had been studying for the ministry and got sidetracked into New Age philosophies for a few years, before going for counseling and volunteering with the organization. He hadn't known about Drew's name change until just before the transfer to Coshocton took place.

"Yeah. The ministry I could have had ten years ago, if I had followed Eve to AME like I promised her I would. I kind of figured the problem with Mason was my fault, after Eve told me what happened. You read enough psych books, you pick up things."

"She told you about Mason?" Kurt smiled, thinking that maybe Drew was right.

"Enough to make me want to pound the loony into a grease spot on the pavement. How could that guy claim he loved her?"

"I think a lot of us don't have any idea what love is, until it's almost too late." Kurt's thoughts shifted to Dani. He wasn't sure why.

"Yeah, that's way too true. You know what I figured out just before I started praying for God to let me find Eve and make it up to her? The best way to be happy is to love someone who's serving God just like you are. Love her so much you're willing to give up just about anything. Except God. And don't ask her to give up anything. That's love."

Thursday, April 17

Thursday afternoon dragged, and Dani would have laughed, but it was torment to sit in her favorite class and watch the clock tick through the hour with painful slowness. All she wanted was to turn in her paper, run down to the cafeteria in the center of campus to grab something halfway nutritious, and jump in Tom's van, which *should* be waiting for her by the theater entrance. They had to be in Fort Wayne by six, to perform by eight.

Finally, the professor passed out the papers listing topics for the essays they had to write. The lecture hall cleared with its usual speed. Dani waved at her professor, who was a member of their church and knew about Firesong's weekend performance. He gave her a thumbs-up as she hurried out the door and down the hall in search of the cafeteria.

Tom's rust-streaked second-hand windowless blue van waited at the far end of the long curving sidewalk in front of Cuyahoga Community College's theater when she hurried outside fifteen minutes later. He leaned against the van with his back to her, talking to someone Dani didn't recognize. She saw the stranger look straight at her. Even from thirty feet away, she saw him grin and look her over, head to foot. Tom turned and waved. She waved with her pinkie, trying to cram her tuna salad sandwich into her mouth.

The stranger hooked a thumb at her and continued talking. Tom straightened up and from twenty feet away, Dani saw a thundercloud fill his expression. He shook his head and snapped out something in a low voice, so she couldn't catch his words. The stranger laughed. The next moment Tom swung, knocking him flat on his back. He leaned over the red-faced boy, built like a football player, visibly daring him to get up.

"What was that all about?" Dani demanded as she reached the van.

"Thought you were straight," the stranger yelped, his voice cracking. "What'd you do that for?"

"What does being straight have to do with not shutting your filthy mouth for you?" Tom growled and stepped back, out of arm's reach.

"You're married. What's it matter what a guy says about other girls?" He rolled over and got up on his knees, very carefully not looking at Dani. "Can't a guy enjoy the view?"

"Do I want to know what he said?" she asked. She stepped around him and headed for the passenger door.

Chapter Six

"Nobody talks like that about my cousin," Tom growled.

Dani caught the stranger's goggle-eyed look as she jumped into the van. Tom stomped around to the driver's side and climbed in. They didn't look at each other as they exited the campus driveway, drove down Pleasant Valley and crossed 130th, where it turned into Sackley. They finally crossed Pearl before Tom broke the silence.

"That was pretty stupid, huh?"

"Thanks for defending my honor, but you shouldn't risk your hands like that. Especially not before a big weekend."

"Dani..." He sighed, and the sound turned into a weary chuckle. "Blame my being married. Makes you see women and think about... well, about sex, in a whole new light."

"That bad?" She didn't know whether to squirm or laugh.

"He wondered how much he'd have to spend on a date to make you willing—" He turned red, which was interesting. It took a lot to embarrass Tom. Marriage to Stephanie had changed him.

Dani rested her forehead on the cool window glass. "Thanks."

"I told him you wouldn't settle for anything less than a diamond ring and he said he could get you cheaper. And that's when I decked him."

"And risked being unable to play all weekend." She reached across the gap between the seats and squeezed his arm. "Thanks."

"Partly your fault."

"Me?" Her voice squeaked.

"You've changed a lot."

"You mean I'm not fat and pimply anymore. It's called puberty. You remember that, don't you? It's when you stopped trying to strangle Stephanie and started drooling over her." Dani rolled down the window to get some cooler air.

"Yeah, you lost weight. And you look great with your hair long. You move different, now. You don't hide behind your books anymore. You don't hang around the edges waiting for people to let you come play."

"Too busy."

"That's part of it. We wouldn't be half as far along as we are without you. You know who to ask and who to talk to and... Remember when we got our first brand-new amp? Jim had it all hooked up wrong and nearly burned down the barn the first time he turned it on. You knew everything was all screwed up and you saved the amp, which was a lot of money for us, back then. I guess all that confidence makes a big change. I don't know." He shrugged and concentrated on navigating mid-afternoon traffic as they passed the hospital.

"If I'm turning into the kind of girl that attracts jerks like that guy you decked — "

"That's not what I meant." He glanced at her, looking uncomfortable. "I'm not supposed to notice, because we're family — "

"And you're a married man."

"And I'm married. But you really are pretty, Dani, and some guys will never stop thinking with their hormones. We're glad you're part of Firesong, even if you do attract slimes."

"Me? I had geeks bugging me all through senior high, trying to be my friends so they could get close to *you*. It's still going on."

"That's stupid." He laughed.

"Yeah, and I'll never tell how many hearts you broke the day you married Stephanie."

"Dani..." Tom sighed. "This is going to be one really long weekend."

~~~~~

"Boring," a tenor voice whined somewhere behind Kurt.

He didn't know which of the White Knights had said it, and right now, he didn't care. Only two hours into his babysitting duties, and already Kurt wished he had been in the car wreck instead of Wade Klinghoffer. He suspected he would only be able to relax while the White Knights were too busy performing to get into trouble, or else asleep. Or else they were occupied somewhere and cut off from all temptation and opportunities for mischief. Meaning no college girls to dazzle and lead off into dark corners. Half an hour ago, he had walked in on the band members speculating on what the college girls here looked like, and making bets on how many each of them could score with.

Remembering his own college days, when he also used his music to impress girls, Kurt could almost sympathize. But he had fallen away from his commitment to God back in college, and his band never pretended to serve God with their music. The White Knights claimed to be Christians, yet they intended to use their music to seduce girls at a Christian college.

No wonder Wade wanted out of this contract.

Kurt had stepped into the dormitory lounge given over to the band and was relieved when they changed the subject. He didn't see any guilt on those faces, and that had made him angry enough to lecture them on the conduct expected of guests on campus. Obviously, his lecture had gone over their heads.

He couldn't trust the White Knights to behave themselves while his back was turned. If they were bored, they weren't heading toward a
~~~~~

lawsuit from some outraged parents.

"Don't you guys have to practice? Aren't you playing tonight?" he asked. It was bad enough he had to sit in the same room with them while he worked on his notebook computer and caught up on paperwork and correspondence. Did he have to think for them, too?

"Nah," the baritone said with a lazy grin. All the White Knights were skinny and blue-eyed, with long blonde hair. Kurt had a hard time telling them apart. "Some other group's driving in from Ohio. We can have a good time tonight."

"Hope so," somebody muttered. Kurt didn't look, but he felt the scorch of angry glances turned his way. He fought a smile and told himself he was performing a good deed.

Then the baritone's words registered. He could be wrong. There were probably hundreds of bands in Ohio. But didn't Katie say something about Firesong performing at a conference for youth leaders this weekend?

Pulling his cell phone from his pocket, Kurt stepped out into the hall. He hoped the White Knights were all too lazy and self-absorbed to listen as he placed a call to Katie.

"Yeah, they're probably halfway to Fort Wayne by now," Katie said, when Kurt asked her. "Why?" She laughed when he gave her the abbreviated version of what he had heard. "What do you know? You and Dani might finally get to spend some time together without a thousand errands pulling you apart."

"Very funny, Miss Matchmaker," Kurt growled. But he grinned at the dormitory door in front of him. She might just be right. This might be the chance he had been praying for, wishing for.

But that meant he had to protect *Dani* from the White Knights. How could they resist someone so alive and vibrant?

~~~~~

Andy claimed the band had a tail wind all the way across Ohio and the border straight into Indiana. They reached Fort Wayne and found the college half an hour ahead of Dani's precise, organized schedule.

"It's a sign," Jason declared, as they hobbled on stiff legs toward the auditorium. "We are going to own this show this weekend."

"It's not a show," Jim said on a sigh. "It's a youth leadership conference and we're only here early to get an extra two hundred. Nothing really starts until tomorrow, anyway."

"Yeah, but we'll impress somebody being here first, huh?"

Jim groaned and shook up the remainder of his bottle of ginger ale and aimed it at his brother, dousing him with most of it before Jason thought to move.

A custodian waited for them, and he knew all about the sound system and what it would tolerate. He answered Dani's questions as they
~~~~~

unloaded equipment onto the cart he had provided and got set up. He had extra cord to patch their equipment into the system, so they didn't have to experiment. Firesong was set up and ready for a test before anyone came looking for them.

Dani busied herself finding the backstage dressing rooms while the guys tuned up. She pulled out their clean clothes and toiletries so they could all freshen up and made sure everything was in place. It took little extra effort to take care of the others along with herself, and this way she ensured everyone looked good and coordinated when they stepped out on stage. She wasn't as blasé about their performance as Jim. Youth leadership conferences were several steps away from coffee houses and youth retreats. Even Danziger agreed it would help their reputation and career, and he had been urging them to stop doing "charity gigs," meaning anything that paid less than a thousand dollars. He had tried to urge them to cancel engagements like this one when they signed their contract, but Firesong had overruled him.

Still, Dani was disappointed to peek between the curtains during the opening remarks and see the auditorium only one-third full. Maybe 500 to 600 people. More than the concert at the Mission, yes, but there was also more room here. She said a quick prayer and stepped out onto stage on her cue. They all wore jeans, the guys in black and Dani in white. The guys wore white jackets and she had black, and immediately broke into a sweat when the stage lights hit. The effect was still nice, though. Dani refused to ruin it. She hit the B above middle C as she passed the keyboard and hummed it while they waited for the audience to fall completely silent.

It only took a few seconds, which was a big difference from youth retreats and coffee houses. Dani smiled, nearly losing the note. These people were interested. Had anyone heard of them outside Ohio? Maybe a lot of people outside Ohio would be interested in them now. She wondered if they had brought enough CDs to sell during the weekend. Then there was no time to think beyond the music and to pray through every number.

~~~~~

Kurt stood in the back of the auditorium with his mouth hanging open and didn't care if anyone saw him. He had been impressed at the Mission, but that had been Firesong having fun with friends. Here, this was Firesong polished and sparkling, professional without being slick. Dani glowed, even when the spotlight didn't track her as the lead.

He wished he had a dozen roses to give her when she walked off the stage. He wished he had the right to kiss her when he told her how wonderfully the band performed.

"Hot stuff," the bass player for the White Knights said in the back row, with a chuckle just loud enough for Kurt to hear. The only reason
~~~~~

they had come to the opening meeting of the conference was because there was nothing else to do on campus. "Think we can get her to quit those dweebs and sing with us?"

"Wonder which one she belongs to?" the drummer said.

"Three are her cousins," Kurt said, leaning over the back of the seats, close enough to smell the musky perfume someone had bathed in. "The one at the keyboard is her big brother. Lay one hand on her, and they'll break more than your drumsticks."

For once, he saw something like respect in the snot's face. Kurt wished he could have made stronger threats. He felt soiled, as if it were his fault these immature hypocrites ogled Dani.

Still, how could anyone not want to get close enough to look in her eyes and hold her hand, put an arm around her and even dare to taste the sweetness of her kiss? Dani was the epitome of the inner beauty Paul had praised in his epistle. It wasn't her fault cretins wanted to own her.

"Please, Lord," Kurt whispered as Firesong slid into their third number of the evening, "keep her safe."

He fully intended to hand the White Knights over to a conference worker at the end of the opening ceremonies and hurry backstage to congratulate Firesong and warn them, but his cell phone rang. The crusade team in Tabor Heights had an emergency. The fairgrounds had been booked eight months ago for the crusade, but now the administrators suddenly claimed someone else had priority. A one-day event in the middle of the crusade week. Kurt wished he could simply pass the task of straightening things out to someone else, but he was the leader of the team for another month, until his superiors came to town and took over. He also knew who to call and what buttons to push and strings to pull.

He handed the White Knights over to another guard and hurried off to do his most important job. He would have to trust God to keep Dani safe.

~~~~~

Tonight's concert was only half an hour. Dani hadn't thought it very long when they planned their selections. The heat made it seem to last a little too long. She was actually glad to link arms with the guys and bow and troop off the stage.

"Let-down, huh?" Andy murmured as they filed out the stage door to the chilly hallway. "Big-time feel, and now the drop."

"I want to drop into a cold shower." Dani peeled off her jacket and shook it, imagining she flicked drops of sweat out of the fabric. Why did she have to try for sophisticated and wear black?

"No such luck. PR time. You want to get fed, don't you?" he added, when she opened her mouth to protest.

Dani definitely wanted to get fed. Her tuna salad sandwich had
~~~~~

evaporated hours ago. She had worked it off with her usual stage gymnastics, as Andy called it.

She thought about Tom's remark about her looks and having lost weight, as she went through the welcoming buffet. One benefit of lower attendance numbers, she reflected, was that it did make for easier access to the food. Dani chose vegetables and cheese and water, avoiding the breads and cookies and sugary drinks, much as her mouth watered at the sight of them.

If she wanted to keep going in this lifestyle at this pace, she had to take better care of herself. She didn't want to end up like some well-known singers who blimped out on junk food and no exercise, and still managed to have marriage-destroying affairs.

Guess it doesn't take flashy looks to sin, huh, Lord?

Dani leaned against a wall out of the traffic and watched people socialize. A few young men, probably unmarried youth ministers, glanced her way. No one approached her and she was grateful. She nibbled broccoli and let her thoughts wander further down that trail.

Success for Firesong meant more and bigger temptations, worse than the idiots in high school acting like rock star groupies. Tom claimed a few of those idiots she ignored had been guys chasing her. Dani squirmed mentally, wondering what kind of thoughts she raised in warped little minds by her very active, physical singing style. She always dressed conservatively. Unless going barefoot was indecent exposure? Some churches refused to let women wear pants. She refused to perform in a skirt, but that didn't make her the Whore of Babylon, did it?

Lord, she prayed, *please protect us from temptation. Andy and Tom would never break their marriage vows. Not consciously, but if we're on the road for long stretches of time...*

Dani shivered at the idea that she could fall away from her values and ideals. She vowed to be careful about everything she did and said while on the road. Never alone with a man not a relative. Never allow a situation to begin that could lead to trouble or compromise or scandal. Purity in all stages.

What good would her singing and songwriting talents do the Kingdom if her personal life contradicted what she sang?

"I won't have a personal life while I'm on the road," she whispered, making it a vow. "That's the only way to stay pure."

She caught one of those unattached men looking her over for the third time. Even if he was a youth minister, Dani couldn't take any chances. She wasn't looking for a relationship, so why waste his time? She would spend the conference writing songs or making contacts to benefit Firesong. Friendships with seminary students and ministers looking for a helpmate were nowhere on her shopping list.

Friday morning meant a breakfast buffet in the building attached to the auditorium where Firesong had performed. Dani had a room in the girls' dormitory on the far side of the quadrangle formed by auditorium, library and two dormitories. The guys were housed in a dormitory next to the auditorium. She didn't mind the walk across the misty, tree-filled green to the building, even though she did grumble that the guys got an extra ten minutes of sleep. When she got to the building, she found a few people picking through the buffet tables, but no family members.

She wasn't surprised. Even though they all grew up on a farm, all the boys were disgustingly flexible when it came to sleeping in.

Taking a deep breath, Dani stepped into the dormitory to hunt for the guys. The inherent smell and mess of male-dominated dormitories were part of the reason she went to a two-year commuter college. If she let them go hungry, she would hear about it until lunchtime. Keeping them on schedule really was part of her job description, after all.

"I'm a doggone babysitter," she mused, and nearly burst out laughing when a young man wearing nothing but boxer shorts, lying on his back on a couch with a pile of books in the lounge, gave her an odd look.

The guest rooms were down a flight of stairs, so Dani didn't have to go through the fire door with a huge sign listing the hours the opposite sex was allowed inside. This was a Christian college, after all. She hurried down the steps and prayed for no more doors or stairs to deal with. A right turn in the little lobby filled with couches and vending machines led into the laundry room. A left turn brought her into a hall lined with doors. Dani paused, trying to remember what rooms Andy said they were in.

"Stupid." She took a deep breath. "Breakfast!" she called, pitching her voice to penetrate.

"Dani?" A door creaked open and Tom looked out, rubbing his eyes. His hair was a tangled mess. "What time is it?"

"The sun is up and has been for an hour. The food is out, and if you slugs don't hurry, there won't be anything to eat." She smiled brightly, turned on one heel and got out of there.

The less time she spent in a male dormitory, even on a Christian college campus, the safer her reputation.

Dani had thought long and hard about her resolution last night. If she set up a routine and a pattern of behavior, no one would believe a word of scandal anyone tried to raise against her. She thought of *Pilgrim's Progress*, where people threw mud at the pilgrims dressed in clean white clothes. The mud slid off without leaving a stain. Dani resolved to be like that.

~~~~~

The morning was filled with seminars on handling youth conflicts, planning events and retreats, and teaching in ways that would reach teens in crisis. Since part of Firesong's pay included entry to every class and event, Dani went over the schedule and picked out the classes she thought would benefit them. Armed with notebooks and pens, she and the boys split up to attend and regrouped at lunch to compare what they learned.

Kurt found them at lunch. Andy saw him first. He stood up at their table in the gymnasium and waved. Dani had her back to the door and turned, wondering what brought that grin to her brother's face. She didn't see Kurt for a moment. He wasn't short, but he walked behind a group of the tallest, blondest, thinnest young men Dani had ever seen.

"Circus act?" Jim murmured, leaning closer to her as the strangers parted, revealing Kurt in their midst.

"Hmm?"

"They're all dressed alike. Either they're with the circus or they're another band."

"They call themselves the White Knights," Kurt said, when he joined them at their table five minutes later.

The Knights sauntered up and down the buffet line, picking at the sandwich fixings and rainbow of cookies and fresh fruit. Dani didn't like the discontent she saw on a few of those long, elegant, too-pale faces.

"This month, anyway," he added with a chuckle, and settled into the empty seat between Jim and Jason. "I didn't know you were going to be here until I talked to Katie yesterday."

"We really didn't have a chance to talk about road tours last weekend," Andy said. "You're managing them?"

"Not one minute longer than I have to. Their manager got laid up and asked me to babysit this weekend. I've been on them like a drill instructor, but I heard them talking about breaking Wade's contract and signing with me." Kurt shuddered.

"So you're why they got bigger and better billing than us?" Jason said. "That's really low, Kurt. You're practically family."

"If I had anything to do with it, they wouldn't be here. The sooner they give up singing Christian music, drop the masks and go secular, the better. I'm glad I'm not signed with them. I can walk out after the weekend's over."

"Think they know that?" Dani said, glancing at the group clustered at the end of the buffet table. She smothered a grin when those narrow, pouting faces targeted on their table like homing missiles.

"They need a nanny mixed with a parole officer, not a manager," Kurt muttered, and stood as the White Knights reached their table.
~~~~~

"We need to talk with you over lunch," the leader of the six said in what Dani enviously admitted was the most gorgeous, rich baritone voice she had ever heard.

"What didn't you say at breakfast?" Kurt returned. "I want you to meet my friends. My family," he added, when the Knight at the far end of the line started to frown.

Dani wondered if they were cousins or brothers, they looked so much alike. Or was that an illusion, created by their matching green shirts and faded jeans and blond hair? Or just the tight look to their mouths and the disdain she saw in their pale eyes?

She sat still and tried not to attract any attention as Kurt introduced the Knights to Firesong. Did those flat mouths sneer when they learned her family was another singing group?

"Suppose it takes all kinds," she murmured, startled to realize she had spoken her thoughts aloud. Andy, sitting next to her, muffled a chuckle.

The White Knights reluctantly and with bad grace allowed Kurt to stay with his friends. They sat at the next table and said little. The talk at the Firesong table was all about the upcoming wedding. Dani wondered if Andy and Kurt kept it that way because the Knights were listening. Were they afraid Firesong would steal Kurt to be their manager?

"Mr. Danziger said he might drop in on us, just to see how we're being treated," she offered. "He's still not too happy about us being here."

"We're a Christian band and it's a paying gig at a Christian college. What's to complain about?" Jim said, not even raising his gaze from his sandwich. He had to concentrate on his food. He had piled together lunchmeat, cheese, lettuce and pickles into a quadruple-decker sandwich that would have made Dagwood green with envy. It was also as difficult to hold onto as a greased pig at the Cuyahoga County Fair.

"He didn't set it up for us. We agreed to it before we signed with him as our manager," Andy said. He met Dani's gaze, nodded in the direction of the Knights' table and winked at her. So, he had deduced the same reason for their stiffness.

She finished eating and left to check out the campus bookstore as quickly as she could, without being rude. Dani felt itchy all during lunch because every time she raised her gaze from her food, Kurt was watching her. She could almost feel the weight of his gaze on her. Admittedly, she liked the warmth in his eyes. Nothing *threatening* about him at all, per se.

Still, it made her feel odd. Especially after he warned her during lunch to be careful of men trying to pick her up because she sang with a band. Something in the way he said it made her think he considered her an especially vulnerable target. Why was that?

She felt flattered by his concern, even as a thread of irritation worked through her. After all, it wasn't like she couldn't take care of herself.

"Hey — you — girl," a slightly breathless voice called behind her.

Dani grinned and thought what wonderfully stupid lyrics those words would make. Or had they been lyrics already during the shoo-bop era, or the sixties with the yeah-yeah-yeah craze? Then she recognized that gorgeous, mellow voice and turned to face him with a crawling sensation up her spine.

The leader of the Knights approached her. She wrapped her arms around herself and braced for an encounter. Dani had the unpleasant feeling this would move far too fast to allow her to think clearly.

"What'd you leave so fast for?" He grinned, displaying perfect teeth that could only have come from thousands of dollars of orthodontic work. "Have a fight with your boyfriend?"

"My brother and cousins, you mean?" Dani distinctly remembered Kurt pointing out their relationships when he introduced the members of the two bands.

"But you've got a boyfriend. Sweet thing like you has to have a boyfriend." He raked his long bangs out of his eyes and leaned a little closer.

"Sorry, it's against my religion."

"I thought you were a Christian."

Dani bit her lip against remarking she could say the same about him. Kurt had been right about the Knights, but he neglected to mention this one's raging hormones interfered with his ability to think.

"I belong to a new sect that believes in no social contact between the genders. Ever. So you're violating my precepts. Please go away." It was all she could do to keep from laughing when he visibly couldn't follow her meaning. Dani sighed. Memories rose, of afternoons grousing and laughing with Max Randolph and other terminally dateless friends at church. "Protestant nuns. We don't date."

"There's no such thing as Protestant nuns." He reached to put a hand on her shoulder.

"Shows how little you know." She twisted her shoulder just enough that he missed and stepped sideways away from him.

"But since we're talking about dating, how about you and me getting together after tonight's concert? Go somewhere quiet, just the two of us, unwind after a rough evening. You know."

Chapter Seven

It was all Dani could do to keep from punching him in that perfect mouth. She didn't need to go to bars or filthy movies to know what that spark in his eyes, the roughness in his voice meant. He thought she was easy pickings.

Because she traveled with a band, the lone girl?

"I know exactly what you mean, and I'm not interested. My idea of unwinding after a concert is to pray and go to bed. Alone," she added, when his smile deepened. "Like I want to be right now." She turned her back on him and hurried away, biting her lip to keep from adding, *I'd rather slit my wrists than spend a moment alone with a hypocrite like you.*

~~~~~

"Man, she's gotta be a lesbo," the Knights' leader hissed.

Sitting on the other side of the dormitory lounge, where he struggled to get some work done, it took all Kurt's self-control not to burst out laughing. He didn't know what was more amusing: Dani's ready wit that had stumped the girl-hunting idiot now conferring with his friends, or the immature snot's conviction that a "real woman" would fall readily into his arms? If he had failed in catching Dani, there was something wrong with her, not with him?

And yet, a few more minutes of thought sobered Kurt to the point his head hurt. Poor Dani. She had found a way to fend off the cretins who thought every woman with a traveling band was easy prey. Yet at what cost? If these pretty-boy White Knights thought there was something wrong with her, what would more critical, self-righteous minds think?

Kurt clutched the sides of his notebook computer so hard he heard the plastic case creak. He couldn't breathe as something dark and fierce rose up inside him. It had been a long time since he had resorted to using his fists to protect the honor of a lady he cared about, but right now, that didn't sound like a bad idea.

What is wrong with me? he wondered in shock.

Maybe Dani meant more to him, after just a few casual encounters and childhood memories, than he had anticipated.

Yes, she was beautiful. Talented. Alive. Intelligent. Gifted with a sharp wit. Dedicated. Focused on one goal.

In the final analysis, there wasn't that much difference between him and the slobs who drooled when they watched her on stage. He wanted
~~~~~

her just as badly, but he wanted *all* of her, not just her body, and for the long run, not just for a single night in the back seat of a car.

Kurt didn't know if he liked that sudden flash of insight. So much honesty gave him a headache.

"Please, Lord," he whispered, and put down his notebook computer so he could fold his hands as he closed his eyes.

"Y'know what we gotta do?" the Knights' drummer said. The couches in the dormitory lounge creaked. "We gotta tell somebody. She's got no right coming to a Christian college and turning other girls into perverts."

"So the only choice a girl has is to either be a lesbian or a slut?" Kurt burst out. He leaped to his feet and stomped across the long room.

The White Knights froze, some standing, others poised on the edges of their seats. They stared at him, wide-eyed, their too-pale, too-pretty faces frozen in shock.

"You hit on Dani, didn't you?" Kurt pinned the leader with a stare that almost burned his own eyes. "You wanted to get her alone somewhere and spend an hour groping her. Didn't you?"

No answer, but the subject of his interrogation blushed and bowed his head.

"Here's a new word for you, boys. *Self-control.* How about another one? *Chastity.* The Bible says for a girl to wait until marriage before giving a boy access to her body. Funny, but maybe you've forgotten that it demands *boys* wait until marriage, too. I'd like to see you convince the college administration that Dani should be thrown out because she chooses to wait until her wedding night."

"But she told Cody—" the drummer began.

"I heard. And Dani is smart enough to know he wanted more than a kiss on the cheek at the end of the night. Of course she's going to put him off. You're lucky she didn't knock you flat." Kurt nearly burst out laughing, even as something inside recoiled at the words coming out of his mouth. "Or worse, break your fingers so you can't play for a month."

"She'd do that?" the bass player whispered. He backed up a step, as if Dani would burst into the room and attack them.

"If her brother and cousins didn't skin you alive for thinking filthy thoughts about her. Dani's a girl worth waiting for. A girl worth treating with respect. She also writes most of the songs they sing, so she's got a brain. That's a shock for you, isn't it? There's more to girls than what's inside their clothes." Kurt leveled them all with a scorching glare, then turned and stomped back across the room to the mini office he had set up.

"You screwed up, big time," he heard one whisper as he gathered up his paperwork, cell phone and computer, and jammed it all inside his carrying case.

Kurt decided to notify the conference's leaders, so they could put guards on the White Knights for the sake of the girls on campus. Then he would call Wade Klinghoffer and report this. Kurt had the sick feeling Wade wouldn't be surprised.

Hypocrites like the White Knights got all the media attention, Kurt knew. They were the ones who made the rest of the Christians in the world look like two-faced, lying, cheating, whoring, money-grubbing idiots. He couldn't stop all the scam artists who painted themselves with a veneer of religion to get what they wanted out of life, but he could stop a few.

"Think it'd work?" one of the Knights said, as Kurt headed down the hall to the guest rooms. "Y'know? Go after a girl's brain before you get —"

Kurt's footsteps echoing on the linoleum drowned out the rest of the words. How was he going to warn Dani without coming across as jealous and over-protective?

On second thought, did she need any warning? She seemed to have caught the entire band's number from the beginning.

Yes, Dani Paul was one smart girl who could take care of herself just fine. Kurt tried to ignore the sinking feeling that gave him.

~~~~~

"They'd go secular tomorrow, if they didn't have bookings to do Christian music almost until the end of the year," Andy confirmed that night after the concert had ended, when Dani told him about her encounter with the Knight. "I talked with Kurt this afternoon. He missed you, but he was sure you were hiding from Casanova."

"He has a reputation already?" she murmured.

"Kurt keeps talking to them about their responsibility to use the talents God gave them. And to at least pretend to be adults. They just look at him like he's from another planet."

"Wish they'd think I was from another planet." She swallowed hard, hating to say what she had to.

"No, they just think you're lesbian."

"What?" Dani didn't know whether to scream or burst out laughing. Or a combination of both.

"Don't worry. Kurt set them straight."

"Oh, just great." For a moment, she couldn't breathe. The image of Kurt riding into battle to defend her made her feel a little dizzy. She liked the idea. But only for a moment.

"How come if a girl says no there's something wrong with her, but a guy can be a snake and he's a 'real man'?" She shook her head when her brother opened his mouth to respond. "Do me a favor, and ask the rest of the guys to help out?" She waited until Andy thought and finally nodded. "I don't ever want to be alone with other guys while we're on the road. If it means we have to take a chaperon, another girl along, that's what we'll do. If that jerk thinks my only choices are jumping into bed with him or
~~~~~

with another woman, what will other people think?"

"Oh." He frowned a little more and nodded again. "Makes sense. Unfortunately. But hey, you have to chaperon us, too."

"I know. But people seem to think guys aren't so prone to sleaze for some reason."

"How do women get sleazy unless a guy helps them?"

Andy had a good point, but Dani knew most people weren't logical. She wondered if she would have these problems if she *hadn't* taken her resolve of purity. Maybe Satan was sending trouble her way, and God allowed it, to make her strong.

Please, Lord, give me the strength, she silently prayed.

Saturday, April 19

"So, which one are you married to?"

Dani kept up her weary smile and clasped her hands behind her back to keep from throttling the pretty co-ed standing before her. No wonder Tom asked her to handle the CD sales table, if he had been deluged with such questions during his stint before the marathon concert that afternoon. She had thought he was a little too nice, freeing her from the take-down chores now that the concerts were over.

"I'm not." She knew she was being cruel, pausing just long enough for shock to touch those big blue eyes. "Three are my cousins and one is my brother."

"Oh."

"Tom is married and Andy is getting married in another month," she added before those too-cute lips could open with the next, predictable question.

"To my cousin," Kurt added, stepping into the square of tables set up in the center of the auditorium lobby.

Dani glanced over her shoulder and saw the White Knights signing autographs and selling CDs at their table, which was three times longer than Firesong's. She wondered if they had roadies or expected the "lesser" bands to pack up for them.

"You want introductions?" he offered.

With a few giggles and blushes, the girl refused. She did buy two CDs before she giggled and blushed her way around the tables to the Knights.

"Thanks," Dani murmured as a knot of football players approached. She assumed they were football players with their crew cuts and wide shoulders and jerseys with the sleeves torn off. It bothered her a little that they had come to the concert looking so ragged. Then again, maybe they hadn't come to the concert but were hanging around trying to figure out what the fuss had been about. Just because it was a Christian college didn't mean everyone attending there believed. Lots of people sent their children to Christian high schools and colleges in an effort to reform or even protect them, while conveniently forgetting that if they had a solid foundation of faith and biblical teaching at home, they might not need that reforming in the first place.

Kurt stayed with her while the students looked over the CDs and some bumper stickers Jim had designed, and the promo flyers/order forms for their upcoming CD. She suspected he was taking a break from the Knights, and she didn't mind being an excuse. How could the Knights even notice he was gone with all the students gathered around them, asking questions, getting autographs and paying hand over fist for CDs and pictures?

She thought nothing about Kurt's company or the football players' smiles, each one politely waiting for a turn, until all six bought CDs.

The last one in line was the tallest. The most human-looking, with no missing teeth or bruises on his face, no tears in his shirt. He took hold of her hand when she gave him his change.

"You sure are pretty," he murmured, gazing into her eyes.

Dani felt Kurt take a step closer. She tugged her hand free.

"Is that your boyfriend?" The player nodded at Kurt.

She could almost see Kurt opening his mouth to say "yes" and she smiled despite herself.

"No. I don't have a boyfriend. Too busy. Between writing songs and studying my Bible, going to college and working a part-time job, well, you can understand." She planted both fists on the edge of the table, just behind the stack of bumper stickers. What was this Godzilla-with-a-shave trying to do?

"So, how much longer are you going to be here? There's a big party for the sports fraternity tonight, and I sure would like the prettiest girl in town to be my date," he hurried on. The widening of his eyes made her think he was afraid of asking her.

The idea of that great big bruiser afraid of someone a foot shorter than him and at least one hundred pounds lighter made Dani smile more. That was a mistake. He tried to take hold of her hand again.

"I mean," he continued, "you need to wind down, right? Just like we need to have some fun after a big game. Right?"

"I'm sorry." Dani stepped back from the table, out of his reach, and nearly stepped on Kurt's toes. "I don't date while I'm on the road."

"But—"

"If I date, people might get the wrong idea about me. People look up to me because I'm a musician. I can't give anybody any openings to point fingers later if something nasty happened. What if somebody attacked me?" she hurried to add, when the player frowned and seemed ready to argue. "He could tell people I led him on. If I don't date while I'm on the road, nobody will believe him. I have to protect my image. I owe it to God to be pure in all ways."

Well, that came out easier than she had anticipated. Dani hoped she sounded calmer than she felt as her explanation slipped through her lips. The football team stood there, listening with various degrees of disbelief, surprise and total lost-ness on their faces. Didn't girls ever turn them down? Was it that much a shock that a girl put her duty to God first?

Dani nearly drowned in a surge of gratitude that she had made her vow of purity. Had God prompted her to do that before such situations hit? She hadn't considered the vow being a defense until now, but it was true. The racing of her heart slowed. She smiled and approached the edge of the table again.

"Are you a Christian?" she asked, softening her voice.

"Well, yeah. I mean, this is a Christian college, right?" one of the guys in the back of the group said.

"Just because you grew up in church or go to a Christian college doesn't make you a Christian. Otherwise, if you were born in a garage, that would make you a car, right?" She laughed with them, relieved that they did laugh. "It's a choice you make every day. I'm a Christian and I owe it to God to consciously choose to live in a way that would please Him, every single day. You owe it to Him, too."

When they finally left, after asking questions about her cousins and the upcoming CD, Dani slumped a little against the table.

"That was something else," Kurt murmured. He rested a hand on her shoulder, squeezing a little.

She knew he meant it in a completely innocent, comforting, supportive way. And she appreciated it. But at the same time, a tiny electric thrill went through her at the contact. It contrasted oddly with the sweat down her back that stuck her t-shirt to her skin. She tried not to move too quickly, shifting her shoulder out from under his hand.

"Talk about being moved by the Spirit," she murmured, and busied herself straightening the disordered table.

"Tell me about it." He settled on the edge of the table and glanced around. Most of the traffic had trickled outside. Even the Knights were losing their twittering flock of admirers. "Sometimes I think this is the best part, you know? The concert or the crusade is over, and the cleanup is almost done. You can relax and know you did a good job and there's nothing to do for a few days until you start gearing up for the next one."

"I just want to head home tomorrow and spend the entire day reading in the loft. Just me and the barn and a good book."

"Would you settle for a pizza?" Kurt laughed when she gave him a puzzled frown. "You still owe me a date."

"I do not. I never agreed to go out with you."

"It seemed to me you agreed to go out with me next time we were both free."

"I did not." She swallowed against a teary feeling that thickened her throat. "For—Kurt, weren't you listening to a word I said to those guys?"

"Yeah."

"I really did make a commitment of purity while I'm out on tour. I can't do anything that will mess up our reputation and our ministry. And it *is* a ministry. We're not glory hounds, using Christian music as a springboard into secular music." She nodded in the general direction of the White Knights. It was on the tip of her tongue to thank him for defending her yesterday.

"I know that. Makes me wish you weren't signed on with Danziger and I didn't have the crusade advance team, or I'd offer to handle Firesong myself."

"That's not a good idea. Not if you want to take me out. Which I will not let you do. Not here."

"Dani—"

"You *didn't* hear a word I said, did you?" Why, she wondered, did she want to cry?

"Yeah, I heard." He jammed his fists into the pockets of his jeans and slumped a little. "I was really talking about back in Tabor, but tonight would have been good, too. Guess I thought I was an exception."

"No exceptions. We've worked too hard for this, and I won't mess things up. Especially now that I've made my vow public. Nobody will ever believe me now, if I tell some guys I don't date while I'm on the road, and then half an hour later they see me on what certainly looks like a date."

"So I need a bunch of chaperons, is that it?" He tried to smile.

"I'm going to my dorm room and die. I don't want to talk to anybody or go anywhere. I want to get a big bag of cookies and a jug of milk from that convenience store down the street, and then pig out and read until I fall asleep."

"A pizza in a quiet restaurant sounds a whole lot more fun." He rested his hand on hers on the table for a moment, sending that electric thrill up her arm and spiraling through her body. "Sorry, Dani. I was listening, but I really didn't hear."

"That's … okay." She couldn't look at him. Did she want to hit him, or give him some hope for the future?

"You still owe me a date," he added, as he stepped back and walked away.

"Do not. I never agreed to go out with you."

"That's what you say." He chuckled.

Dani sighed and bent to pull a box from under the table so she could get to work packing. The weekend really was over, all but for the sunrise service tomorrow morning. Firesong had lodging for one more night, one more breakfast, and the freewill offering taken at the concert was even now being tallied. They needed that money for new equipment, after all.

She wondered if, in their own way, Firesong wasn't just as mercenary as the White Knights. Or was it really mercenary to be concerned about bills and the future?

"Lord, please, show us what's the best road to take," she whispered as she cleaned up the table. She continued to pray, in whispers, as she packed everything away. She prayed for her cousins, for Andy, for Katie, for Nikki and the pressure she was under because Brock Pierson had followed her home, for the upcoming wedding, for her friends in Tabor Heights and her college classes. She prayed for the other musical groups, that they would see their music as a ministry and not a steppingstone.

She had just started praying for the White Knights when their drummer crossed the empty square between the tables and blurted an invitation to go out with him for a burger and to talk about writing songs. Dani was glad she had her back to him. She bit her lip against laughing and paused a few seconds until she could get her face under control.

Three's the charm, she thought, as she turned around to give him the same speech she had given the football player and Kurt.

Sunday, April 20

"He's still following us," Andy murmured, glancing in the rearview mirror of his truck as he pulled off the main road and headed down the long lane to the Gibson farm.

Dani slouched lower in her half of the seat. She closed her eyes and wished the whole world would go away, especially Kurt Green. Her reaction earned a chuckle from her brother.

"He's pretty persistent, got to admit that. What's wrong with the guy, Dani?"

"He could have any girl he wants, so why does he keep chasing me? There were plenty of girls just begging for him to walk over and charm them, back at the college."

The day had started far too early. She could barely keep her eyes open during the sunrise service and breakfast. The crowded conditions in Tom's van had made it impossible to sleep. She had hoped she could catch a short snooze between Tom's apartment and home, but she had been conscious of Kurt following them the entire time.

"That's probably why he wants you. The only girl in the entire state of Indiana who wasn't throwing herself at his feet." Andy reached over and slapped her arm, startling her into sitting up and opening her eyes.

Dani looked in the mirror. Kurt's dark green sedan was still there, where it had been since they left the campus half an hour after breakfast.

Somewhere between the sunrise service and the end of breakfast, Kurt had finagled a yes to a future date. She blamed that moment of weakness on the fact that she was half-asleep. Dani suspected he wasn't the kind of guy who would wait a day or two. Which, she admitted she rather liked about him. She suspected Kurt was going to walk up to her before she even got out of Andy's truck, inform her that she was no longer on the road, and half-drag her to his car for their date over Sunday lunch. Which, she was honest enough to admit, might be rather fun. And frightening. Because what if he asked her on more dates, and she wanted to say yes? Part of her wanted to tell him to leave her alone forever. It wasn't just because of her vow of purity and devoting herself solely to her music ministry. There was something very safe about the whole idea of never dating, never getting involved with anyone.

Never making any changes in her life.

Which was ridiculous, she knew. Life was change. If she stopped changing and growing, that meant she was dying.

Firesong was a good reason to never date. She couldn't let anything distract her from the band and her ministry. This was where God wanted her. She knew that like she knew her own name.

Yet the idea of being alone for the rest of her life kept threatening like a black cloud on the horizon. Sometimes Dani still woke from foggy-painful memories of her parents' deaths and scrambled across the hall to Andy's bedroom to talk to him. She had that dream last week and nearly burst into tears when she found his room empty of everything that was Andy, before she remembered he had moved into his apartment. In that moment caught between sleep and remembering, she had nearly drowned in the utter conviction that Andy was dead, too. And if she checked out Jim and Jason's rooms, and Aunt Betty and Uncle George's room, she would find herself totally alone in the house. Alone in the world.

Maybe she was just afraid of being alone, and that was why she seriously considered Kurt?

Dani sighed, rubbed hard at her eyes, and tried to tell herself she was just worn out from the trip. Kurt was a nice guy and dedicated to serving God. It wasn't like he would demand she give up Firesong and settle down to play house. How could he, when he spent most of the year on the road in ministry, too?

"I'm losing it," she whispered. Why think about marriage to Kurt? They hadn't even gone out on one date yet!

"What's that?" Andy asked as the truck turned down the gravel driveway.

"Nothing. Hey, what's up?" She pointed at the house. "Why aren't they at church?"

Their aunt and uncle came out onto the front porch of the farmhouse as their truck, followed by Jim and Jason in their truck and then Kurt's car pulled into the big gravel turnaround between the house and the two barns. They looked genuinely worried. How long had it been since they worried about the band on road trips?

"Something bad happened," Dani whispered.

"Like what?" her brother replied, just as softly. "I haven't seen them look like this since Mom and Dad..."

Her entire body felt jangled. Dani jumped out of the truck almost before Andy had it in park and ran to the porch.

"What happened?" she demanded, as her cousins came running.

"The Randolphs were in a horrid accident last night," Aunt Betty said. "Joel and Emily — the children were all at home, thank the Lord."

"They were hit broadside by a drunk idiot in a construction truck. He ran a red light," Uncle George said, taking up the thread.

"Are they—" Dani choked. For five horrifying seconds, she was eleven years old and standing at the railing of the waterfowl refuge, looking out over the sunset-streaked water while Andy told her their parents were dead.

"They're both alive. Joel's laid up with a shattered leg, but Emily's in a coma. Seems like half the church is there, but Max is your friend." Aunt Betty gave Dani's shoulder a squeeze. "I know it'd help her to have you there."

"Right." Dani swallowed hard, afraid the knot rising in her throat was a shriek of denial.

"Let's go," Andy said as he slid an arm around her.

Dani gladly leaned into his support as they headed back across the gravel yard and climbed into the truck. She clenched her hands together so hard, they tingled and went numb.

Please, God, why is this happening? How could You let this happen to them?

Chapter Eight

Dani knew she should look at the positive side: Max's parents were alive. But she couldn't. A wedge of ice sharper than a knife lodged in her chest as Andy drove to the hospital.

It wasn't right. It shouldn't happen to anyone. Max was twenty-five, not eleven, and she could probably handle it. But Joe was sixteen and Jeremy was only fourteen. They shouldn't have to go through the fear of loss and the worry and the sleepless nights. Dani huddled in the seat and shivered, remembering. The news about their parents had come on a gorgeous day like this. Her life had changed forever, in so many subtle and blatant ways. What changes would fall on Max, now? Probably half the church had already been to the hospital or dropped off food, but who would really be there for Max? Who could she lean on and dump on, like Dani had with Andy during those tumultuous, aching months after their parents died? There was Tony Martin, Max's writing partner, but he was in California on a writer-in-residence stint.

"Please, God," she whispered. And choked. Dani had no idea what to pray.

~~~~

"You okay?" Kurt asked, finally daring to slide across the wooden bench in the hospital hallway.

Dani turned to look at him, and for a moment, he was positive she didn't recognize him. Maybe she wasn't even there, mentally. She had dark smears under her eyes, as if she had been sitting vigil for days, not an hour or two.

"Fine. Thanks." She tried to smile, and turned her head to watch Max leave the big waiting room filled with friends from the university and church. For some reason, she had been unable to sit in the waiting room with everyone else who had come to support the three Randolph children and wait for news on Joel and Emily.

Kurt vaguely remembered Max Randolph, who followed two doctors down the hall with her brothers to another room. The somber looks on the faces of both doctors made him feel helpless and useless, and made him ache to be able to do something.

He wanted to fix things because Dani seemed so distraught by the whole situation. Maybe he was selfish, but he didn't like the way she seemed to shrivel up into herself, growing paler with every passing hour.
~~~~

As if those were her parents in the hospital.

Maybe Dani was reliving the days after finding out her parents were killed? Kurt could only imagine what it had to be like for her, to be slapped so hard with the news and have no hope. At least Max had hope.

Dani had changed after her parents died. She was still strong and focused, but some of the happy-go-lucky had fled. She had grown quiet and didn't reach out to every stranger who came to the church. Kurt hadn't liked it, the few times he spared any thought for the quiet girl who seemed more Katie's shadow than her twin after that.

"Please, Lord, don't let her..." Kurt flinched, surprised to have his prayer become audible. Dani didn't react, all her attention on the door that Max, Joe and Jeremy had passed through. "Sure looks like the whole church is here, doesn't it?" he said with a forced chuckle. "Who's that?"

He pointed at a dark-haired man in a BWU sweatshirt, leaning against the wall in the hallway, accompanied by a gray-haired, bearded behemoth in a green beret. They watched the door, waiting for Max and her brothers, too.

"Dr. Morgan and Dr. DeFiore. They teach theater at Butler-Williams with Mr. Randolph." Dani attempted a smile. "What do you want to bet they take over building the set, so Homespun's performances start on time?"

"That's the way things are done in Tabor Heights, isn't it?" Kurt murmured. "You don't realize how great a place is, and how much you miss it, until something like this happens."

"You never do," Dani whispered, "until it's too late."

She shivered, as if the hospital's air conditioning had dropped ten degrees. Kurt slid his arm around her, to offer comfort and warmth. Dani leaned into his support, but he suspected she didn't even notice what he had done.

He nearly snatched at her, to keep her seated and in the shield of his arm, when Dani leaped to her feet a few seconds later. Then Kurt realized the door down the hall had opened and the doctors and the Randolph children were coming back to the waiting room.

"Dad's awake," Max said with a choked voice and grinned, tears in her eyes.

Kurt slapped himself for feeling jealous when Dani hugged Max and her brothers. He followed when she went with them into the waiting room, to share the news with the rest of the friends and supporters. Joel was awake and stable, and the doctors could work on piecing together his shattered leg. Emily was in a coma, but other than her head injury, she was fine. Kurt didn't think that was such good news, but he decided to be encouraged with everyone else.

Some of the people who had been waiting seemed to take the news as permission to leave. Dani settled in the waiting room with Max, but from where he stood by the door, watching her, Kurt was positive it hurt her to be in the room. She didn't speak, except to offer to help, to run errands, offering tissues or reaching to hold Max's hand when the struggle to be organized and coherent got to be too much for her friend.

When more people poured into the waiting room, after the church service ended and people from the university joined them, Max urged those who had been there longest to go home. Dani stayed. Kurt watched how she concentrated on Max and her brothers, holding a hand or giving a shoulder to lean on, making sure they weren't alone. Kurt knew with so many friends offering help and sympathy, Dani's presence or absence wouldn't make a bit of difference. He wondered if did more good for Dani to be here.

A brainstorm hit, as he watched Dani helping Max, with her ever-present notepad and pen. He had been doing a lot of thinking about Dani in the last week or so. This was how Dani coped with everything; she organized, she supported, she kept everything running smoothly. She kept so busy she didn't stand still long enough for anyone to see into her eyes and soul.

It was the craziest thought, but what if Dani used her activities, her dedication and ministry, as a shield?

Against what? he immediately asked himself.

Pain, for one thing. Loneliness. Maybe against all the harsh realities of life in a distinctly anti-Christian world.

Maybe she was trying to buy God's favor?

No. Kurt pushed that thought away the minute it hit. Dani wasn't like that. She knew salvation came through grace, not works. She knew, she taught in her songs, that no one could buy God's love.

But still, he couldn't push aside the conviction that Dani kept a lot hidden from the world. And maybe pushed a lot of the world away. He thought he was getting to know her, but what if all he ever saw was the veneer, the public Dani-face?

The thought chilled and saddened him. But what could he do?

He was so caught up in his epiphany and trying to find some solution, he almost missed it when Dani left the hospital with several other girls to take care of errands. Kurt left soon after, sure that Dani wouldn't be back. She would keep busy, helping, pushing away the pain and supporting others.

Tuesday, April 22

Dani was relieved when Tom and Andy called a meeting Tuesday night to discuss the latest news from Danziger. She needed to get her mind off the Randolphs. Max and her brothers would be fine, if concerned friends didn't drive them crazy. Joel was sitting up and already itchy to go home and back to work on *Shrew*. Emily was still in a coma. Dani hated knowing there was nothing any of them could do for Miss Emily except pray. And call twice a day to find out if there was anything she could do to help.

In between hazy, twisted dreams about her parents' deaths, Dani grumbled about Kurt. She knew he had been about to ask her out, but things got in the way. She didn't know whether to feel relieved that he hadn't or guilty that she wished he had. What were her petty personal problems compared to the larger catastrophes hitting her friends?

Maybe she should extend her vow to include no dating, period. Look what thinking about dating did to her emotional balance, and she hadn't even had one yet.

When Andy showed up for dinner that night, he seemed more distracted than usual, more than Dani could blame on the upcoming wedding. She said nothing about it as the family ate dinner in the big kitchen and talked about the wedding and how much easier the farm was on Uncle George between his new equipment, his hip replacement and fewer acres to tend. Band business could wait until everyone was there.

Tom and Stephanie showed up in time for dessert, just as Aunt Betty put out the pie plates. Dani scooted over to make room for Stephanie to slide in a chair next to her and Tom pulled up a chair on the other side of the corner.

"We've got a big decision to make," Tom began, after everyone had been served pie. He pulled a thick sheaf of papers from his back pocket. Dani recognized Danziger's dark gold letterhead, and her back muscles tensed.

They suspected Danziger would send another contract, just because they were getting more requests from low-paying ministry events. He hadn't been happy when Xander Finley at Common Grounds Legal Clinic insisted on a clause giving Firesong veto power on anything their manager arranged, and the right to make ministry commitments without his input. Even before Kurt's word of warning, they had feared Danziger would sign them up for dates they already had plans for. Sometimes Dani wished they had never met Troy Danziger, though the man had certainly lined up some good-paying dates already.

There was something hard about the man, though he was highly regarded in music circles as a competent, reliable professional. People in the Christian music arena said Danziger was a man who knew what he was doing, and knew how to get what he wanted.

But what if he wanted Firesong out of Christian music?

"Wait a minute." Dani looked around the table. "Where's Katie? She's part of the decision, too."

"Katie isn't feeling good," Andy said a shade too quietly. He picked at the crust of his cherry pie and looked at a spot in the center of the green checked tablecloth. "She said whatever I decide is all right with her."

"Okay." Tom frowned, visibly wavering between asking for more detail or letting Andy keep his silence. He took a deep breath and spread the papers out on the table. "These arrived this morning. Danziger wants to activate the option to revise the contract because of new opportunities. He claims the one we just signed limits what we're able to do, and what he can do for us."

"Sounds good. At first," Jason murmured, reading over his brother's shoulder. "What's all that legalese stuff about?"

"Do we want to stay a weekend band, or be available for concerts full-time? It might mean switching jobs, finding bosses more likely to let us take off in the middle of the week. It'll mean more time on the road. But the upside is we'll be traveling longer distances—"

"That's a good point?" Jim said with a crooked grin. "I'm the one who has to drive while the rest of you bums sleep."

"And we can fly and charge the concert promoters for the tickets," Tom finished.

"Fly for free?" He nodded, his grin smoothing out.

"Not for free," Dani said. "It could get exhausting. Fly out in the afternoon, set up, do the concert, fly home on the red-eye flight and try to go to work the next morning."

"Exactly. Danziger warned me what it'll take for the first few years, until we really catch on." Tom paused, visibly swallowing hard. "Until we start making the kind of money that'll let us quit our jobs and play full-time. He's negotiating with three labels. Two are considering us as part of the tours for some big-name groups."

"Like, ride in the bus and open for them at every concert?" Jason said in an awed voice.

"Kind of like that, yeah."

Dani glanced at Andy, who picked at his pie. He didn't seem surprised by anything Tom said. Either his mind was far away from this conversation, or he knew everything proposed by Danziger and tried not to influence the vote. Maybe her big brother didn't really care?

Jim and Jason were all for making sacrifices: jobs, health, time, even relationships. That amused Dani, because they had become more serious about their sporadic dating after seeing Tom and Andy find stability and happiness in Stephanie and Katie.

She might have to give up college if the professors wouldn't let her skip lectures and take make-up tests. Dani chose Cuyahoga Community

College over Butler-Williams because the fees were lower and she could trickle along as a part-time student with part-time jobs. She worked at the Mission several days a week, considering it ministry work since it didn't pay much. Could she get by on her savings and what Firesong made? Should she give up trying for a college degree?

Dani listened to the pros and cons that went across and around the dinner table. They finished off the pie and two pots of coffee before they were ready to move on.

"Okay, that's settled," Uncle George said, when they had worked out all the good and bad points of the proposition. "You wouldn't be wearing that grim look if there wasn't a catch hidden in there. What's Danziger trying sneak past you?"

"He wants to throw out our veto clause, while setting up one of his own," Andy said a little too quietly. He didn't glance up, just kept picking tiny bits off the crust of his uneaten pie. "We ran the new contract by Xander this afternoon, and he said it's cleverly hidden, but Danziger wants the right to cancel anything we set up without him, including dates we're already committed to, not just future dates. It'd mean better-paying jobs on those dates, with more money —"

"If we only cared about money, we would have ditched our commitments the first time he asked," Dani said. "I'm not signing anything that lets him cancel out on people depending on us."

"Ditto," Jason said, raising his hand.

"Right now, we have the right to make commitments without Danziger being involved — and he doesn't get a cut of the pay, either. That might be the biggest motivator," Tom said, pausing for emphasis. "But Xander warned us of the repercussions. We're free to walk out on Danziger after one year, with the current contract. Once we sign this new one, we're stuck for five years. Danziger says he has the right to get some profit from all the hard work he's going to put in on us."

"Sounds like he thinks he's the only one doing any work," Andy offered in that same, not-quite-there voice.

"Exactly."

"Does it give him an option to dump *us*?" Dani wanted to know. Her brother nodded, with no change of expression. Tom's somber look darkened a degree or two. "Then I say we stick with our current contract, and if we're not happy together when it expires, we run for our lives."

"That's what Xander said. But in lawyer-talk," Tom added with a snort of what could have been amusement.

It only took another ten minutes to come to agreement. Dani felt a little more relieved than she liked to admit when the others followed her decision to stay with the current contract. Danziger would not be happy. He wouldn't have sent this new contract unless he had big plans and wanted to force them down a specific path.

Maybe Katie was right. He had been worried by Kurt's appearance at the Mission concert and feared he would steal them.

Maybe she should ask Kurt for everything he knew or had heard rumored about Danziger, so they could be properly warned for a battle royal down the road.

Tom and Andy, as the leaders of the band, went to Uncle George's office and got on the speakerphone to talk with Danziger about their decision. Dani went outside, needing some fresh air and to walk out some of her nervous feelings. Something felt wrong with Andy. He should have led the discussion, instead of offering comments from the sidelines. She needed to talk privately with her brother.

Kurt drove up to the house as she came out the side kitchen door and headed for the barn. He nodded to her and sat for several seconds in his car after he had turned off the engine. Dani changed direction and wandered over to lean against the hood, feeling that same sense of wrongness in him that she had felt in Andy. The same brooding, heavy, almost betrayed shadows in his eyes. What would cause the same reaction in both of them?

"Katie?" The sudden suspicion made her feel like someone had punched her in the stomach. "Is something wrong with Katie?"

"Oh, great," Kurt sighed. He slumped and looked away. "I thought Andy had told you already."

"Told me what? We've been busy with band business until now. I know something's wrong." She stepped around to the side of the car as he got out and caught hold of his arm. "Tell me."

"She's sick." He finally looked at her. A hint of tears in his big eyes surprised her and made her ache. "Not sure what it is yet, tumor or viral or just some stupid anomaly that's been building up all her life."

"Her headaches? She said it was just nerves and not eating right. She's not gonna die, is she?"

"We don't know," Kurt said. "She had a really bad attack while you guys were gone, just passed out. Her folks were furious when they found out she's been having headaches and bad spells for weeks now and didn't tell anybody. The tests are just starting. When Andy came over today... She offered to postpone the wedding."

"No wonder he's so down. What did he say?"

"Well, Katie seemed a lot happier when he left. Whatever he said was the right thing. I'm just worried how he feels right now. Sometimes when you take up somebody's burden, it just makes yours twice as heavy." He caught hold of Dani's hand and squeezed it. "Can I talk to him?"

Kurt went inside to wait for Andy and Tom to finish their phone call with Danziger. Dani got in her car and drove to the Greens' house. Katie was outside, watering the tall green stalks of lilies. Dani thought of all the years Mrs. Green had brought her prize lilies to church to decorate for Easter. The flowers always made her think of funeral parlors and death, even if they did also symbolize resurrection.

Katie didn't turn to look when Dani drove up. No surprise. Her best friend's mind and heart were probably too full to let her notice the outside world. Dani got out and crossed the lawn and waited until Katie turned. She let out a yelp and dropped the hose when she saw Dani. They nearly knocked heads as they both dove to retrieve the gushing hose and turn off the faucet. That brought awkward grins to them both.

"Hi." Katie looped the hose around the caddy instead of winding it. "Told you already, huh?" She looked away, blinking against tears for a few seconds.

"You know how Andy is. He's still chewing it over. I knew something was wrong at dinner, but he hates telling anybody when he's hurting."

"So how... ?" Katie settled down on the front steps.

"Kurt came over to talk to him." She sank down next to her. "Guess we were both wrong about the nerves and all, huh?"

"Big time." She knuckled at her glistening eyes.

"You know, I'll be really ticked at you if you've been soaking somebody else's shoulder. That's my job."

That earned a hiccupping chuckle. Then the torrent.

Dani held Katie, rocking her, and they clung to each other as they had when Dani's parents were killed. The big difference, Dani realized with a sharp throb in her heart, was that her parents' suffering was over quickly. They probably had no time to think of those left behind. Katie could suffer for years, and witness the sorrow of those she loved and who loved her.

"How come we're all so positive it's all going to end in doom and gloom?" Dani asked, as Katie's tears slowed to a trickle and her nail-digging hold began to relax.

Around them, dusk had settled into chill evening and automatic lights came on in gardens and along walks up and down the street.

"What?" Katie sat back and scrubbed away the last tears.

"They don't know what's wrong, do they? You still have tons of tests to take. They could be way wrong. You could just be allergic to something, for heaven's sake."

"Allergic to what? Happiness?"

"I refuse to let anybody give up on you. Especially *you*. I need you too much. Who else can talk me into wearing dresses and make-up instead of jeans and Ts?" A choked giggle was her reward. "You're my best friend. What am I going to do without you to keep Andy in line?"

"That's what he said," Katie whispered. Her lips trembled, but she did smile.

"You didn't really tell him—"

"That we should postpone the wedding? It seemed like the only sensible thing to do."

"Since when does 'sensible' apply to that brother of mine? The smartest thing he ever did was fall in love with you. He wants to take care of you."

"How can I marry him and then die a few months later?" Katie asked in a remarkably steady voice. "I can't do that to him."

"He'll be happy for the time God gave you."

"That's what he said." Her voice dropped to a whisper. "He said he wants us to spend the rest of our lives together, whether it's a long time or a little bit. He told me we were going to have a big fancy wedding and nobody was allowed to cry because love is stronger than death or sorrow and no matter what—" Her voice cracked. "No matter what happens, we have to remember we'll be together for eternity. What does that compare to a few years separated down here?"

"I thought I was supposed to be the poet in this family," Dani grumbled. She felt painfully close to more tears.

"If I wasn't in love with the big jerk before, I'm definitely lost now," Katie said with a sputtering laugh. She hid her face in her hands several long moments until the shaking left her shoulders. She took a big breath and raised her head and wiped her face. "Promise me something, Dani?"

"Anything. Except wear that goofy sunbonnet with the green sunflowers you keep looking at in those bridal magazines," she hurried to add. The tightness in her throat eased when Katie grimaced and slapped her shoulder, just like normal.

"Promise me Firesong will be a success. When I'm gone, I want him to have something to hold onto. You know? Promise me?"

"I swear." She raised her hand, palm facing Katie. "Nothing is going to get in the way of Firesong being the best band in the entire world. And you're going to be there to see it," she added, wrapping her arms tight around her friend.

~~~~~

"Lord," Dani whispered as she drove down the dark streets of Tabor Heights an hour later. "Please, Lord, don't let Katie die. Don't do that to her or Andy. Or me. They're so happy. They're so sick in love with each other. I'll never be that much in love with anyone." She sighed and a shiver ran up her spine.

"Please, God, do I love my music too much? Is this a wakeup call? I mean, we'll never be arrogant jerks like those White Knights, will we? Why Katie? She hasn't done anything..."

Dani drove in silence, until she realized the blurring of the streetlights came from tears.
~~~~~

"Do I love my music more than You?" she whispered, the words catching in her throat. "Please, God, help me figure out what's going on inside me. I'm scared." A sob escaped her tight-clenched control. "Please, don't take her away. Don't do that to them. To us. Take me. Wake me up any way You want, but just... don't take her away."

Kurt waited on the porch when she got home. Dani almost didn't see him, a shadowy lump sitting on the steps inside the darker shadows of the big, uneven bushes Uncle George never got around to trimming. She started down the flagstone path from the driveway to the porch and he stood, wringing a tiny yelp of surprise from her. Dani didn't know if she wanted to punch him or hug him for a moment.

The very thought of flinging herself into his arms and letting go the tears that threatened to choke her sent a shock through her that drove away those tears. Dani remembered crying in Andy's arms and Aunt Betty's arms, after her parents died. It hadn't done any good, had it? What good would it do leaning on Kurt Green, of all people? Why had she wanted to? Was she that disturbed by Katie's problems?

"What are you still doing here?" she asked, and forced a chuckle to wipe away the ungracious sound of the question.

"I figured you were with Katie, so I thought I'd hang around and see if you needed to talk." He shrugged and leaned against the support post next to the steps. In the shadows, his eyes looked huge. Like warm, soft black holes she could fall into and lose herself forever.

For half a second, Dani felt the tug of the temptation and wanted to give in. She was so tired. She wanted someone to lean on, someone who only thought about her. Maybe even someone she didn't have to look after. *Is that selfish, or what?*

Dani took a mental step backward and a physical step to the side, so she could climb the steps without tripping on Kurt. The way she felt right now, if she fell down — into his arms — she might never get back up.

And that was wrong, too. What had happened to her vow of purity, of avoiding even the appearance of looseness?

Chapter Nine

"I'm not going to fall to pieces, so you don't have to worry. Thanks anyway," Dani added, just a few degrees softer.

"Didn't think you were. But sometimes even the strongest person needs to let go, let it loose."

"That's what I do on stage. Didn't you see us all weekend?" She reached the top of the steps and turned, to walk backward to the door while talking. She hoped Kurt would take the hint.

"Not that kind of letting loose. Thought maybe you could use a shoulder to cry on. Katie dumped everything on Andy, so my shirt's nice and dry." He moved down to the bottom step, so he had to look up at her.

"Thanks, but I ... I'm not going to do any more crying for a while."

"Too much to do, huh?" His smile thinned. It wasn't his tone of voice, but something about Kurt changed, making Dani shiver.

"There's always too much to do. Number one on my list right now is sleep. Thanks for waiting, Kurt. I don't mean to be rude, but... Goodnight."

"You're not the savior of the world, Dani," he said, as she turned and reached for the doorknob.

"What?" Dani flinched, hearing her voice rise just enough to disturb the crickets out past the apple orchard.

"You try to take care of the whole world, but who takes care of you?"

"Andy. And Aunt Betty and Uncle George." She shook her head, feeling slightly dizzy. Almost lost. What had brought this on?

"As much as you'll let them. I think you keep busy to block everybody out. No one is meant to go it alone, you know."

"Kurt, what the heck are you talking about?" She wanted to go to bed, not start an argument that might wake the whole sleeping house.

"Why are you scared of letting me in?"

"Scared of—for Pete's sake. Just because I wouldn't go out—"

"You don't even know what you're doing, do you? I saw it in the hospital. One minute you're warm and bright and keeping everybody smiling. The next, someone touches you as a person and not the Salvation Army, and you pull back. What's with you?"

"Kurt, you're more tired and upset about Katie than I am. Go home and go to bed."

"Just think about this, will you? Are you leaning on God, or using

Him as a shield to keep the rest of the world away? Is your music a ministry, or an excuse?"

For five long, aching heartbeats, they simply stared at each other. Then Kurt jammed his hands into his pockets, turned on one heel and stomped down the path to his car. Dani leaned back against the wall, one hand on the doorknob, and watched him. Something inside her begged to run after him, pound on the hood of his car and make him stay until they got this whole stupid, incomprehensible problem ironed out. Part of her wanted to punch him in the mouth for suggesting such a thing. Another part of her whimpered and curled up tighter in the darkness.

Dani wasn't at all surprised when she dreamed of her parents' deaths when sleep finally, reluctantly came.

Wednesday, April 23

A little past midnight, Dani woke and scooted down in her bed so she could see out the low window that let her look down on the side yard between the Gibson house and the barn that served as Firesong's studio. Light seeped between the old boards. Andy's truck sat inside the pool of floodlight between the barn and house. That hadn't been there when she got home two hours ago and argued with Kurt.

She lay still several long moments, listening to the quiet of the night. A faint whisper of keyboard music came through the chill air and the closed window. Andy dealt with his heartache and questions with music. He had taught her that trick.

Dani got up, wrapped a blanket around herself, and slid her feet into her sneakers. She grabbed the notebook that always sat open on her desk, with sticky notes all over it and filled with notes in pen and pencil.

When she stepped into the barn a few minutes later, the music had stopped. Andy leaned over the keyboard, both elbows resting on the surface just clear of the keys. From the few chords Dani had heard, he had been working on the song everyone simply called "the wedding song." It had no title yet. Andy had been working on it ever since Dani could remember. He had the basic melody notated back when he first suggested Dani help him write words for his music. The song had been there without a name all these years, and Andy had started working in earnest on it after he proposed to Katie, to play for her at the wedding.

The irony of the connection between their parents' deaths and Katie's illness nearly choked Dani. She paused in the doorway, waiting until she could be sure she wouldn't burst into tears. Andy needed her. She had to be strong for him, and for Katie.

She watched her brother until he sat back and ran his fingers up the keyboard in a muted glissando.

"I wondered why I kept it in a minor key," he said after a momentary glance at her. He didn't seem surprised to find her there. "Maybe I sensed something was wrong. Maybe my subconscious knew and was trying to tell me something."

"It's still good." She hitched the blanket a little higher up around her shoulders and crossed the packed dirt and canvas floor, stepping over power cables.

"What are you doing out of bed? You've got a test tomorrow, don't you?"

"Yeah, but it's so quiet tonight, I can hear you playing even with the amp turned down."

"Sorry."

"No, it's good. It reminded me." She held out her notebook. It was blue. She always used blue notebooks to record song ideas.

Andy looked over the scribbled words for a few seconds. He glanced up and met her eyes. Dani held perfectly still, leaving the decision up to him. She wanted to help, wanted to do something to release the pressure they were all feeling. She hated feeling helpless and useless. She had found solace in the music others wrote. Maybe she could offer some help and encouragement to them all, even herself, with her own words.

Andy set the open notebook on the music rack on the keyboard and kept studying it. His fingers moved a scant fraction of an inch above the keys, as if playing the music to match the cadence of the words.

"New poem?" he asked.

"Not really. I've been working on it for years. Put it away, take it out again, nothing ever felt right. They have to go with the tune, you know?"

"Yeah, I know. I'm coming to realize this isn't the wedding song I intended to give Katie. This melody needs words. It's a thinking song, not a feeling song."

He resumed playing, speaking the lyrics, stumbling as he fit the words with the notes.

"How do I know when God is speaking? Has He ever spoken—just to me? Have I ever truly listened? Do I know how? Do hopes and fears—scream to close my ears—to Him? Or does my voice, my pride and selfish choice, drown Him out?"

"That's just the chorus," Dani murmured when he came to the end of the page. "I'm still working on the verses."

"Needs some tightening."

"But?"

"It's sure coming at the right time. God's speaking through you."

"You think? What if all this is a punishment?" slipped out before she could think to stop herself.

"Was our parents' deaths a punishment? If so, for who?" He waited. Dani could only stare at him and wish she could take back those words. He shook his head and seemed to wilt. "It's late and we're both stressed."

"Andy—"

"It's okay. I've been skirting around the edges of that one myself. I guess it needed to be said. Better you than me, maybe."

"Sometimes I wish we were little kids again, and we could talk Mom and Dad into not going on that mission trip."

"Me, too. But there's still no better way to go than serving God. I'll always believe that—and you better believe that too, little sister."

"I'm not that little."

"I know..." He yanked her down on the piano bench next to him and hugged her one-armed. "Mom and Dad would be really proud of you, Dani. I know they would."

"Oh, yeah, we raised each other pretty good."

"Hey, I raised you, not the other way around."

"Don't say that too loudly." She thumped his shoulder. "You don't want the blame for the way I turned out, do you?"

"You bet." Andy sighed and hugged her close, then released her. Dani stayed on the bench next to him. She wished she knew how to get her mind off that evening's revelations for a while. Maybe the only way to get past it was to get it out in the open?

"Love hurts too much—" she began.

"Hey, don't get that way."

"But we can't survive without it, can we?" She rubbed at her eyes and tried to smile. "I guess pain is how we know we're still alive."

"There's more to life than pain, dummy." Andy wrapped his arm around her again and shook her. "Falling in love is worth it. I'm going to marry Katie and do my best to make her happy, no matter what all those tests say. Someday, you'll know how I feel and it'll be great—even when you're miserable."

"No way. Not ever. This is where God has called me. Music, not marriage." Dani winced as an odd little pain went through her, as if she had irrevocably shut a door with her foot caught in it.

"You can mix ministry and marriage. Look at Pastor Glenn and Rita, for one thing."

"It's different for guys. What if you have kids? Katie can stay home with them, but I can't if I had kids."

"Take them with you."

"It's not that easy."

"Well... if you're called to be single, that's fine."

Dani groaned, hearing that note in his voice she had hated all her life. It meant he tried to give her the benefit of the doubt, but he thought she was being particularly stupid.

"What if God has different plans for you?" her brother offered after a few moments of silence.

"Considering, I've never had a date in my entire life? I don't think so."

"You're twenty. It's a little early to call yourself an old maid." He snorted. "Not if Kurt has anything to do with it."

"What?" She thought back to those hard words exchanged only a few hours ago.

"Oh, he was real apologetic," Andy continued with a lopsided grin. "Asking me about you when he really came over to give me some support. I gave him a few tips on catching your interest."

"Andy!" Her normal reaction would be to punch him, but she hesitated. Yet she and Katie *had* agreed they would live as if they had years, and not ruin the time they had with doom and gloom and regrets.

Dani hauled back with her notebook and slapped him hard across the chest, with a resounding whack. Andy yelped and toppled backward off the piano bench.

"Kurt should buy you a tranquilizer instead of flowers. Why he's interested in you, I have no idea."

"Neither do I." Dani slapped her notebook down on top of the piano. "I can't have both, Andy. Right now, music is more important than anything else."

"Better make sure God actually wants that kind of a sacrifice before you make it."

"It's not a sacrifice. I know what's more important. Right now, that means getting a decent night's sleep for my test tomorrow. G'night."

"Night," Andy murmured. He made no move to get up off the barn floor. When Dani was halfway to the house, through the crickets chirping and the soft rustling of leaves in the night breeze, she heard him singing her lyrics, softly, but with more confidence.

Monday, April 28

"So, things are on target?" Kurt asked, cradling his phone as he adjusted his position. He stifled a groan as he stretched out on his couch, toed off his shoes and reached for the ginger ale he had put down when the phone first rang.

"Looks good from this end. You're the one who always catches the mistakes before anyone else sees them coming," Ned Vandewitt said with a chuckle. "If you think things look good, that means they are. You won't have to make any trips up here to report on problems solved."

"And that's a good thing because?" Kurt prompted, hearing an odd catch in his supervisor's voice.

"Seven letters, on the prowl, whimpering to all her friends that her fiancé is too burdened with his duties to take time for her."

"Belinda." He swallowed a heartfelt sigh that might just turn into some foul language he hadn't indulged in since his rebellious, backsliding days in college. "Wait a minute — fiancé?"

"Well, to give her credit, the word has never left her lips. But that doesn't mean other people aren't saying it. She isn't flashing a diamond ring, but people assume you're making big plans."

"*She's* making plans. I'm on the road and on the run, remember? And it isn't that I *can't* take the time — I refuse to *make* the time. For the love of — Ned, I respect you as a man of God and an asset to the team, but that niece of yours doesn't take after your side of the family at all!"

"Yeah. Sorry about that," Ned said with a chuckle that sounded forced through the angry pounding in Kurt's ears. "Just thought I should warn you. And congratulate you that things are working out so you don't have to come anywhere near her."

"Lucky me."

"Something else bothering you, son? Your last e-mail said something about some family concerns, but you didn't want to elaborate until you had more information."

"That's the problem. No more information." Kurt slid down further on the couch. His tension ratcheted up again as his mind switched back to worrying about Katie.

A week now of tests and still nothing positive. An MRI showed a shadow in her brain, but another scan denied it, and a third test gave different information. Katie had roses in her cheeks, full steam ahead with wedding preparations — and an hour later collapsed, whiter than paper and shaking, nearly blind from nausea and pain.

Slowly, the words scraping at his lips, Kurt told his supervisor and friend what had happened. Tears pressed hot and hard at his eyes as he finished, and he sat up to keep them from overflowing into his ears.

"We have a neurosurgeon or two and a few other specialists among the board of directors," Ned offered after a few moments of silence. "Just give me the go-ahead, and I can send out a call for help. Katie'll be in the best hands in a day or two. We'll use the team's private jet to fly her anywhere."

"Hey, thanks, but this is Cleveland Clinic territory. If her doctors think they're in over their heads, they'll send Katie there. I trust them." Kurt swallowed hard and nodded for emphasis. He had to trust these doctors to save his cousin's life.

He had to trust God, too. Did he? Or had he been taking everything on his shoulders, just as he had accused Dani of doing last week?

"Between the prayer warriors here at church and Dani—" Kurt choked. "Well, whatever's dragging Katie down doesn't stand a ghost of a chance."

"Who's Dani?"

"Katie's best friend. Her fiancé's sister."

Ned offered a chuckle that sounded a little more convincing. "Does she have anything to do with your lashing out at Belinda?"

"I didn't—"

"Kurt, usually you just groan and roll your eyes when Belinda's up to her tricks. You just about blew a gasket when I told you what she's done. That's not like you." He took a deep breath, and Kurt could almost see the man grinning. "Unless you have another lady on your mind."

"I wish. Can't even get her to go out for pizza." He swung his legs off the couch and sat back against the cushions. "Ned, how come the whole idea of settling down with someone makes me want to head for the hills, until I get home to Tabor and see a girl who was just a background pest all my life? Is it just Belinda who makes me run from the idea of marriage?"

"Or did you finally find the girl who makes you want to settle down?" his friend offered.

"Settling's the last thing on her mind." Kurt went on to explain about Firesong and what Katie had said about Dani being dedicated to ministry over marriage.

"Are they any good?" Ned wanted to know.

"Hot and getting hotter. They're years away from their peak and the long slide down."

"Are they genuine? They aren't using the less-crowded arena of Christian music to make their mark, and then switch over when the secular world is ready to notice them?"

"Suggest that, and they'll beat you senseless with their Bibles," Kurt said with a chuckle that surprised him.

"The whole band? Or just your lady love?"

"She's not mine by a long shot." His slowly rising mood dropped again. "Ned, how do you know when you've met the one? How do you know she's a gift from God and not a trap set by Satan?"

"By their fruit you shall know them. Let go and let God." Ned chuckled. "Sorry about that. You want solid advice and I'm offering up clichés and platitudes."

"They don't become clichés unless they're true."

"Point." The older man sighed. "I wish I could help you, Kurt. Other than pray. Sometimes, that doesn't seem like very much, does it?"

"Not right now. But if you could send up a wall of protection for the next couple weeks... The wedding is Saturday. I'd be glad if Katie and Andy could have some purely good memories, you know?"

"You got it. And we'll be praying about your other problems, too. Maybe your concern about Dani will cancel out Belinda."

"Or send her into hysterics and shred my reputation at headquarters for being a Casanova." Somehow, Kurt could smile at that mental image.

Saturday, May 3

Gold candles lit the church from baptismal to podium, in stands down all four aisles, and across the narthex. Lilies and pale pink and gold roses filled the vases dotting the platform. Lilies and roses decorated the ends of the front four pews in the center and on both sides.

Jeannette Marshall walked down the aisle, followed by Stephanie, followed by Jeanette's son, BJ. The bridesmaids wore pale green knee-length dresses, their hair studded with baby's breath. BJ, the ringbearer, wore a tiny dark green tuxedo.

From the front side door, Pastor Glenn led Tom, Jim and Jason to the front of the aisle where a long, white runner crinkled under the bridesmaids' steps. Andy came in, nearly tripping as he climbed to the top of the platform to wait in front of the podium. He stared at the door leading into the narthex, where Dani peeked around the corner, watching the progress of the other two bridesmaids. Brother and sister exchanged nervous grins. Dani's heart fluttered at her brother's mixed nerves and joy.

She hoped she was the only one who could see the slight darkness in Andy's glow today and the way he hunched his shoulders in the black tailcoat. She knew where the darkness came from; the same bitterness that clutched at her sometimes. Bitterness at the uncertainty and doom that hung over Katie's tests. Every time the doctors thought they had a diagnosis, which could mean a treatment, something appeared that threw their calculations out of whack. Dani was almost relieved when the wedding put a halt to the tests. Let Andy and Katie have some happiness while they could take it, was her reasoning.

"All set?" Bruce Coleman, the church's sound technician whispered as he stepped up to Dani and gave a final tug to the wireless microphone she wore in a headset. She rolled her eyes and grinned and hoped the microphone wouldn't pick up her thudding heart.

"You better do a good job," Katie muttered in the hallway behind her. That prompted a snort of laughter from Dani. She nodded and Bruce gave the signal to his partner in the sound booth in the balcony.

So that every member of Firesong could participate in the wedding, and to reduce the fuss of instruments cluttering the platform, they had recorded the background music. Only Dani and Andy would perform today. Dani concentrated on matching her footsteps to the beat as the opening strains of Pat Terry's *That's the Way* filtered through the sanctuary.

As they had practiced, she came through the archway between narthex and sanctuary as she sang the first line. All her nerves vanished as she slid into the well-rehearsed music. As long as Dani told herself this was just another performance and not the wedding for her brother and her best friend, she would do just fine.

Andy took up the second verse, letting her catch her breath. Walking and singing somehow took more out of her than all the jumping around she did during a concert. Dani smiled, trying not to laugh as she realized that strange, illogical truth.

She looked up and straight into Kurt's eyes. He sat in the second pew, right behind Katie's parents.

He smiled as he looked her up and down, and up and down again. His eyes widened and his lips parted a little and then his expression grew totally unreadable. Dani lost her pace for a moment as her heart skipped a few beats and she couldn't seem to look away. Kurt turned to follow her with his gaze as she passed the pew.

Dani swallowed hard, relieved to be torn free of his imprisoning, electrifying gaze. And nearly missed her cue to start singing again. Worse, she had to turn and climb the steps to the top of the platform to sing with Andy — and that meant looking at Kurt again.

She focused on the rest of the guests as she poured her heart into the song. On the last refrain, Katie rustled into the narthex, leaning on her father's arm.

The bride glowed, surrounded in a mist of gauzy white and lit from behind by the first rays of afternoon sunshine slipping through the back windows. It was hard to believe Katie was sick, with her pink cheeks and sweet smile and the glow in her eyes. Still, the signs had been there, visible when Dani had helped her get dressed. The wedding dress that had fit perfectly a month ago now had an extra inch of room in it.

Please, God, I'll give up everything and spend the rest of my life on the road, singing, if You'll just let them stay together until they're both old and gray. Please?

Andy missed a note. Dani let go of her bouquet of roses and trailing ivy with one hand and gripped his hand. His palm was sweaty and he squeezed her hand hard enough to hurt, but they got through the last few lines of the song without either one faltering. As the last recorded note died away, Mrs. Ogden slammed the organ into a triumphant, blaring rendition of the *Wedding March*.

~~~~~

The bridesmaids laughed about the glitch in the song while they sat at a corner table, barefoot, during the reception at a party center in
~~~~~

Stoughton. Hannah Blake sat with them, keeping little BJ busy with paper animals she folded for him out of napkins, giving Jeannette a breather. Claire wandered over to join them, having done her duty attending the guest book.

Kurt proposed the first toast after Tom did his duty as best man. Dani busied herself picking up crumbs off the table with a damp fingertip, to keep from looking at him. Her face burned when he spoke of "others following in your footsteps of love and devotion."

Please, oh, please, don't let him be looking at me.

Dani wondered if she would have felt so uncomfortable if Kurt had taken her out for pizza or a movie at least once. She had been too busy the last two weeks to think of anything but schoolwork, wedding plans and rehearsals. It was a legitimate excuse, but she also knew she could have pushed everything aside for an hour or two and not fallen behind.

If Kurt had asked her.

He hadn't avoided her the last dozen times they met up, but he hadn't made any effort to talk to her, either. Dani supposed she should have done or said something. He probably felt awkward after their heated discussion. It couldn't be called a fight, could it? Maybe that was why she felt so uncomfortable. She knew most of the trouble was her fault.

Why couldn't things just go back to normal?

Why did Kurt have to be so nice? Why did he have to be so persistent? Why did he have to be Katie's cousin, and in town until the end of the summer? Why did he have to be so heavily involved in the music industry, which meant Firesong would meet up with him on the road occasionally?

"Oh, no," Claire moaned. "They talked Tommy into doing some comedy after all."

Chapter Ten

Dani smothered a chuckle as she turned to see Kurt and the three groomsmen deposit Tommy's wheelchair on top of the short platform in front of the table where Andy and Katie sat with the Greens and Aunt Betty and Uncle George. Tommy clutched the microphone and wore a particularly evil grin. He had taken off his nice, sedate, dark blue sport coat to reveal a baby blue tuxedo t-shirt underneath it, with rippling muscles bulging out from the short sleeves.

"Hi, folks, I've been asked to speak a few words of encouragement to the happy couple." Tommy paused, waiting for the audience to quiet down. "But doggone it, I can't think of a single thing to say. Why me? I'm not married. And if I ever do get married, somebody please check for a lobotomy scar!" he added, a note of desperation making his voice squeak.

"I keep checking, believe me," Claire muttered, just loudly enough for those at her table to hear.

"Now honestly, folks, asking me to have some sort of inside knowledge on marriage, well, why not go all the way? Why not ask me to be a track coach?" He waited, face exasperated but eyes sparkling with laughter, while the audience held its breath a moment, collectively stared at the wheelchair he sat in, then visibly caught the joke. Laughter bounced off the ceiling. "I mean, I tried it. I went out for hurdles." Tommy shook his head as giggles and snorts bounced around the room and people muttered comments to each other. "I just couldn't do it. I kept crashing and burning — the ramps just weren't long enough!"

Dani settled back, letting herself relax and enjoy the afternoon. Claire's brother always gave a clean joke that made people stop and think and re-examine how they saw the world. Most of his material did come from the waist-level perspective of someone caught in a wheelchair.

Andy and Katie smiled and laughed and leaned closer together. He had his arm tight around her back, she rested her head against his shoulder, and they looked at each other more often than at Tommy or their guests. Dani watched her brother and best friend so happy together and suspected that slightly bitter taste in her mouth was jealousy. She mentally slapped herself. Who was she to be jealous, on this day of all days? Andy and Katie belonged together. They needed each other.

She had committed herself to her music ministry, hadn't she? Purity in all thoughts and actions and words; purity in her emotions, too. Dani clenched her fists and resolved not to feel jealous. Envy, if not a sin, would pollute the joy she did have.

Maybe it had already done some damage, because in those dead tired moments before sleep claimed her, she found herself wondering what life would be like if she gave up Firesong. If she stayed home and worked a nine-to-five job and finished her college degree in four years instead of ten. In the morning, Dani always felt sick over even considering giving up the ministry that had called her since middle school. This was where God had placed her. Wasn't it?

Besides, Dani admitted, if Kurt hadn't asked her out since coming back from Indiana, what kind of relationship would they ever have? Neither of them, obviously, valued it enough to put in any effort.

After Tommy finished his routine, amid waves of laughter, the music resumed and couples moved out onto the floor to try a few waltzes and slow dances. Dani sighed. It would be nice to dance, she admitted, but she didn't know how. She had hated square dancing in elementary school gym class, because back then boys were icky. Ever since then, she had been too busy. Besides, why need to know how to dance when she never went anywhere, never did anything, never dated?

Tom came over and claimed his wife, promising her she was safe, because how could anyone, even the inexperienced, mess up a slow waltz? Stephanie laughed and let him lead her away, in her stocking feet. Xander came over to claim Hannah, saying they had to practice for their own wedding, if she would ever set a date. To which she retorted that he hadn't put a ring on her finger yet, and he still had two months to go on their agreement. Dani didn't think she wanted to know what agreement they were talking about, but it was nice to know Xander and Hannah were thinking marriage. Two people who looked as in love as they did had to eventually get married, didn't they? Jeannette and Claire took BJ out with them and made a trio, spinning slowly around in a corner, out of everyone's way. The little boy laughed, black curly head tilted back, mouth wide in a bright grin.

BJ put an aching hunger inside Dani's heart, sometimes. Jeannette had been widowed just after she found out she was pregnant. The thought of having a little boy like BJ made Dani wish she could have it all. She would never have children, because the life of a musician meant too much time away from home. Jeannette's estrangement from her vicious in-laws had long ago prompted Dani to vow she would never marry unless the man was an orphan.

Or he had really great relatives. Like Kurt did.

Stop that! she scolded herself.

"So this is where you've been hiding," Kurt said from behind her.

Dani glanced up at him, then around the table. Her face burned when she realized how stupid that was. She was alone.

"Don't give me that innocent look. Don't you know it's tradition for the bride's cousin to dance with the maid of honor?" He held out his hand. Dani shrank back in her chair, making it creak.

"I can't dance—I never learned how—I'm clumsy."

"I've seen you on stage, Dani. You're not clumsy," he said, his voice thickening with a warmth that made her face hotter.

Dani was very glad there was no one else there to hear that particular note in his voice or see her reaction. For several seconds, she could only stare into his warm, deep eyes. She had to clutch at the seat of her chair to fight a momentary sensation of falling. Falling into his eyes?

That idea created an oddly compelling, yet ridiculous image in her mind. Smiling, she shook her head.

"Come on." Kurt grinned. "I mean, you've never fallen off, right? Let me teach you. Just one song." He moved closer, his hand only inches from her face, and Dani knew he wasn't going to leave.

"How would it look—"

"I already talked to Pastor Glenn. Special dispensation. Once a year deal." He gestured across the room to the table where Pastor Glenn and Rita sat chatting with Stephanie's parents. Pastor Glenn looked over at them at that precise moment. He waved to her, and winked.

"But—"

"We'll go outside, okay? We can still hear the music with the windows open, but nobody'll see you."

"It's raining." She smiled as she said it, somehow knowing Kurt wouldn't let something like rain stop him.

"I happen to know there's one humongous porch out there, with plenty of room and no witnesses. Now, are you coming or do I throw you over my shoulder and carry you outside, kicking and screaming?"

"Cave man," Dani muttered. She leaped to her feet, then snatched up her discarded slippers when Kurt reached for her hand. He muttered under his breath, but the scowl he wore as he herded her toward the door couldn't hide the sparkle in his eyes.

The chairs on the porch were all pushed up against the wall and stacked, leaving plenty of room on the redwood-stained boards. Dani sighed and looked around and considered for several seconds the damage to her bridesmaid dress if she made a dash through the raindrops to the front door, around the other side of the building. She grinned and shook her head, and knew Kurt wouldn't give up that easily.

Besides, she really did want to know what it would be like to dance with someone, period. The fact that it was Kurt Green didn't have anything to do with it. She hoped.

"When I stomp all over your feet, don't say I didn't warn you," she said, when he took hold of both her hands and backed her into the cleared center of the porch.

In response, the rain drummed harder on the roof. They could barely hear the music coming through the open windows in the reception hall.

"I've seen you on stage, Dani. You can dance just fine." That note of rough warmth returned to his voice.

"You've seen—you've really watched me?" The dropping sensation in her stomach was pleasant, yet terrifying.

Kurt just smiled a little wider and nodded. He adjusted his hands, holding hers so their fingers were interlaced. She flinched a little when an electric sensation ran up her spine at the innocent yet intimate touch.

They danced that way, slowly turning around the porch floor, with six inches of empty air between their bodies. Dani found it hard to find some place to focus her eyes. Kurt's chin and lips were on the level with her eyes and looking at that soft, satisfied, slightly smirking smile made her sway between laughter and discomfort. She knew his lips would be warm and soft—but there was no way she would ever let him kiss her.

Would Kurt want to?

No. We haven't even gone on a date yet.

Not that she had ever let him take her out.

This is a test, right, Lord?

Dani focused her gaze on Kurt's shoulder, just the right height to rest her head. But when would she ever get a chance?

Stop it! she scolded herself. She flinched back a little, and Kurt let her move away without letting go of her hands. That made it easier to look into his eyes. The laughter had faded, though he still smiled. That warmth, that glow she had seen during her walk down the aisle, filled his gaze now, and her knees went wobbly.

The funny thing was, she liked it.

~~~~~

Andy and Katie slipped out of the reception hall, grateful when their many guests pretended not to notice their brief escape. They sighed in unison as a cool breeze from the open door washed over them. Laughing, Andy drew his wife into his arms and held her close. They swayed together for a few seconds.

"This is kind of nice," he whispered. "Think you could get used to it?"

She didn't answer right away.

"Katie—"

"Look." Katie stepped back. She smiled, and that stilled the sudden chill that washed through Andy all too often lately. He turned to see where she pointed.

A wide plate glass window filled the wall behind them, floor to ceiling, giving a glorious view of the rolling lawns behind the party center.
~~~~~

The view also showed them the porch.

Dani and Kurt swayed slowly in a small circle in the shadows of the porch. They looked into each other's eyes. Kurt smiled, but Andy thought his sister definitely looked stunned.

"I think she likes it, though," he whispered after a moment.

"Oh, I hope so," Katie said with a chuckle. "The way that cousin of mine keeps trying not to ask about her, but asks about her, you'd think he came into town to see her and not put together a crusade."

"That bad, huh?" Andy drew her up against his side. Kurt Green was all right in his book. There weren't many men he considered good enough for his little sister, but Kurt was one of them. "From the looks of things, I think Dani finally figured out what guys are for, besides moving equipment."

"Is that relief I hear?"

Andy just grinned and answered his bride with a long, sweet kiss.

~~~~~

When it came time for Katie to throw the bouquet, Dani preferred not to get up with the other single girls. She knew better than to try that, though. Her pale green bridesmaid dress was impossible to miss. She let Stephanie drag her from their table and walked up front with an equally reluctant Claire.

"Hold it, folks!" Andy called, as Katie climbed up on a chair to get some height for the toss. "We've received a judgment from higher authorities, and we're allowed to use a little help with this ancient custom."

Groans rang through the reception hall, followed by laughter and whispered comments. Dani groaned, too, as she saw Tom and Jason stroll back into the hall with a four-foot-long rectangular mirror.

"Isn't that the mirror from the girl's bathroom at church?" Claire asked, her voice starting to crack.

"I wouldn't put it past them." Dani considered protesting, but the last thing she wanted was to draw attention to herself.

Amid laughter and comments from the guests, Tom and Jason adjusted the mirror so Katie could see the nearly three dozen single girls standing behind her. She winked and wiggled her fingers in Dani's general direction.

"I don't care if she is my sister now, she's going to pay for this," Dani muttered, earning laughter from Claire.

As soon as Katie raised her arm to toss the bouquet over her shoulder, Dani darted to the right, aiming herself out of the path of the flowers.

The bouquet hit her in the face.

Despite herself, Dani grappled for the bouquet. Later, she claimed she had been worried about saving it for Katie's memory box. At the
~~~~~

moment, the only thing she was conscious of was clutching the bouquet against her chest and looking up to see Kurt watching her with that slow, secret, warm smile lighting his face.

Then her watch buzzed and she nearly laughed aloud. Time to start Andy and Katie's escape. Dani, as maid of honor, had to get things rolling. Timing was important, or the newlyweds would miss the plane to their honeymoon in Hilton Head.

"How far are we behind schedule?" Katie gasped fifteen minutes later, as she raced into the women's lounge with Dani right behind her.

"Four minutes, twenty seconds."

Dani didn't even look at her watch. Her glib tone earned a scowl from her new sister-in-law. She just smirked and guided Katie around the modesty wall so anyone entering wouldn't treat the people in the hallway to a view of the bride disrobing.

"Did you have fun?" Katie asked after Dani helped her step out of her dress. She spread her arms and turned slowly in the cool air. Dani imagined how good it felt to be free of that dress, almost weightless, feeling perspiration evaporating.

"Oh, sure, I love spending the afternoon in a crowded party room, wearing the fanciest dress I hope I ever own." Dani slid the dress onto its hangar and hung it on a stall door. She hunted around for the plastic storage bag she had stashed in there before the reception started.

"I meant, dancing with Kurt."

"You saw us?" She crumpled the bag, nearly popping it.

"Oh, just for a little bit. How did he talk you into it? I was sure you'd say no."

"I tried."

"That cousin of mine is *very* interested in you." Katie sat down on the couch against the far wall and sighed. "Oh, if I could just sit for the rest of the day, that would be heaven."

"As long as Andy was right next to you?" She knelt and yanked Katie's slippers off her feet.

"Of course." The new bride smirked, eyes sparkling, and scooted forward on the couch so she could slide out of her stockings. "What do you think of Kurt?"

"He's a nice guy, I suppose."

"You suppose? I think you two are perfect for each other."

"That's because you have marriage on the brain right now." Dani yanked the stockings out of Katie's grasp and stuffed them into the gym bag that had contained the getaway clothes.

"I just want you to be as happy as I am."

"Are you?" She caught hold of her hands, making Katie look her in the eye.

"Deliriously."

"Are you really happy? Because if my brother doesn't take good care of you—"

"We'll take care of each other. That's the way it's supposed to be. And I bet Kurt would like to take care of you, too. He's never looked at anyone the way he's been looking at you."

"No." Dani shivered, which was odd because she was still perspiring inside her fancy dress. She bent over and picked up Katie's sweatshirt and tossed it to her. "We're seven minutes behind schedule now. Get moving."

"What's wrong with Kurt?"

"It's not Kurt. It's me. I made this vow..." For the first time, her pledge of purity seemed like a wall instead of a shield. Dani pushed that feeling away. She would only make herself miserable wishing for something she knew was wrong for her. She had chosen the path she knew absolutely God wanted her to take.

"I know you joke about starting an order of Protestant nuns, but honestly, Dani, you and Kurt would be great for each other. What's wrong with encouraging him?"

"I have to be careful. There's a lot of temptation, out on the road, singing. A lot of opportunities for something innocent to turn into something really wrong."

"Kurt is not—" Katie paused as she tugged her sweatshirt down over her head, catching it on the roses and baby's breath in her hair. Dani helped yank the collar free, then got to work loosening the decorations she should have removed first. "He'd never hurt you."

"I know, but we both know how easy it is for people to get the wrong idea. I made this vow that as long as I was on the road, I wouldn't date, wouldn't let myself be alone with a guy who wasn't a relative. I've dedicated myself to a totally pure lifestyle. I have to, if my ministry is going to have any effect. You know what I mean?"

Katie slowly nodded as she scanned Dani's face. She stayed silent as she changed into her getaway clothes: sweatshirt, jeans, cowboy boots and baseball cap.

"You think that's the right thing to do?" she asked, as Dani finished cleaning up the debris from the hasty costume change.

"I've prayed about it, and I know this is what God wants."

"Then why are you miserable?"

Dani's mouth dropped open. She started to deny the idea, then something caught in her chest. She thought of the hypnotic, warm brightness in Kurt's eyes, the electric jolt of his fingers laced through hers, his palms pressing warm against hers.

"I'm not. I'm just tired. And a little teary. I mean, it's not every day my best friend and my favorite brother get married."

"You're sure?" Katie stood.

"Positive." Dani opened the door just wide enough to look out. She nearly yelped when she saw Kurt leaning against the wall opposite the bathroom door.

"Coast is clear," he said in a stage whisper. "Better hurry before the guests start looking for them."

Dani wondered who had the bright idea to bring Kurt into the plot without telling her. Nodding, she yanked the door open.

"I think you're afraid to let yourself be happy," Katie whispered as she hurried past her and out into the hall.

Kurt gave her a nod and a thumbs-up. Dani leaned out into the hall as Katie scurried away. Andy appeared just before she reached the corner. He wrapped an arm around her waist and they vanished around the corner.

Monday, May 12

Dani never knew there were so many professional recording studios in the Cleveland area until Firesong started researching how to put together their CD. Danziger still had no contract with a Christian label, and Dani suspected he had given up on that market as "narrow" and "limiting." He used those words frequently since they had refused the new contract. If they wanted to record the CD they had been promising their growing fan base, they would have to do it themselves. Danziger did arrange for a loan for them. Tom and Andy looked over the contract and did the calculations and seemed happy with it. Firesong would be responsible for the lion's share of the marketing, but that suited Dani. She knew just how fast their homemade CDs sold after each concert. In the last year, they had been packing more each time and always came home with at least two dozen orders taken after they ran out.

Since Danziger no longer went beyond the requirements of their current contract, as he had done before, all the legwork and arrangements fell to Firesong. When Andy and Katie came back from their honeymoon, tanned, relaxed and glowing, they recommended turning to Kurt for advice and introductions to the right people. Dani was so relieved to see them looking happy and healthy, she didn't protest.

Thursday, May 15

Kurt scrambled through a mountain of paperwork on his tiny dining room table, trying to find his notebook. He had exactly five minutes to get out the door, down three floors to meet up with Andy and Katie at their apartment, then get in the car and swing by the Gibson farm to pick up Dani, before heading downtown to meet the rest of Firesong for the first of several appointments lined up today with possible recording studios. Part of him was aghast at having agreed to take on this huge project. He knew from experience, putting together a recording took more time and effort and headaches than he could spare right now, as the date for the crusade drew closer. But Firesong was *family*. And he admitted only in the deepest, darkest recesses of his thoughts that this was a chance to spend more time with Dani.

The doorbell rang, prompting a groan just as his fingers closed over his leather-bound notebook. Kurt yanked it free, sending four folders sliding to the dull brown carpeting. He stomped to the door and tried to rake his shower-damp hair into place. Less than three minutes left.

"Kurt!" Belinda Kain giggled like a child delighted with her newest trick. "Aren't you happy to see me, sweetheart?" As always, she was color-coordinated and groomed as if she expected to be on camera. Today she was a vision in blue, making the ebony of her hair darker by contrast.

"Stunned." Kurt glanced over his shoulder, into his chaotic apartment, his mind racing through his options. The last time he had let Belinda stay alone in his apartment, she had totally rearranged it, hinting how much she wanted to rearrange his life. He couldn't find vital papers, books and music for nearly a week without her help. He was positive she had hidden things specifically to force him to call her.

He wasn't going to leave her here half the day. Belinda might find that folder with the lists and diagrams he had made, trying to decide if he should pursue making Dani Paul a part of his life. He hadn't written Dani's name anywhere, so Belinda might think all his scribbles and doodles and prayer requests dealt with deciding on his relationship with *her*, rather than Dani. She might call home with the "good news."

Then again, there was no time like the present for shocking her into some common sense and removing her hooks, permanently.

"How did you get here? Where are you staying?" He sent up a silent shout of thanksgiving that she didn't have any luggage sitting next to her in the hallway. He wouldn't put it past Belinda to try to shame him, even maneuver him into a compromising situation, to force him to marry her.

"The Marriott. Near the airport," she added with a careless shrug. "You wouldn't believe how hard it is to find a taxi that knows how to get out here."

"I can believe it." He wondered if he had used up his quota of answered prayers for the week. What were his chances the taxi was still downstairs if he hurried? His mental clock shrieked that he had two minutes, twenty seconds left. "Look, I'm on my way out."

"Important meeting?" she cooed, with as much pride as if she had arranged the meeting herself.

"Very. And I wasn't expecting you. I can't just rearrange my schedule to suit you, so—"

"Well, then, I'll just come with you. Where are we going?" She hooked her arm through his.

"I'm helping some friends start arrangements to record their next CD. If you had bothered calling and telling me you wanted to come for a visit, I would have told you I don't have time to spend entertaining you. I'll take you back to your hotel."

"No." She stomped her foot and took a firmer hold on his arm. "I came here to talk with you, Kurt Green. We're going to get some things straightened out in our relationship if it's the last thing we ever do."

"We don't have a relationship. I told you that multiple times."

"That's what we need to talk about. I think this time apart has been good for us, let us both do some clear-headed thinking. Now we need to settle things. Is that too much to ask for?"

Kurt bit his tongue to keep from pointing out that their relationship *was* settled—as in terminated, dead, and buried. He was glad his jobs kept him away from headquarters, so he could avoid Belinda, who refused to accept that anything was settled unless it was settled to her satisfaction.

What would happen if he let Belinda come along on his errands, and made her see just how little time he had for her? Would she finally see that she had no part in his life, and he wanted no part in hers?

Chapter Eleven

"You're going to be bored, and I won't let you get in the way of this meeting," Kurt warned, as he yanked his arm free and stepped back into his apartment to get his jacket and keys.

"Don't worry. I know exactly how to behave at important meetings. I've sat in on a few recording contracts, remember?"

Unfortunately, he did remember. And Belinda did know exactly what was going on. With his luck, Belinda would finagle a better deal for Firesong and charm her way into everyone's hearts, and he would have to be nice to her because he owed her.

I deserve it, if it happens, he scolded himself as they stepped into the elevator. *Just because Belinda's oblivious to anything outside her version of reality doesn't mean she'll mess up everything.*

A moment later, he felt a stab of guilt. Maybe he wasn't as heavy-handed and bull-headed as Belinda, but wasn't he doing the same thing to Dani? Hadn't he decided Dani was the one for him, just like Belinda had set her sights on him? He and Belinda had honestly tried out the idea, had spent time together. He knew it wouldn't work unless they both made changes in their lives. Belinda only wanted to change him.

He was never going to find out if he and Dani would fit for the rest of their lives until they spent more time together. Private time, serious time. Like a flare of light inside his head, Kurt admitted he wouldn't mind changing to have Dani part of his life. Or was that more accurate to say, be part of *her* life?

That had to be a real sign of love. Yet how had he fallen in love when they spent practically no private time together? He admired and respected and wanted to be with the woman he saw working and singing and giving, the woman in the family situations he had shared, his cousin's best friend. Kurt sensed Dani would be the same person in private. He could spend the rest of his life with the woman he had seen in the last month.

Okay, Lord, get me free of Belinda and open Dani's door a little bit today, please?

~~~~~

Dani did not want to ride with Kurt, even if Andy and Katie were going to be there as buffers.

And yet she did want to ride with him — alone.

It drove her crazy, to want to work some things out while at the same
~~~~~

time she wanted to stay away from Kurt Green for the rest of her life. How could she get her head on straight?

Maybe it's meant to be, she mused as she sat on the top step of the porch and drummed her heels on the bottom step and watched the gravel driveway and the haze of morning heat above the fields. Jason and Jim both had to work the early morning shift and they would meet the gang downtown, so she couldn't ride with them. Tom and Stephanie had gone to Kelly's Island yesterday to help her parents with the pre-camping season inspection, before they started cleaning and making repairs. They would come from Sandusky and couldn't backtrack to pick her up. Dani hated driving downtown, and the fares for the bus and Rapid were ridiculous. No, it was better if she rode with Kurt. Even if they weren't alone in the car to clear the air. And if he finally asked her out on a date, most likely with some urging from Katie, she decided she would say yes. Maybe. Depending on how he asked her. If he asked her at all.

Could she handle it, one-on-one in a social setting instead of thrown together as they worked on something? Katie and Andy both seemed to think they were perfect for each other.

Dani grinned as Kurt's familiar, dark green sedan appeared over that rise in the fields that partially shielded the house from the road. She stood, clutched her notebook and stepped back into the house to let Aunt Betty know she was leaving.

When she stepped back outside, Kurt had already turned the car around so the passenger side door lined up with the flagstone walk. With mixed disappointment and relief, she saw the back door hung open. No one was making her sit in the front seat with Kurt.

"Get a move on, shorty!" Andy called, sticking his head out the front passenger window.

Dani's retort that the honeymoon was over died on her lips, as she bent to slide into the back seat. Katie sat in the middle and a stranger sat directly behind Kurt.

"This is Belinda Kain," Katie said when Dani paused. "She just showed up, a surprise visit. Kurt couldn't leave her all alone, could he?" She wore her "I'm only being nice because it's the Christian thing to do" smile.

"Hi," Dani muttered, and pulled the door closed behind herself. Katie slid over a little so their hips bumped. The two friends exchanged glances—Dani's, questioning, and Katie's, resigned.

Belinda was gorgeous, with her glossy, curly black hair and violet eyes—those had to be contacts, right? Who in the world wore make-up at this time of the morning? She just got into town? She didn't look like she had been traveling. She looked like a magazine ad for "country club chic." That simple little blue gingham sundress was disgustingly modest, with its wide straps and high, square neckline and the lace-edged hem falling past her calves. Dani didn't want to know if Belinda wore nylons. She suspected this newcomer wore high-heels and had polish on her toenails.

Then Belinda opened her mouth, and her voice was gorgeous. Rich and flowing, sweet but not verging on being so high only dogs could hear. Dani knew she could have liked the newcomer better if she had at least one flaw.

"Fiancé?" Dani blurted, realizing she hadn't heard a word Belinda said, until *that* word.

"We're not engaged," Kurt said, almost growling, when Belinda started to nod. "I never asked her."

Dani could almost hear him thinking, "and I never will." She felt dizzy with the relief that slammed her.

Belinda pouted, sticking the tip of her tongue out at Kurt. She winked at Katie and Dani, as if Kurt's words were a joke, then changed the subject. Dani barely listened to the story about a singing group where Belinda and Kurt had been the leaders. It cast Kurt in a very good light, but Belinda talked about herself every third sentence.

From her vantage point in the back seat, Dani saw Kurt and Andy exchange discreet looks. Rolling their eyes, frowning, raising an eyebrow. Belinda couldn't see their reactions. Then again, Belinda was lost in her memories, seeing herself and Kurt on stage in all their glory. She couldn't see Kurt's white-knuckle grip on the steering wheel, or the rippling of muscles in his jaw as he clenched and unclenched it. Dani saw it all, and she felt sorry for him, even as that sympathy mixed with amusement.

"So, you really miss that kind of life, don't you?" Dani interjected, when Belinda's story had run down and she paused for more than a breath. "Did the ensemble break up?"

"I have no idea." Belinda shrugged and gave a perfect little smile and harp-like chuckle. "I haven't kept in contact with the others. They all used it as a steppingstone in their careers. I don't miss it at all. It's so draining. Living out of a suitcase, never knowing where you're going to be the next day, never eating right, sleeping in uncomfortable beds. I'm still trying to talk Kurt into taking a better job at headquarters so he can settle down and have a normal life, but his sense of duty is stronger than his common sense, sometimes." She chuckled again and reached over the seat to squeeze Kurt's shoulder.

Dani could see him turn to stone — couldn't Belinda feel it, before she let go? "Headquarters?" she asked.

"Belinda's father and uncle both work for Allen Michaels," Katie offered.

"Oh." Dani mentally filled in the information gaps. Belinda and Kurt had met while singing with the crusade ensemble. Belinda had found some position at headquarters and she expected Kurt to "settle down" one of these days.

As in—marriage? Maybe she had a real reason to expect to be Kurt's fiancé.

From Kurt's silence and the growing thundercloud in his expression, Belinda's visit was both unexpected and unwelcome.

Dani leaned back in the seat and fastened her gaze on the view outside the window as they followed I-71/I-90 into Downtown Cleveland. Amazing how breathless and even a little giddy that realization made her feel. Was that relief? Joy?

Did she feel jealous about Belinda's connection with Kurt?

She mentally shook herself and forced her mind back onto the business at hand: finding the right studio to record the CD. That was the only reason for this trip. If Kurt wanted to clarify things with her, she would be willing and waiting, but he would have to make the first move.

~~~~~

The studios they visited that morning and afternoon were a far cry from the basement studio in a friend's house where they made their first recording. Dani missed the acoustic tiles on the walls and ceiling, the padded floor, the makeshift control booth and the wires strung everywhere with a constant threat of fire. She told herself to be grateful for this step up, to pay attention and learn all she could so the next CD would be less work. This was going to be part of her life.

Belinda, of course, had a dozen amusing little anecdotes to relate about recording sessions, impossible engineers, and all the miracles Kurt had managed to pull from the teeth of disaster.

Dani glimpsed Kurt clenching a fist for control or a muscle twitching in his jaw as he made gentle-voiced corrections. He corrected her constantly, especially references to their future together. Dani wondered if the day was as exhausting for him as it was for her, by the time they had a contract and a date set to get to work.

"Why are we going there?" Belinda asked, as Kurt turned the car into the parking lot of the Marriott.

"You did say this was where you were staying?" Kurt didn't even look in the rearview mirror as he spoke.

"Well, yes—"

"Why should you take another long cab ride back here?"

"But, Kurt, I want to spend the rest of the day with you. Now that your very important business is over." She glanced around the car, offering a little smile. Dani suspected Belinda wanted them to notice what a sweet, unselfish creature she was.

Creature, yes. What kind, I have no idea, Dani mused. She didn't even feel shocked at her catty thoughts. *He's too patient. He should have strangled*
~~~~~

her a long time ago.

"I don't care what you want," Kurt said on a weary sigh.

"Kurt! What will people think about our relationship?"

"Maybe they'll see what you refuse to see—we don't have one. Stop lying to yourself."

"Lying?" Her face flamed.

Dani had to look away to keep from cheering. Finally, Kurt was letting Belinda have it, and she didn't feel a bit of sympathy for her. Dani wished she could record Kurt's voice. She had never heard a razor so clearly in a soft, dog-tired tone before.

"Ned told me something very interesting." Kurt glanced in the rearview mirror once, his gaze flicking from one side of the back seat to the other. Dani flinched when their gazes locked. "Rumors are going around headquarters that we're engaged. He knows it isn't true, and you know it isn't true, but you haven't done a thing to stop them. Have you?"

"Well, Kurt, I thought it was only a matter of time..."

Dani wanted to cheer. Belinda—speechless for the first time all day.

"It's not." He punctuated his statement with a final jerk of the car as it stopped before the hotel entrance. He put it into park, got out, and opened Belinda's door. "If you have any trouble changing your tickets to leave, someone at headquarters can help you much better than I can. I have work to do." He took a deep breath and glanced once over the other occupants of the car.

Dani read an apology in that glance, and something else. Embarrassment. Relief. Anger. Maybe a little pity.

"This is the last time I'm telling you this, Belinda. I want witnesses because you never listened any of the other times I told you. I *like* being on the advance team and traveling. I have no intention of trading in my suitcase for a briefcase."

"But you don't know how happy you could be. How happy we could be," Belinda added, her voice dropping to a whimper.

Andy turned to look out his window, suddenly interested in the architecture of the hotel. Katie rummaged in her purse. Dani held her breath, unsure if she wanted to burst out laughing or if she was angry at both Kurt and Belinda.

It sounded like they had had this discussion before. And Belinda had never listened. Maybe she needed to be embarrassed so it would stick. Dani didn't know who to feel sorry for, and who to be angry with. Belinda for being so oblivious or Kurt for letting her go on so long like this? He must have been miserable.

"*You* might be, but I wouldn't. I'm not in love with you, Belinda. Why should I give up the life God called me to, just to please you?"

"That is the most selfish thing I've ever heard!"

Dani stifled a giggle—Belinda sounded like a fishwife.

"Go away, Belinda." Kurt reached for his car door. "We are not getting married. I am not changing job assignments. When I finally do get married—"

Involuntarily, Dani glanced at Kurt. He was looking straight at her. She felt like her heart had dropped into her shoes and her lungs didn't want to work. Shaking, she glanced out the side window again. Katie reached over and caught hold of her hand.

"When I finally do get married," Kurt finally continued, after what felt like a year of tense silence, "it will mean *both* of us compromising and sacrificing for each other and serving God together."

Belinda turned white and let out a tiny wail. She reached for Kurt as if she would fling herself into his arms and hang there. Kurt put up a hand to block her and glanced at Dani again.

"You!" Belinda shrieked. She lifted a foot as if she would climb back into the car, and her hands curved into claws. Katie yanked the door closed, nearly catching Belinda's hand in it. "You stole him from me! You call yourself a Christian?"

"Do you?" Kurt grabbed her wrist and half-dragged her away from the car, toward the sidewalk.

"She—"

"I was never yours to be stolen." He stepped back, leaving her in front of the hotel entrance. "Go home. Go talk to Uncle Ned. Better idea—sit and *listen* to Uncle Ned for a change." Kurt turned and stomped back to the car.

Belinda stood there, eyes glistening, her mouth opening and closing like a stranded fish. The wailing and screaming Dani expected didn't emerge. How much was theatrics, how much a desire not to break down in public, and how much was just plain shock?

"Sorry about that," Kurt muttered as he slid into the driver's seat and slammed the door.

"She had it coming," Katie said as she moved over into Belinda's side of the seat. "You've grown up a lot, Kurt. Ten years ago, you would have slapped her against the wall, and you wouldn't have been so nice when you told her off."

"Thank God I've grown up. Some." He managed a lopsided smile as he looked into the rearview mirror, right into Dani's eyes.

"She's good at the guilt-trip," Andy said. He slouched down in his seat as the car pulled away from the hotel. Nobody looked back. "She's got to learn guys don't want to be hunted down and snared. Even a wimp wants to feel like he worked hard to get his lady."

"Absolutely," Katie said. "I made Andy chase me until I caught him good and tight."

"Now she tells me!" he wailed and slapped a hand to his forehead with a loud enough smack to make Dani wince.

The resulting laughter helped clear the shards of tension filling the atmosphere.

~~~~~

"Sorry about that," Kurt said when he dropped Dani off, after taking Andy and Katie to her parents' home for dinner. They planned to walk back to their apartment afterwards.

"For what?" She didn't know if he meant making her wait until last or the scene with Belinda. She had been grateful it was only a ten-minute drive from the Greens' house. She hadn't known whether to climb into the front seat or stay in the back, which she had. What message did it send Kurt, and was it the one she wanted to send?

"I shouldn't have been so nasty."

"Katie said she deserved worse." Dani stepped over and leaned against the driver's door. "Thanks for your help today."

"I feel kind of guilty."

"For what?" This time she could smile.

"If I wasn't here, Danziger wouldn't be pushing that new contract and being such a stickler over the current one. He's worried I'll snatch you out of his hands. You won't sign, so he's being a spoiled brat."

"If you weren't here, we wouldn't know what to avoid." She took a deep breath. "I'm glad you're back in town, Kurt."

"Yeah?"

That smile that bloomed across his face wasn't the tight, business-like expression he had worn all day, but something that sent a warm flood through her and melted her knees. She gripped the edge of the window to keep from falling inside.

"How glad? Glad enough for... skating at Roller Bowler?"

"The what?" Dani snorted, trying not to laugh. "They tore that place down eight years ago to build the new rec center. It's called The Drop now."

"Do they still have roller skating? And those mini pizzas that taste like cardboard soaked in sauce and wax cheese?"

"You know, I think they do."

"Wanna go?"

She did want to go. Dani surprised herself with how much she wanted to just take off and skip balancing the band's books tonight, and a dozen other chores she had to do.

"I'd love to," she began, drawing out her words.

"But?" Kurt still smiled.

"We're doing an all-day spot with the Eagle this weekend, and I have a ton of things to do and a test tomorrow and... you could stay for supper."
~~~~~

"Sounds good." He turned off the engine and yanked the keys from the ignition. "You're saving my life, you know."

"Belinda's going to barrage your phone until you give in?" Dani waited until he got out, then headed for the porch.

"Probably. She gets her mind set on the way things ought to be, and she doesn't let up for anything. Which can be really good, in the right situation. But bad in a ministry like ours."

"Or in a relationship." She shivered, sensing echoes and implications from those words.

"Yeah." Kurt paused with his foot on the bottom step. "But I can understand how she feels. I almost sympathize."

"Kurt!" Aunt Betty called, appearing in the door. "The boys were just telling me how much help you were today. Can you stay for supper?"

"I just asked him," Dani said.

"Good. We're having barbecue chicken and corn on the cob. George, set another plate!" she called, and turned to bustle back into the kitchen.

Kurt and Dani stood on the porch a few seconds longer. Dani wanted to ask why he sympathized with Belinda, but the words clogged in her throat.

Was she jealous? That was stupid—she had just turned down another date. They had no relationship whatsoever to speak of.

"I know how Belinda feels," Kurt said, as he reached for the door. "There's a lady I want to get to know... and sometimes I think she doesn't even know I'm alive."

"Oh. That's too bad." Dani ducked her head and hurried through the door as Kurt held it open for her. She mentally kicked herself for such a lame response.

No wonder Kurt wasn't trying harder to date her. There was someone else he would rather be with. Dani swallowed down the choking sensation that came from a dozen emotions she couldn't identify, all of them unpleasant.

~~~~~

Katie had come back from the honeymoon browned and glowing and full of energy. Her headaches had stopped completely and didn't return as the days turned into weeks and then a full month. Dani and Katie both believed that validated their theory that the stress of the wedding had contributed to her problems, aggravating what the doctors theorized was a chronic, long-term condition. No one said her problems weren't life-threatening, but the fact that she hadn't had any symptoms in weeks encouraged everyone. Andy was much happier as a result, easier to work with, more like the carefree guy in love Dani knew before Katie got sick.

The days grew warmer and the CD came together and Firesong spent at least two nights a week on a stage somewhere. Katie came with them
~~~~~

and the hours spent riding in the van or truck didn't seem to bother her.

There was something to be said for happiness as the best medicine. Dani also put a strong reliance on the heavy band of prayer wrapped around them, by friends and family and the regular group of prayer warriors at church. She was ready to believe in miracles, even before Katie's testing moved over to the Cleveland Clinic and the anomalies in her blood didn't re-appear and follow-ups with the MRI revealed nothing had changed.

Miracles seemed to be the norm in Tabor Heights. Nikki James had been assigned a permanent position with the Mission, as the Arc Foundation's liaison. All the repairs and renovations and new programs that Tabor Christian had dreamed of when they established the Mission could become reality in months instead of years. Nikki would help run the Mission in partnership with Tabor Christian, as well as doing regional work for the Arc Foundation. Brock Pierson, whom Nikki had run away from home to be with four years ago, had followed her to Tabor to win her back. While it was true that he had turned his life around and worked with the DEA to take down his former boss, and he was a Christian now, Dani wasn't sure if that was good for them. Even if it did strike her as romantic.

Even more important, all was well with the Randolph family. Dani felt guilty that she hadn't been able to spend more time helping, thanks to her overloaded schedule and concerns with Katie. The Randolphs certainly hadn't missed her presence or support, with half the church rallied around them. Joel was out of his cast and getting around with just a cane. Emily had emerged from her coma and seemed to be suffering no ill effects.

Even more amazing to Dani, Max's natural father had suddenly appeared in her life. Carlo Vincente, who had starred opposite Emily in a handful of films. Dani had almost choked the first time she recognized the elder statesman movie star. Max and Tony had simply been walking around town, giving Carlo the tour, talking and laughing as if they were old friends.

Max and Tony, however, made Dani feel odd. She had been teasing Max about her friendship with Tony for years. They were so good together, so mentally tuned into each other, the perfect couple. They had stayed at the "best buddies" level for so long, Dani had given up all hope for them. Then, somewhere between the Randolphs' accident and Carlo coming into Max's life, they discovered they were in love.

Dani admitted she was jealous. Not that Max and Tony had finally found some common sense. But jealous that their lives worked together so well. There would be no disruption, no major sacrifices either one had to make when they got married.

She knew if there was ever anyone special in her life, she would have to sacrifice so much. And she couldn't do that. Her music and her ministry came first. That was the way it had to be. She had made her vow long ago. God would forgive her if she changed her path, but she never could.

Friday, June 13

Dani took one summer class that year, an independent study course in English that would let her be flexible with her schedule and take off whenever Firesong had concerts or road trips. With the infusion of money from the Arc Foundation, her hours helping at the Mission had grown. If she wanted to put in eight and ten-hour days, she was welcome.

She was all-around pleased with her life and situation that first long weekend Firesong took off to do a three-day Christian music festival in Pennsylvania. The organizers arranged for her, Stephanie and Katie to share a cabin with a five-girl puppet team. She wasn't above smirking when her brother and cousins complained about the damp tent and uneven ground. They had elected not to bring cots, to have more room in the tent. Dani knew better than to say she told them so.

Chapter Twelve

Kurt arrived during set-up for their first concert Friday afternoon. Dani held her breath when he walked into the backstage area, just waiting for him to paralyze her with that look she couldn't interpret.

He had other matters on his mind. First, he fed them, bringing in pizza and buckets of barbecue chicken to gorge on after the concert. Then, when they were tired and relaxed, licking sauce from their fingers in the somewhat damp, mildewy privacy of their tent, he let them have it.

"I need your help with two big events I'm helping put together," he said, after he had refilled his cup with ginger ale. Kurt very carefully didn't look at any of them as he said it. Dani, Katie and Andy exchanged curious glances.

"Should have known he wouldn't have come just to see us," Katie chirped. She had been feeling unusually lively, and her high spirits had rubbed off on everyone.

"On the contrary, favorite cousin of mine," Kurt retorted. "I just love rubbing shoulders with you down-to-earth types. Seriously, I'd kill for a chance to relax like this, exchange business suits for jeans and Ts and sit around. The most fun I've had in months. Not counting your wedding."

He didn't look at Dani, but everyone else did. Dani held perfectly still and prayed her face wasn't as red hot as it felt.

"So, what are these two big events?" Andy prompted.

"Well, I got handed the organizer's job for the big Jesus Fest in Goshen, Indiana. Joe Mayser has been pretty sick and couldn't follow up on a lot of folks. He's lost some big name acts. I got together with the sponsors and they've agreed on a new angle: give a chance to some worthy, up-and-coming—"

"Cheaper," Tom prompted with a grin.

"Less expensive, newer Christian bands," Kurt corrected him, matching his grin. "How would Firesong like to be the main act for the entire fest?"

"You're kidding," Jason whispered. When Kurt just shook his head, face solemn, he whooped.

"I know you," Katie said, when the others had reacted loudly and joyfully. "You always save the big news for last. What could top that?"

"How about the Allen Michaels crusade in August? Would you guys be interested?"

"Interested?" Andy's voice cracked. "It's the chance of a lifetime. I'd do it for free!"

"Forget free," Jim broke in, "I'd pay to perform at an Allen Michaels crusade. And in our own backyard, too!"

When Kurt left half an hour later, to make a long string of phone calls related to everything they had arranged, they were still excited. Dani nearly couldn't sit still. She wished she knew how to turn cartwheels, to work off some of the exuberance she felt.

She had to go for a walk. The entire backstage area was full of people and Dani needed to be alone. She headed for the open meadow some distance from the main fields holding the stages and concession tents.

"Where can we go from here?" she said, not meaning to speak aloud. She glanced around, relieved to find she was alone, but for some birds and squirrels and any critters hidden in the knee-high grass. Dani spread her arms and spun around a few steps, until she lost her balance. Chuckling, she stumbled and caught herself and raised her arms to the sky. "Okay, Lord, now what? This is what we dreamed about when we first started singing for You, reaching thousands of people. Now what do we do? Where do we go from here?"

Dropping her arms, she sat and then stretched out on her back in the high grass and squinted up at the sky. It was more than enough to be alive and breathe the sweet air and feel the warmth of the late afternoon sun beating down on her. And envision a lifetime making music and helping people get to know God a little bit better.

She must have dozed off, after imagining scene after scene of success at the crusade. Dani blinked and opened her eyes and sat up, startled to see the sun had dipped down toward the horizon in what felt like a few heartbeats. Then she heard voices, coming her way. Unfamiliar voices.

"Hey, where'd you come from?" a laughing male voice called out. Dani got up on her knees and turned around and saw three skinny blond boys with their guitar cases in hand, stomping up through the high grass almost directly toward her.

"Just trying to be alone for a little while," she responded, and got to her feet.

Dani smiled, recognizing them as the warm-up trio who played when the first speaker was late that afternoon, and filled in while the puppet team set up their stage. They were good sports, and flexible. They seemed like nice boys, grateful for any pointers the more experienced bands felt like giving them.

"Oh, hey, sorry," the green-shirted one said.

"No, it's okay. I should head back before the guys get worried about me. We've got an evening concert, anyway." Dani nodded to them and started back down the shallow slope.

"You're with Firesong, aren't you?" the one in the tattered Petra shirt asked.

That was the only way Dani could tell them apart, by their clothes. They were so skinny, with the same angular faces and buzz-cut blond hair and blue eyes, she couldn't see any other differences in them. She liked them because they struck her as real; not like the pretty boy White Knights. Dani said a quick prayer these three would never become like them.

"Yep, but if I miss tonight's concert, I won't be."

"Are you busy after?" Green-shirt asked. He licked his lips in a distinctly nervous gesture.

"Sleeping, probably." Dani continued down the slope. They didn't take the hint. All three turned and followed her.

"We're heading into town for a movie. Want to come?" His eyes flicked away from her for a moment. Dani sensed someone approaching from behind her, but didn't turn; probably one of the organizers, trying to gather up wandering performers.

"Thanks, but I make a rule of never being alone with someone who isn't a relative."

"Huh?" The three nearly spoke in chorus. Their mouths dropped open in identical quizzical expressions.

"It's a purity vow," Kurt said, nearly startling Dani out of her shoes. "To protect her ministry from unfounded accusations. Something every Christian performer should do."

"But it's just a movie," Green-shirt said with a sigh.

"I have to establish a habit of purity and caution now, so when false accusations come, people will believe me and not the person trying to damage my reputation. Does that make sense?" Dani asked.

"Sounds kind of extreme," the one in the blue muscle shirt muttered, looking at his feet instead of Dani.

She suspected he entertained some not-quite-pure thoughts toward her and he felt embarrassed.

"What if—like—one of your cousins came along?" Green-shirt asked.

"You'll have to ask them."

That seemed to satisfy the three. They slung their guitars over their shoulders on their long, ratty straps and headed out into the field. Dani sighed and let her shoulders slump. All the good her private time had done her was completely gone.

"That was a good idea, making that vow. Saves you from a lot of well-intentioned dorks," Kurt muttered, watching the three ragamuffin musicians trudge away from them.

"Dorks?" She sputtered a giggle.

"Fits, doesn't it?"

"Maybe. Never thought I'd hear you use a word like that."

"There's a lot you don't know about me." He glanced sideways at her. "Come to think of it, there's a lot I don't know about you, either."

"And I'm alone with someone who isn't a blood relative." Dani stepped away from him and walked double-time toward the far-distant cabin where she hoped to find shelter.

"I'm willing to wait until you're at home, Dani." Kurt didn't have any trouble keeping up with her. They were both silent as they dodged several groups of performers warming up or backstage workers making adjustments on power cables or wires or moving barrels of supplies.

"Kurt—"

"Somebody would think you didn't like me, the way you keep avoiding me."

"Of course not!" She nearly stopped.

"Then why won't you go out with me?"

"You always ask when I'm super busy."

"When *aren't* you super busy?"

She dared a glance at him. To her relief, Kurt grinned. It amazed her how her heart skipped a few beats in very definite relief. It mattered to her, she realized, if Kurt was angry with her or not.

"Try me between summer school and fall semester, okay?"

"You better believe I will. And you'd better not leave the country," he added with a chuckle.

Somebody called his name and he stopped to turn and respond. Dani kept moving. She knew, without having to look, that Kurt glared at her. A moment later, he burst out in that hearty laughter that made her feel warm inside.

It wouldn't do any harm to go out on one date, would it? It wasn't like he wanted her to marry him. He had even said the lady he wanted didn't even know he was alive. Dani told herself that hollow feeling was relief.

Saturday, June 14

Katie collapsed the next morning with a sudden, massive headache that left her shaking, white, and vomiting. Dani was grateful she had driven separately, so she could bundle Katie into her little car and drive her and Andy to the nearest hospital. After consulting with Katie's doctors in Cleveland, the local doctors flew her home. Andy would have gone with her, but Katie insisted both he and Dani stay and do their final concert of the festival.

The MRI scan showed the dark smears inside Katie's brain had returned just as mysteriously as they had vanished. And still no easy or fast diagnosis available for anyone.

Tuesday, June 17

Dani wondered if the return of Katie's headaches was a sign that nothing would go right anymore. She had at least one a day, triggered by something as harmless and common as a strong odor, bright sunlight, or a change in humidity or temperature.

The day Danziger showed up at the barn during a rehearsal, Katie was at home. Dani and Andy leaned over his keyboard, trying yet again to smooth out the lyrics for Andy's everlasting melody. Jim and Jason sat in a corner, playing with the amplifier they had bought at an estate sale the week before.

"Okay, kids, here's the scoop," Danziger announced, walking through the ajar door with enough energy to stir up dust clouds from the gravel in the yard outside and bring it in with him. "Your CD is coming along nicely and we have a major emergency with the cover artwork."

"We all agreed Lisa's art was perfect," Jim said, with a tone that clearly said "is he crazy?"

"Yeah, it was perfect for a backyard, part-time band. Which you definitely no longer are." Danziger struck a lecturing pose. "You kids are getting too big for home-grown artwork. Friendship is fine and dandy, but this is business, folks."

"We like Lisa's artwork. She drew exactly what we told her we wanted," Andy said slowly, as if speaking to a particularly stubborn child.

"Extra, extra!" Tom shouted, rushing through the door so quickly he almost ran into Danziger. "Read all about it!" He held an envelope in one hand and waved several sheets of paper in the other.

Stephanie followed him through the door. They were both sweaty and dusty, meaning they had come on Tom's motorcycle. She just grinned.

"Hey, Mr. Danziger, you're here to hear the good news!" Tom continued. He held the papers up higher. "Guess who's going to the crusade?"

"You're kidding!" Jim shouted. He raced up and tried to grab the papers from Tom's hand. His older brother grinned and twisted nimbly aside, and handed them to Dani.

"Would I kid about something so utterly fantastic as performing for an Allen Michaels crusade?"

"So, how many evenings do we open up?" Jason demanded, stepping around behind Dani so he could read over her shoulder. He rested his chin on her shoulder and grabbed hold of her upper arms to steady her when his weight pushed her off balance.

She barely noticed, feeling as if her feet were about five inches off the floor. She read the key paragraph again, just to be sure.

"We're not," she said, feeling her breath leave in wonder. "We're performing. The main act... two nights in a row, and leading the singing the rest of the time, and for the all-day youth crusade on Saturday."

"Excuse me, folks," Danziger said through his bared teeth, his voice going nasal, "but don't you think you should tell your manager what's going on?"

Dani glanced at Tom, who nodded. She handed him the pages of the letter. The others stood around grinning, vibrating with excitement, while Danziger read it.

"It's for an entire week. How often does a big crusade like this come to our own hometown? It's the chance of a lifetime."

"There's nothing here about how much you get paid." Danziger handed the papers to Tom.

"Love offering," he said, taking the papers and shrugging.

"Is there a guarantee with that?"

"It's called trusting in God," Dani muttered. She shivered, frightened by how quickly the high-flying feeling of excitement and delight could vanish.

"Yeah, well, I like things in writing. Like contracts. And checks. Guaranteed pay for work performed. And I'll tell you something, folks, I got people asking for you on those dates. Big-time promoters, big-name bands and big-time pay."

"They'll understand. I mean, what Christian band or event would grudge us performing for Allen Michaels?"

Danziger's face went too quiet, and Dani thought his lip twitched into a sneer. She knew then, all those big-name bands couldn't have cared less about serving God. And neither did Danziger, for all his fine words when he first approached them.

"No," Tom said in the quietest, yet the most penetrating voice Dani had ever heard him use. "We already talked about this, and we agreed that if the chance came, we would do whatever it takes to perform at the Allen Michaels crusade."

"It's all your fault!" Danziger snapped, turning on Dani.

"Me?" she squeaked.

"You got some tabor romance going with that Kurt Green. Didn't I warn you to stay away from him, or he'd ruin your careers? He's got you sweet on him, so you risk your careers to help him out. Well, I ain't buying it, folks."

"You're delirious," Andy said, putting himself between Dani and Danziger. "Sure, Kurt's interested in Dani, but he wouldn't use a relationship to blackmail us into performing for him."

"Yeah, then he's an idiot."

"Besides, there's nothing going on between Dani and Kurt. She doesn't encourage him at all."

"Maybe not, but does she discourage him?" their manager shot back.

"Don't you understand?" Dani nearly whispered. "It's a chance to do something really worthwhile."

"I understand a whole lot more than you kids do. So understand this: my job is to protect you and make sure you get all the recognition and the perks your talent deserves."

"Some things are more important than money," Andy said.

"I hope you can tell me that when your honey is dying and you don't have the money for the doctor bills and your insurance won't renew." Danziger glared at them all, meeting their gazes and trying to intimidate them each in turn. No one would look away, and his face grew darker with every second that passed. He muttered something under his breath and stomped to the door of the barn. "Remember, kids, you got a *paying* festival coming up. Better earn every penny you can. Missionaries and monks don't make much money."

Then he was gone. They stared at each other, waiting for the subliminal echoes from his outburst to fade away.

"He just doesn't understand, does he?" Stephanie whispered.

"He's doing what we hired him to do," Dani said just as quietly. They all flinched when the roar of Danziger's engine starting up ripped through the humid air.

"He's trying to scare us into doing what *he* wants," Andy said. "When it comes time to sign the new contract..."

"We shouldn't," Tom said. His words echoed through the barn and Dani shivered, despite the humidity of the day. "We won't."

~~~~~

"Green? Yeah, you hide, you slimy crook," Danziger growled from Kurt's voicemail.

Kurt sat down in his dark apartment, wondering where Danziger had got hold of his phone number. It was unlisted. Maybe he had called crusade headquarters and conned someone into giving it to him?

Panic flashed through him as Danziger let loose a string of obscenities Kurt had never heard of, some of which he couldn't follow. Had Danziger called to cancel the band's appearance at the crusade? What damage had he done to Firesong's reputation with the organization?

"You keep your hands off Firesong. They're going places and *I'm* taking them there. I got a contract, you sanctimonious—" The air turned blue. "Think you can sweet-talk Dani into giving you anything you want, is that it? You preachers are all alike, talking all straight and narrow until you can get a girl into a dark corner. Yeah, well, you might be inside Dani's
~~~~~

pants, but I got control of the music, buddy-boy. That's where she lives. You ain't ruining anything for my band."

Danziger continued on in that vein for another minute or two, then abruptly hung up. Kurt held his breath as he checked for a second message. Danziger was just the kind of man to catch his breath, then call back to continue the abuse.

But nothing else waited on his phone. Kurt moved his thumb to tap for delete, then paused. Maybe he should save it? But what good would that do, exposing others to Danziger's filthy mouth and accusations?

Well, at least he knew Firesong had received the official invitation to perform at the crusade. It sounded like they were all for it and Danziger was against it.

"Please, Lord," Kurt whispered.

This could be the breaking point for Firesong, the moment of decision. Danziger would force it on them. Could they weather that crisis? Kurt believed they were dedicated enough and would come out winners in the process.

But what about those accusations about him and Dani? How could Danziger believe he and Dani were doing anything? The closest they had ever come to a date was dinner with the entire family. And yes, he *had* entertained a handful of daydreams about kissing Dani — and more.

What had Kurt confused was how Danziger could get that idea, when the man had rarely, if ever, seen them together. Did Dani say something that made Danziger think she and Kurt were serious about each other?

"I am in big trouble," Kurt whispered to the quiet room. The glee he felt at such an idea wiped away the weariness of an especially long, hard, draining day.

Yet he felt guilty, too, if he was the cause of Firesong's friction with their manager.

And confused. If Dani was interested, why didn't she let him know?

But that helped him make a decision. Situations like this were serious and needed to be addressed immediately, instead of relying on the "ignore them and they'll fade away" attitude of years ago. Kurt regretted having to write up a report like this and send it in, with the voicemail file attached, but reporting such accusations against him and Dani and Firesong as soon as they occurred would protect them all in the long run. And he would get friends to start praying big-time, to head off any damage Danziger would do or try to do.

As for him and Dani and whatever relationship they might have... Kurt just didn't know yet. But he decided to be hopeful.

Wednesday, June 25

Two days before they were to head to Indiana for the next festival, a new concert schedule came from Danziger, with performances every night of the crusade, a different state each night. He had confirmed with the concerts' organizers and took deposits without verifying the dates with Firesong first, as their contract specified.

"It's a power play," Tom said, looking around Andy and Katie's tiny living room, where they had all come for an emergency meeting.

Katie and Stephanie sat on the couch, with Andy and Tom perched on either side of them. Jim and Jason sat on the floor. Dani sat on the deep windowsill Katie had turned into a reading nook with a piano bench cushion. Aunt Betty and Uncle George had the only other chairs.

"What it comes down to is this," Tom continued. "To perform at the crusade, we have to refuse all those jobs Danziger lined up for us. It'll be bad for our reputation. And you can bet he'll dig his heels in about returning the money. If the story goes around and nobody knows the truth, we could lose a lot of prospective jobs. People will think we're unreliable."

"But if we told the right people—" Jason began.

"Who are they going to believe? A bunch of kids who don't know anything except how to play and sing? Or Troy Danziger, who has all the right connections?"

"Oh." His brother nodded and bowed his head over his clenched fists again.

"On top of that," Andy said, taking up the subject, "we'll lose paychecks, from all the time we have to take off work."

"Consider the up side to it," Dani offered. "We'll actually have more time at home, plus we'll cut down on the wear and tear on our cars."

"Our contract states we have the right to refuse jobs and to accept jobs without Danziger's go-ahead," Jim added. "He signed the contract, and he's the one violating it."

"And we're doing something important," Jason said.

"Is it any different from what you've been doing before?" Katie asked, her voice a little softer than usual.

"Heck yes! It's the crusade. How many chances does anyone have to do this big a production? With all the prep work put into it, and the publicity and the amount of people they can fit into the fairgrounds... they can't do more than three crusades a year. It's the chance of a lifetime."

"But is it any better than the ministry you've had already? You'll reach more people, but I don't think God has ever worried about the numbers game."

"You think we're wasting our time, hon?" Andy asked, resting a hand on her shoulder.

"I think we're putting too much emphasis on the glamour and forgetting the end results are the same, whether you're playing for thousands or just a hundred."

"Well, that is why you keep her around, isn't it?" Uncle George said, when flickers of chagrin touched nearly every face in the room. Smiles and a few chuckles met his words.

Tom's phone rang and everyone flinched. He slid it out of his pocket and looked at the screen.

"Danziger," he said and winced.

"For heaven's sake, kids," Uncle George growled, "you're not criminals. The man works for *you*, remember? If what you need to do doesn't fit his plans for fame and riches, he has no right to bully you into doing what he wants, understand?" He looked around the room, waiting until he got a nod from everyone. "Go face down that sneak-cheat, son. You know what's best."

Tom nodded slowly, managing a half-smile for his father. He and Andy went into the kitchen to face Danziger over the phone.

"Well," Aunt Betty sighed, "I think it's safe to say this is the watershed moment in your careers."

"If what we think God wants us to do goes against what our manager wants..." Jason shook his head.

"How do we know this is what God wants?" Dani had to ask.

"Come on," Jim groaned, "how hard of a choice is it? We go after our own fame and glory, or we give up a few concerts to work at the crusade."

"That's what I mean. Have we been chasing our own fame and glory all these years, or have we been trying to glorify God? Are we really doing what God wants by chucking everything to do the crusade?"

They were all still considering that question when Tom and Andy returned to the room.

Chapter Thirteen

Friday, June 27

Dani drove separately to the festival in Indiana. She had a half-day at the Mission on Thursday she wanted to squeeze in, and Andy only agreed to leave on Thursday with the rest of the group if Dani went with Katie to the Clinic for her latest tests that evening. The Greens were well able to take care of Katie, but Andy felt better knowing Dani was there. Katie had bullied him into agreeing to work the festival by promising to have Stephanie stay with her until Firesong got back into town.

On the four-hour drive to Indiana, Dani had plenty of time to think and wish she had some valid excuse to stay home with Katie and Stephanie and have a pajama party. Their plans for their nights alone sounded more fun than camping out, eating bad food and trying not to let the dampness of the outdoor stages ruin their equipment and instruments.

When she arrived at the sprawling farm that had been dedicated to the festival instead of that year's crops, Dani found the excitement contagious. As she drove down the gravel lane, she could see across acres and acres; taking in three different stages, what seemed like miles of tents and trailers, two ponds equipped with slides and rafts for diving, huge temporary water towers, and row upon row of outhouses. It was like a very comfortable refugee camp—with music thrown in.

She arrived just after noon. All the opening festivities had broken up so people could get something to eat. Dani had to stop dozens of times for traffic on her way to the performers area, set apart by high walls of black and green plastic and canvas, to give a semblance of privacy. She wondered if that had been Kurt's idea, or something already established before he was asked to bring order from chaos.

She had to identify herself to the balding, spectacled man in army surplus fatigues and waist-length ponytail, who stood guard at the gate. When she got over the novelty of the experience, Dani was grateful. How many other festivals had she worked at where there was literally no place she could go to have some quiet time, some privacy, some freedom from those who were agog over anyone who performed on stage? Or the wannabes who thought if they could ask enough questions, she would reveal the secret to instant success in the music industry. Dani smiled at the man as he let her through the gate.

Almost instantly, she had to stop. The performers area was filled with vans and mini buses, tents and trailers and cars and a sprawl of equipment in every direction. Fortunately, she recognized the long tent the guys shared, with a large enough space blocked off next to the van for her to park her car. She pulled up to it and simply sat for a few seconds after turning off the engine. She had arrived.

~~~~~

Firesong had the first concert that night; one hour of music before the main speaker. Another band would finish up the evening with another hour of music.

Three songs into the evening, Dani looked across the rolling field as dusk moved in and could see the entire audience was tuned into them. Listening and intent, ready to have fun. Still throbbing with the final chords of *Witch Hunt*, in a slightly mellower rendition than Petra's original. She smiled at Andy as the last notes faded into the night. Her brother bowed to her and winked as the applause crashed up from the audience, across the stage, nearly throwing them against the makeshift walls of pipes and plywood and faded red threadbare curtains.

Tom tossed the wireless microphone to Dani, who barely managed to catch it. She mimed terror, fumbling the microphone for a moment. The audience roared laughter.

"Isn't it awful how we get sidetracked?" Dani said, sauntering to the edge of the stage. "We're so busy trying to get rid of the bad things in our lives—and other people—" More laughter from the audience. "We forget to look for the good things. We forget to be thankful for all the blessings God loaded on us. Or else we go in the other direction, and we get kind of arrogant."

"No! Not you!" Tom shouted, still several steps away from his own microphone.

The audience reacted appropriately.

"I used to be a rotten speller," Dani continued, when they had calmed a little. "How many here hated English class until you got past all the spelling and grammar and finally started reading stories?" She raised her hand. Hands shot up through the audience, out beyond the spot where all those faces and bodies turned into a blur. "Remember the old song, 'Dare to be a Daniel'? I used to sing it this way: 'Dare to be a Danielle, dare to stand alone.'" She grinned as groans swept the audience, rippling out into that blurry darkness.

Is this where You want me, Lord? Reaching people? Speaking what's in my head and on my heart and getting through to them where nobody else can? I'll give up anything You want, Lord, to stay here, doing this, for the rest of my life.

That prickling sense of being watched went up her neck. Despite her resolve not to, she turned. Kurt leaned against the big support pole for the
~~~~~

sound system, hidden by the side curtains, grinning and watching with that "look" in his big, dark, mesmerizing eyes.

What was she going to do about him?

~~~~~

After they cleared off the stage, Kurt followed them back to their tent. He brought pizza and salad and more buckets to haul water for cooking and drinking, or bathing in the roofless bathhouses scattered throughout the campgrounds. He kept them entertained for nearly an hour, talking about the near-disasters that had come with this sudden, eleventh-hour responsibility. He joked that he couldn't decide if it was a good thing that the rest of the crusade advance team had come to town, freeing him up to help out his old friend. Dani could see he enjoyed the stress, the challenge. He enjoyed making things work and helping people and bringing it all together. She thought back to her Spiritual Gifts class and tried to classify Kurt. He fit the other definition of Shepherd — someone who led and organized and kept people out of trouble, not the teacher-type definition. He was a definite leader, yet someone who preferred to work in the background, who gloried in keeping things running smoothly and didn't seem to live for the praise that could come with big accomplishments.

She admired that in him. She almost suggested a few times that Firesong ask Kurt to become their manager, since they were breaking free of Danziger. He hadn't backed down on his contract-breaking actions. Rather, he defended what he had done. He implied Firesong was in the wrong because they stuck to their principles instead of doing what he wanted. He did say Firesong didn't know what was best, so he had to grab it for them. The fact that no court in the land would let him get away with such clear-cut contract violations meant nothing to the man.

Andy told Kurt about the problems with Danziger and their fear that the man would blacklist them. He wanted advice on how to handle the problem. Dani was proud her brother didn't mention to Kurt that it was their desire to work at the crusade that had caused the split.

"Yeah... Danziger let me know I was ruining your careers by forcing you to work the crusade," Kurt said with a wry grin.

"Oh, man, we are really sorry about that," Tom groaned. "How bad was it? Sometimes I think the guy could get violent. What did he say?"

"Well, he burned out the circuits in my phone." He shrugged and looked away. "If you guys are serious about doing the crusade, I'll be more than happy to spread the true story. Who do you think the movers-and-shakers in Christian music circles are going to believe? A guy who only jumps into the pool when he wants something, or someone who belongs?"

"Thanks," Dani said with more intensity than she intended. Kurt met her gaze for the first time since they sat down to eat. He looked away a little too quickly, with something like guilt clouding his eyes.
~~~~~

She cringed. Danziger hadn't accused Kurt of romancing her to get control over the group, had he? It was bad enough he thought she was a silly little girl who let her hormones overrule common sense, but did he have to throw it at Kurt, too?

And why did she feel thrilled as well as guilty?

In the silence that spread through the tent for a few seconds, Dani strengthened her vows. Nothing mattered more than singing for God, no matter how tiny or large the audience, no matter how inglorious or spectacular the venue. If important people in the music industry laughed at Firesong for choosing to sing at a crusade over pursuing their careers, they weren't the people she wanted to be involved with, anyway.

"So," Andy said, breaking the silence before it started to throb, "what's fun to do around here when we're not on stage?"

"What's fun?" Kurt frowned, as if thrown by the question. He glanced at Dani again. She tried to meet his gaze. It was hard when she felt flustered and grateful for Andy's distraction. "Well, right now I haven't the foggiest idea. I'll tell you what other people consider fun, though. You were planning on keeping your equipment in that second tent?"

He pointed to the old dome tent that had gone through a dozen too many wild camp-outs with the Gibson family. Plastic covered multiple much-mended tears in the canvas sides. Most of the netting had been torn out and replaced with more plastic. The zipper doorways still worked and everything had been sewn up tight. The band had brought plastic sheerts and some boards to keep their equipment off the ground and dry when it wasn't in use.

"Sure. What's wrong with that?" Andy asked.

"Keep it in your van, and check it at regular intervals. I bet you laughed at how tight security is when you came in, right? Well, we've had an interesting time the last week, setting things up around here. Every time we turned around, equipment was stolen, tent lines cut, outhouses knocked over like a row of dominoes. Someone doesn't want this festival to succeed." Kurt's eyes darkened and new lines appeared around his mouth and he turned to look at Dani.

Everyone automatically focused on her, and she tried not to flinch at the creepy-crawly feeling up her spine.

"Where are you sleeping, Dani?" he asked, sounding tired. She saw the gnawing fear trying to get hold of him, a darkness at the back of his eyes, a few new wrinkles around his eyes, tension in his voice.

"My pup tent, same as always when I can't get a cabin."

"Would it be too much trouble to sleep in your car? I've been warning all the women performers to find some place where they can lock the door. You guys didn't hear the fuss, way over here, but last night over on the eastern perimeter, right next to the woods, two women and a little girl were pulled out of their tents. Whoever did it just cut through the canvas. They were all sleeping alone." A crooked grin caught his mouth for a moment. "At least, their attackers thought they were alone. The little girl had a dog in the tent with her. He went after the creep and the noise woke up other people, who rescued the two women before anything worse happened."

"Are they okay?" Dani whispered.

"They're fine. The worst damage was scaring them, and the cuts in their tents. We're warning everyone not to be alone when it gets dark. Can you sleep in your car? If not, I'll rent you a hotel room in town. I mean, heck, you're my family, right?" He tried to shrug, but he looked stiff. "If I can't take care of you, what good am I?"

"Thanks," Andy said. "Dani's slept in the back of the car plenty of times. You're used to it, huh, shorty?"

"Yeah. Fine." Dani shivered, realizing just how much Kurt worried about her, personally. It went beyond his sense of responsibility for everyone in the festival.

What did I ever do to make him care so much?

Saturday, June 28

Kurt's worries were easy to forget the next morning. The sun shone down bright and warm, sparkling on the last of the dew on the grass. Laughter, strange sound effects and silly music came from the stage for the children's programs. The performers area was half-deserted and more organized than it had been the night before. Cars were lined up along the officially designated driving lane, with other areas set apart for playing or relaxing.

Dani found a few dozen sunbathers around and people playing catch when she came back from the bathhouse at nearly eleven. It had been too jammed up that morning, so she had settled for washing her face, brushing her teeth and extra deodorant before hurrying to the first Bible lesson of the morning. She had to hurry to bathe before their early lunch and heading over to the main performance stage to set up again.

She smiled ruefully and rubbed at her sore neck when she went to her car and deposited her soap and towels and dirty clothes in the front seat. She groaned softly as she discovered new stiffness in her back when she bent to straighten out her sleeping bag and pillow in the back seat. Just because she fit into the back seat didn't mean it was a comfortable place to sleep. Dani told herself to be grateful she had a safe place to sleep. She retrieved her comb and settled down on the back bumper to comb out her wet hair. It dripped everywhere.

Andy emerged from the tent and sauntered over to settle on the bumper next to her. He gestured at the quiet semi-village around them.

"Not as great as you thought, huh?"

"Oh, sure, I love taking a bath standing in a little hut with no roof, dumping buckets of cold lake water on myself. Wouldn't miss it for the world. If it was anyplace else, I'd expect to see a dozen creeps looking over the walls." She chose not to mention the young women with security badges and radios walking patrol around the perimeter of the bathhouse, making sure no one climbed over the top to spy on or do worse to the women and girls washing inside.

Her attention momentarily caught on two women in long dresses stepping through the gate area that led out into the main concourse of the festival. Why would anyone wear long dresses in this heat?

"That's not what I meant, brat. Maybe you should have taken Kurt up on his offer of the hotel room."

"It's fine. I'm a little old for sleeping in the car like we used to when we were kids, but it's fine." She flipped her comb at him, spattering him with drops. "Besides, where would I sleep? In the tent with you guys?"

"Hey, I'm just worried about you. I promised Mom and Dad I would look after you." He put an arm around her, shaking her a little. "You know I love you, even when I yell, right?"

"Tom snores and Jim talks in his sleep and Jason has gross breath in the morning."

"Huh?"

"You want to sleep with me, right?"

"I knew it!" a scratchy voice trumpeted from behind them.

Dani and Andy turned, nearly falling off the bumper, to see two shriveled, gray-haired women coming around the side of the car. Their hair was twisted back in buns so tight, Dani wondered how they could think when their brains were squeezed like that. They wore long-sleeve dresses despite the heat of the day, heavy shoes and dark stockings, and carried Bibles bigger than phone books. Their eyes were bright coals in nests of wrinkles as they glared at brother and sister.

"Huh?" was all Dani could manage. Where had these two come from? Only performers were allowed back there.

"The minute I saw you on that stage, I knew you were here for no good reason," the tall one said.

"Besides keeping the sound system together?" Andy said with an innocent tone so fake, Dani elbowed him. Couldn't he tell these two sourpusses were nothing to fool with?

"The festival has their own sound system," the dumpy one declared in a voice so high and baby-dollish, Dani had to hold her breath to keep from laughing. "They don't need any outside help."

"Tell them that," Dani couldn't help muttering.

"Don't you use that tone with me, you little slut." She hefted her Bible as if she would club Dani with it.

"Little what?" Andy got up and took a step toward them, and Dani grabbed his arm to stop him.

"It's disgusting," the tall one growled. "You ought to be turned out of the festival immediately. The idea of you filthy musicians parading around in front of impressionable children. Isn't it bad enough you brought this tramp, you're sharing her among the four of you?" She gestured disdainfully at Dani, who automatically looked down at herself.

What was wrong with shorts and bare feet? True, her T-shirt was slicked to her skin in spots with water, but it wasn't like she was running around without a bra. Dani had seen far more skin at church camp.

"Even ten years ago," the baby-voiced one squealed, "we'd have you whipped out of town!"

"You don't know what you're talking about," Andy growled.

"Don't you take that tone with us!" the tall one snapped and slapped at him as if he had attacked her. "The gall of you hypocrites, coming in here and claiming to be Christians and sleeping with this little tramp where everybody can see you."

"My sister is not a tramp!"

"Your sister?" the dumpy one shrieked. "You don't feel any shame in what she's doing, do you?"

"If you'd just shut up—"

"I'm going to the directors right this moment and I'll have your entire group thrown out of here so fast you won't know what hit you!"

"We haven't done anything!" Andy shouted. The tightness in his voice shocked Dani out of the dazed feeling that paralyzed her. "Kurt would know that better than anyone!"

"Lying, on top of fornication. What is this world coming to?"

"Is fornication worse than incest?" Dani asked, after taking a few deep breaths to get her head clear again. "The other three are my cousins. Which sin is worse: fornication or incest?"

"Your—cousins?" The dumpy woman visibly wilted.

"And Kurt Green, who is *running* this show, is my wife's cousin," Andy added, as he wrapped an arm around Dani. "He made Dani sleep in the car because he's worried about her safety. There's a lot of crazies running around this place. Even if everybody here is *supposed* to be a Christian."

The tall one seemed to sink into the ground about six inches. "Why didn't you say anything?" she whimpered.

"Did you give us a chance?" Andy asked. "You saw one girl with four guys and assumed we brought a hooker with us. To a *Jesus* festival. That takes a lot of gall."

"But we have to protect the children here," she said, trying to rally some of her former self-righteousness.

"We should go complain about harassment," Dani said. "You're definitely not performers, so you have no business being back here in the first place."

"You know, there's been vandalism, people damaging equipment and cars. People who go where they don't belong are the first suspects," Andy said.

"We didn't mean any harm!" the tall one protested, visibly shuddering.

The dumpy one seemed to have lost her voice completely. She edged toward the gate and didn't seem to care if her friend came with her or not.

"Prove it," Andy said in that implacable tone that got snotty junior high kids moving and silent, back at church. With a rustle of skirts, the two women scurried away.

Dani let out a heavy sigh. "Why did they even come here? They don't fit in."

"Oh, please, God, don't ever let us become stiff and nasty and self-righteous like them!" Andy said, lifting his hands to the sky. He sank down onto the bumper again and Dani joined him. "I have this awful feeling we're going to run into more jerks than good times if we keep going."

"If you're trying to discourage me —"

"Just promise me you'll get an education and a career to fall back on, okay? I mean, what if Danziger wins and we're finished as a band?"

"But if this is what God wants me to do, to serve Him —" Dani gestured around, taking in the entire festival grounds. "Can anything stop me? Us?"

"Are you sure music is what God wants?"

"How can anybody be sure?" Unbidden, Kurt's face flashed in front of her mind's eye. She thought about the interesting talks when he was around, the insights gained when he joined them in Bible studies before their concerts. He was an all-around great guy, even discounting the things Katie said about her cousin. "I mean, it's not like the clouds roll back and an angel comes down with a message on a golden scroll, right? How can we know what Tabor wants us to do?"

"Well... Dad always used to say, you do what you already know God wants you to do." Andy shrugged. "The things that are just common sense. The right things. What's spelled out already in the Bible. You get used to doing things God's way, and when that big decision comes up, you'll know what's the right choice."

"Is it easy for you?"

"Not as often as I'd like, but... yeah."

"So, I should listen to the voice of experience, huh?" She smiled, teasing.

"Plan like you'll serve God for a thousand years and live like you'll be taken home tomorrow. That's how Mom and Dad lived and died. I bet leaving us behind was their only regret."

Friday, July 11

Andy's words still rang in Dani's mind two weeks later. She was working alone, doing a last few checks on the sound equipment in the Tabor Heights High School gym. The rest of the group had gone off to do last-minute errands or help set up dinner in the room off the stage. They were helping with a rally for all the high school church groups in the county. Dani kept mulling Andy's words, wondering at times if she had misinterpreted what seemed like clear signs from God, and at other times kicking herself for doubting. If she kept looking back, second-guessing herself, she would only be miserable.

But what if she blinded herself? What if she had thrown herself into music and serving God with music because it had saved her from the black, devouring loneliness after her parents died? What if this wasn't what God wanted from her life, and He allowed the troubles with Danziger, the possible destruction of Firesong, to get her back on track?

"No," Dani whispered as she taped down a cable that had come loose yet again. "God isn't cruel."

But that tiny voice of doubt, which she tried not to listen to, whispered that God was often very hard to understand except in retrospect.

She moved on to double-check the contacts between the mixer and the first bank of speakers, and tried not to imagine what kind of a life she would have if she left Firesong. What could she do? She loved children — maybe get a degree in education? Work at the Mission? Lead the choir at church?

That sounded too much like something a pastor's wife would do, which dragged her thoughts to Kurt. He had said nothing more about the elusive woman in his life. Had he given up on her, or was he making headway and not inclined to brag?

"Don't you ever take a break?" Kurt asked, stepping out of the darkness of the gym, into the pin spots set up on the stage.

"From what?" She stayed on her knees, trying to get one last twist of the wire around the contact posts. It was hard when her hands shook at the shock he had given her. Almost as if her thoughts had conjured him.

"Steph sent me to get you — it's time for supper."

"Is Andy here yet? He went to get Katie from work."

"So you don't eat without your big brother? Boy, you really are tied to him." An edge to his voice made Dani turn away from her work, finally. She saw his teasing grin, but there was still something about his voice that bothered her.

"What are you talking about?" She got up off her knees and put down the screwdriver. Anything to get her mind off Kurt and those looks he gave her, that could turn her upside down and melt her knees. His heart belonged to someone else, so she obviously misinterpreted what she read in those unsettling glances.

"Nothing. Come on and eat. You're getting as thin as Katie."

"Hah! I just look at ice cream and I gain ten pounds."

"Keep dancing around on stage, you'll never get fat."

"I don't dance."

"Yeah? What do you call it then?" He settled down on the edge of an amplifier and crossed his arms, daring her to defend herself.

"Interpretive movement." She stuck her tongue out at him.

"Hair-splitter."

"Nope, got rid of those at my last haircut."

"You're hopeless, you know that?"

"Nope. And as long as I don't know it, I still have hope. That's what I learned in logic class, by the way, so public education is not a total waste of time."

"I give up. Come on and eat, okay?"

"Hey." She almost laughed as she realized Kurt was supposed to be in Los Angeles today — not that she kept up on his schedule. Not on purpose, anyway. "What are you doing in town?"

"She finally noticed I'm here!" Kurt raised his arms to the ceiling. "Take me home, Lord. I can die a happy man."

"You are a lunatic."

"Takes one to know one." He flipped her a salute and turned, vanishing into the darkness.

Chapter Fourteen

"What did you mean, about waiting for Andy?" Dani asked Kurt twenty minutes later, as they stood over the buffet table set up two rooms down the hall from the stage.

They were the only ones there, everyone else having served themselves and settled down at the long cafeteria tables. There was enough noise from excited chatter and laughter, Kurt knew no one would overhear their conversation.

"Nothing." He tried to shrug and smile and concentrate on the coleslaw as if the words he had said weren't still ringing through his mind.

It had struck him like an epiphany, as he walked away from the gymnasium. Dani clung to Andy. Not from jealousy, to control and monopolize her brother's life. She wouldn't have been so delighted for Katie to marry him, if that were the case. But Dani definitely molded her life around Andy's. She probably wasn't aware of it. She would argue strenuously if he suggested it. Why else would Dani throw herself so heartily into Firesong? Andy loved his music, lived for his band, and Andy was all she had when their parents died.

Andy had told Kurt about the promise they made to each other the night they got the news about the plane crash that killed their parents, and how he felt guilty sometimes about making a life of his own that Dani couldn't share. At the time, Kurt had thought Andy was giving him permission to step into Dani's life. What if it wasn't? What if it was a warning that Dani wouldn't let anyone else in?

The relationship between brother and sister was healthy. But what if there were roots hidden in the darkness neither one knew about? Would Dani fall apart if anything happened to Andy?

"That wasn't 'nothing', and you know it," she said. "You think I'm a baby and I need my big brother to lead me around everywhere and take care of me?"

"Not what I said at all. You're a big girl, Dani." Kurt swallowed hard and forced himself to look at her. She was too busy with the broccoli salad to look at him, which was a relief. "I was just teasing. I mean, any idiot can see you're standing on your own two feet just fine, and you let Andy have his own life. And... I think I should stop before you hand my head back to me."

That got her to look at him. Kurt felt something go hollow with relief when she grinned.

"Smart man." She winked and sauntered over to the table to join the others.

Kurt waited a few seconds, swallowing the lump that had formed in his throat at the thought of Dani furious with him.

But what if that was the problem? What if she was so tied to Andy, and to the band and ministry for Andy's sake, she didn't have a life of her own? And what if she couldn't see that? Was there any hope for them, together?

"Hey, Kurt, what's up with the damage control with Danziger?" Tom asked, as he finally joined them at the table.

The only open spot was two seats down from Dani, on the other side of the table. Kurt accepted that as a mixed blessing, put his plate down, and sat before answering. He was glad to get his mind off Dani for a while, before he twisted his brain and his heart into further knots.

How could his thoughts get so wrapped around a girl who hadn't even gone on a date with him yet?

"Well, first off, the damage isn't as extensive as he wanted you to think. He was a little too pushy, getting that advance money, and a couple people suspected something wasn't right. I sent out copies of the contract you gave me, and the dated letter from the crusade office, stating they want you to perform." Kurt smiled around the table. "Nothing like hard evidence to prove Danziger signed those contracts without your consent, *after* you had already committed elsewhere. His reputation is smeared, not yours."

Maybe the dinner conversation wasn't as light and relaxing as he would have liked, but Kurt welcomed it. It would be good to get overloaded with the last-minute crusade details, to push all other thoughts out of his mind. This dithering over Dani and his own uncertainties was driving him crazy.

Could he give up the crusade work, to travel with Dani and support her career?

Would she ask him to? Probably not.

Could he ask Dani to give up Firesong and travel with him?

Was he thinking only of himself? He really had to sit down and think things through, and then sit Dani down for a long, intense, serious discussion.

Just not now.

~~~~~

Two hours later, the high school gym was packed. The collapsible bleachers had been pulled out from the wall to their full extent and there still wasn't enough room. Wrestling and tumbling mats had been pulled out of storage and were jammed with students sitting on the floor. Others
~~~~~

stood against the walls, sometimes five and six deep in places. Firesong had them singing along, swaying in time to the music, emotionally revved up with fast-moving, fun songs like they sang at church camp.

Dani looked out at the sea of faces when her spot came in the program, and she hesitated. She wasn't that much older than the majority of the young faces shining in the darkness, but suddenly she felt as if a huge gap existed between them. What could she say that would make a difference to them, help them rededicate their lives to Christ?

"Please help me, Lord," she whispered as she stepped up to the front of the stage.

Dani opened her Bible, adjusted the microphone in the stand, and took a deep breath. This was no time to hesitate. This was what she was born to do, and if she didn't do it, then what was the use of anything?

"Paul wrote in Philippians that to live was Christ, and to die was gain. Did you ever think about that? It means that whatever we're doing here on Earth, we do it as if we're working to please Jesus only. And when we die, it's a *promotion*, the reward for all our hard work. Think about it! Anything we do outside the goal of pleasing God — it's useless. Paul, when he wrote those words, was in prison. He didn't see anything wrong with where he was, because he left it all in God's hands and knew that no matter what happened to him, he would come out the winner. If he was released, it would be a miracle of God. If he died, he would be in Heaven. Can we say that in our everyday lives? Can we say that no matter what happens, it will be for God's glory?"

Softly, Andy slid into the opening notes of what the group now called the "Question Song." This would be the first time they would sing it in public. Danziger hadn't wanted them to put it on the CD and had discouraged them from performing it, saying their audiences weren't ready for deep philosophy. Free of him now, they planned to sing it whenever possible.

As the music built up loudly enough to be heard, Dani stepped out of the spotlight, which shifted over to Andy. He closed his eyes, opened his mouth, and sang with his soul.

Saturday, July 12

The next morning, Dani took the box with the rally decision cards to church, to have the pastoral staff go through them and make contact with the youth who had signed them. She was tired, having stayed up until nearly 2 a.m. talking with people and putting away equipment, and then getting up before 8 a.m. to meet with her extremely flexible professor at Stay-a-While for a summer class conference. Yet she felt like she flew, a foot off the ground and ready to burst into song. She took the box into the church office and waved to Rita Carson and Jeannette, who were busy in the next room with the copy machine. Probably some copying project for a teacher who waited until the last minute. Rita waved and rolled her eyes in exasperation. Dani grinned and pressed her hands together, miming prayer and headed back out the door.

The VanGaars were just parking their car, two tires over the edge of the handicapped parking slot, when Dani skipped out the door. She nodded to them as she floated over to her car.

"You. Danielle Paul," Mr. VanGaar called, jerking himself out of his car. "What's this I hear about you preaching?"

"Preaching?" Dani blinked and felt like she had been jerked back to Earth with a bump.

She had never expected to hear that cold tone from Mr. VanGaar. He was one of the pillars of the church. Even if he did smell of mothballs half the year, the children liked him. He did corny magic tricks for the toddlers—the only ones who couldn't see through his flawed sleight-of-hand—handed out king-size chocolate bars at Christmas and Easter, and sponsored camp scholarships for those who memorized reams of Bible verses.

"You've never been to seminary, so who told you that you could preach?" he continued.

"I don't preach—"

"My grandson was at that concert of yours last night. He was all excited about what you talked about in between the songs."

"That's right. I was talking, not preaching." She offered a shaky little smile and tried to edge around him toward her car. Mr. VanGaar headed her off. Mrs. VanGaar stood there in her tiny rosebud print dress and matching hat. The sad disappointment on her face said Dani had done something blasphemous, like spray-painting profanity on the walls of the church.

"You had a Bible in your hand," he snapped, "and you were reading verses and you had the gall to tell people how to live their lives."

"I shared what I had read in my devotions. That's all."

"Some people think it's perfectly fine for women to preach to men," Mrs. VanGaar said in that sad, guilt-inspiring voice she did so well. "I can't imagine what this world is coming to."

The VanGaars, Dani remembered, still found it hard to accept women wearing pants to church during the week.

"Women can teach in Sunday School, can't they?" Dani offered with a smile. She didn't want to get them angry with her, though it was hard to remember she liked them.

"What does that have to do with it?" Mrs. VanGaar asked.

"It's all right to teach infants how to live their lives—but not teach immature Christians how to live?"

Mrs. VanGaar looked as if she had never considered the idea before. Her husband shook for several seconds before he could continue.

"You'd better watch your tongue, young lady."

Dani knew better, but she let the words come. "Did your grandson tell you what I talked about? Or did you get so upset at a woman—who's four years *older* than him—teaching him, that you didn't bother to listen?"

"No one so arrogant could say anything worthwhile. Your brother is a saint to let you travel with his band."

"I'm arrogant?" She wasn't ashamed to admit she shrieked. "Get the plank out of your eye before you criticize the dust in mine, you nasty old Pharisee!" Dani stomped across the parking lot to her car while Mr. VanGaar gaped like a stranded fish. She trembled as she jerked the car door open and jumped inside. As she pulled out of the parking lot, she saw the VanGaars stomping toward the door of the church.

~~~~~

Andy and Tom were in the barn when Dani got back to the farm. Any other time, she would have thought it amusing that the married members of the band spent more time at the house than the sons who still lived at home. Right now, she was just grateful for someone to talk to. She spilled out her frustration over the VanGaars to them, with a sick twist of shame. True, they had no right bringing her down from such a wonderful, high feeling after last night's success. That still didn't give her the right to snap back at them. They were elders in the church. They had been friends of her parents. She owed them some respect, even if she didn't agree with them.

How was she supposed to serve God on stage if she couldn't control her tongue?

To make matters worse, Andy and Tom found the whole situation funny instead of a tragedy. Emotions plummeting, she felt like crying. She felt like giving up.

"I'm really ready to junk it all and abandon ship, you know? I can't do anything without some self-righteous jerk immediately accusing me of doing wrong. You guys could stand there on stage and preach yourselves hoarse and nobody would bat an eyelash. I get up there one time and tell them something I learned in my devotions and—"

"The VanGaars coined the phrase, 'but we never did it that way before.' Bob wouldn't have talked about the concert if he had known they'd get upset about something so small," Andy offered.

"But there have to be thousands of self-righteous jerks out there. What if my being with you guys hurts the group?"

"What are you going to do?" Tom asked. "Quit? Get your English
~~~~~

degree and teach fourth-grade snots to conjugate verbs? Get married and have lots of kids and forget your music?"

"Well, Kurt would probably go for the get married and have kids part," Andy said with a grin, "but who says you have to give up your music?"

"An—deee," Dani groaned. The last thing she needed to add to the churning inside her was the fluttery feeling she got whenever she thought of Kurt lately.

"Would you really quit if you thought you were hurting the group?"

"Yeah." She thought she would throw up as the word slipped from her lips.

"Do you want to?" Tom asked, his voice soft.

"Not in a million years."

"How did you get the VanGaars on the warpath?" Jim asked, coming through the door. "They're in the kitchen with Pastor and the folks."

"Shoot me now!"

"Whatever it is, it has to be hilarious. You know how Pastor gets when he's trying to be serious, but he's busting not to laugh?"

"Oh, that'll help." Dani stood up and braced herself to face the lions. What could she say? What could she do? She had never prayed so hard about anything since Katie first got sick.

"Head for the hills," Jim said, glancing out the door. "Here they come!" He slid out the door and she heard his running footsteps on the gravel.

Andy and Tom came over to stand on either side of Dani. She appreciated that gesture of support, though she couldn't make herself look at either of them.

Pastor Glenn followed Uncle George and Aunt Betty through the door, followed by the VanGaars, who looked more sour than they had in the parking lot. Dani thought Mr. VanGaar's fedora looked crumpled and sat crookedly on his head. As if he had crushed it in anger and jammed it back on without thinking. She immediately quashed that thought, or she might start laughing.

"Dani. Andy. Tom." Pastor Glenn looked around the barn. "I'm sure you know why we're here."

"I was rude," Dani said, trying not to let her voice tremble. "I shouldn't have spoken the way I did, and I'm sorry."

"You're too full of yourself." Mr. VanGaar stepped up, leaning forward until his nose was only a few inches away from her. "First you take it on yourself to teach when you have no right or training, then you have the gall to resist when you're being disciplined."

"Henry," Pastor Glenn said gently, that resisting-laughter brightness in his eyes. "She didn't apologize for what she said at the rally last night.

She apologized for being rude. That's all."

"But she was in the wrong!" Mrs. VanGaar said. Her voice wavered slightly, with a hint of uncertainty.

"I should point out that my office window was open and I heard everything that was said, on both sides." He smiled. Aunt Betty and Uncle George relaxed a little bit. The VanGaars didn't react at all. "Tell me something, Andy. What do you think was the average age at the rally last night?"

"Oh... fifteen or sixteen," her brother said after a moment of thought. "It was geared for teens. A lot of churches came."

"Exactly," Mr. VanGaar snapped. "Where does she get the authority to teach?"

"Where do you get the authority to criticize when you don't know what she said?" Pastor Glenn returned.

"It's the fact that she dared to speak at all!"

"I have three things to say, and then I want this subject dropped." Pastor Glenn looked around, including them all. "First, Dani has been teaching Sunday school and helping out with the Middlers since she started high school. Everyone will vouch for her spiritual maturity. Second, I was at the concert, and I saw nothing wrong with what Dani said or how she said it. She spoke for five minutes, tops. No self-respecting minister I know would call it preaching. They'd call it warming up."

Dani and Andy smothered chuckles. Tom just rolled his eyes. Aunt Betty and Uncle George sighed and gave the VanGaars wearily disgusted looks. Dani had the sudden, heartening realization that these "pillars of the church" had made similar accusations against other people, and been found similarly wrong.

"Third," Pastor Glenn concluded, "a lot of teens gave their lives to Christ last night. Including your grandson."

"But he never told us!" Mrs. VanGaar blurted.

"You probably never gave him a chance," Tom said, not bothering to smother his grin.

"How long have you two been praying for him, Madelaine?" Aunt Betty asked.

"Ever since he was born." She gave them a trembling smile and dug in her suitcase-sized purse.

"The way I see it," Pastor Glenn said, in the tone he used to wrap up his sermons, "your grandson listened because Dani *wasn't* preaching."

"I know what it's like," Dani said, finally able to breathe freely. "So I tell them what I understand... Look, Mr. VanGaar, Mrs. VanGaar, I apologized for being rude. I don't take criticism really well sometimes."

"Try all the time," Tom offered. Everyone but Mr. VanGaar smiled at his teasing.

"I shouldn't have reacted the way I did. But I won't ever apologize for anything I do to bring people closer to God."

Mr. VanGaar glared at her, his jaw working, as if he tried to build up steam to start yelling again. Pastor Glenn tapped him on the shoulder and gestured for him to leave. Uncle George crossed his arms and took a step closer to the man. Huffing, Mr. VanGaar squared his shoulders and stomped out of the barn. His wife watched him go, dabbing at the tears in her eyes.

"Bobby really did... You have no idea how glad I am..." she whispered, then scurried after her husband.

Aunt Betty followed after her, and Uncle George winked at the four left behind before he made his exit.

"Wow," Andy gusted on a sigh. "What's with people like that?"

"Nasty old Pharisee," Dani said. She sank down on the piano bench and wrapped her arms around herself.

"True," Pastor Glenn said. "The problem is, there are a lot of sincere, kind Pharisees who don't realize the damage they're doing. Don't you turn into one, Dani. God's using you. Don't mess up His plans."

Monday, July 14

Dani was working at the Mission, supervising the craft room, when what Tommy Donnelly laughingly referred to as "green alert" went through the building. At that signal, everyone was to evacuate the children onto the playground as quickly as possible. She herded a half-dozen four-year-old girls out through the side door of her classroom and tried not to think about the jar of green tempera paint that got knocked off a counter as one of her charges passed. She managed to snatch up a plastic box of damp wipes and kept her girls busy wiping paint off their hands and faces, then got them out of their plastic raincoats, worn backwards, to protect their clothes.

"What's up?" she asked Tommy, when he wheeled around the perimeter of the playground with a clipboard on his lap, checking with the various teachers and taking a headcount.

"Pray hard." His normally laughing face had never looked grimmer. "Jeannette's ex-in-laws just stomped through the front door with a lawyer and enough paperwork to choke a mule."

"Where's BJ?" she immediately demanded and stepped away from her gaggle of girls to look around the crowds of laughing, running, playing children filling the playground.

Dani had often speculated on the reasons for why Jeannette Marshall never talked about her dead husband's family and took back her maiden name. She had been in high school and heard whispers about the bad taste the Evans family left in everyone's mouth, when they swept into town like a storm cloud for Jeannette and Brody's wedding. There was only one reason she could think of for the Evans family to show up after five years of silence, with a lawyer and paperwork.

"He's fine." Tommy pointed to the slide, where a long line of children snaked around the equipment, waiting their turn. "Do me a favor?"

"Depends." She had learned long ago to expect the unexpected with Tommy. There was a reason he was a popular comedian in the surrounding counties, even though the comedy scene seemed to be dying in the Cleveland area.

"If you see a bunch of suits get past the folks standing guard in the office, you shriek as loud as you can. You got the lungs for it." He smirked.

"Thanks ever so much."

"Then you grab BJ and run for it. I'll do my impersonation of a roadblock. Jeannette's on her way over, so hopefully we won't have to do anything."

Dani hoped so, too. She was pushing all her girls on the swings, trying to keep an eye on BJ, when Jeannette showed up and took her son away.

"Okay, God, I get it," Dani whispered, when the signal finally came to bring the children back inside. "There are some things a whole lot more important than my problems. But please, don't let them take BJ away?"

Nikki and Claire had a meeting of all the teachers and staff that evening, after parents came to take their children home and the Mission could close up for the night. They explained the situation, what they had heard from the church, and the advice from Xander Finley at Common Grounds Legal Clinic. Anyone who was not an official member of the Mission's staff, or a documented parent or guardian of a child under their care, was to be kept away from all the children. It didn't matter how well known they were to the staff and the children. Until it was known what the Evans family was going to do about their claim on BJ Marshall, and who in Tabor Heights would support them or even try to help them get hold of the little boy without his mother's permission, the Mission would act as if every child was in danger. Teachers were to carry cell phones at all times and wear police whistles, and Nikki was looking into the legalities and hazards of issuing pepper spray to all the members of the staff, just in case.

No one asked if it was overkill. Everyone had heard horror stories of non-custodial parents snatching children from daycares and schools, or strangers who walked into a safe, open atmosphere to randomly steal children, or child molesters who wore false names and joined churches so they could work in Sunday schools to gain easy access to their victims.

They refused to let it happen at the Mission.

Dani didn't sleep well that night, alternately raging against the cruelty and selfishness of the Evanses, and wondering what had happened to the safe, quiet town she had grown up in. She didn't know whether to laugh or cry or be angry with herself when she woke up with an idea for a song.

Then she did laugh at herself when she realized she wanted to call Kurt and talk it over with him. That wouldn't be good at two in the morning. It might give him the wrong idea about their friendship.

Chapter Fifteen

Tuesday, July 15

"I really appreciate this," Dani said, as she settled down at a table in the Bluebird Cafe.

She and Kurt had a table for six because they needed the room to spread out all the proofs for posters and the CD cover and interior designs. Today was one of the few days he would have partially free until the crusade was over. Dani was the only member of Firesong able to get free in the middle of the day to meet with him. Only two weeks until Firesong's first CD was to be released.

Kurt had offered his connections and expertise to help with the last-minute details, since Danziger had pulled out of the entire process. He had even caused some trouble with the studio and the company that would burn the CDs, by passing on contradictory information. Kurt had made an official call to both, updating them on the situation and making it clear that Troy Danziger was no longer Firesong's manager.

"Hey, what are friends for?" He grinned and nodded yes when the waitress asked if they wanted water.

"You're more than a friend."

"Yeah?" That warmth gleamed in his eyes.

"You're family."

"Oh." Kurt looked away for a second and fussed with spreading papers and folios across the table between them.

"No matter what, you're going way beyond the call of duty. We'd be lost without you."

"Sometimes I wonder if you'd all be better off if I hadn't stuck my nose into things." He tried to smile as he picked up the stacks of artwork and slid them over in front of her to peruse instead of her menu.

"We wouldn't be doing the crusade. That's the greatest thing we could ever do."

"But you'd still have your manager. Danziger is one of the best. He knows talent, and he can take you to the top."

"What if God doesn't want us at the top?" she asked softly. "What if He wants something totally different for our lives? Sometimes what's best isn't what's right."

"That's highly philosophical. Or is that theological?" Kurt tried to smile.

Dani flinched when he put his hand on top of hers, but didn't move her hand. For four long heartbeats, they just looked at each other. She knew in another moment, something struggling deep down in her soul would finally burst forth into the light and she would understand. The hungry, sometimes lonely feeling inside would have an answer.

"Well, if it isn't the lovebirds," Danziger sneered as his shadow dropped across their table. "You're faster, Green."

"Faster?" Kurt sat back, withdrawing his hand. He scooted his chair sideways a little to look up at Danziger without craning his neck. "What are you talking about?"

"I've seen the dodge played out a dozen times before. You move in, separate the real talent from the rest of the band, and then you make her your meal ticket. Make her think she can't live without you, career and heart-wise." Danziger sneered at Dani, who stared at him with her mouth slowly dropping open. "Got to admit, you're good, yanking them with the religious angle. What's the rest of the band gonna do, sweetheart, when their careers are shot and you and lover-boy here take off on your own?"

"You're crazy," was all she could manage.

Danziger just cackled and continued out of the Bluebird.

"I thought he was long gone," she muttered.

"He's probably sticking around to see what happens when the CD is released," Kurt offered.

"You think he'll keep trying to sabotage us?"

"You're the best band he's ever lost." He glanced at the door, finally swinging shut behind the other man. "Ah, about the other things he —"

"I'll never leave Firesong. Not for anything or anyone. So don't even ask."

"I wouldn't."

"Then what are you hanging around like this — Forget it." She pressed her palms against her face, feeling it grow hotter. "Let's just get this business taken care of, okay?"

"Sure."

All during their meal, discussing the samples of artwork, making final decisions, choosing how many posters they would need for the grand release party at McCready's Music, every time Dani raised her eyes to look at Kurt, he glanced away. She knew what she would see if their gazes ever locked, and she was grateful, yet strangely disappointed, when he avoided looking at her.

Suppose Kurt didn't have that mystery woman in his life? What if he did ask her to leave Firesong for him? Singing and writing songs for Firesong was where God had called her.

Falling in love, marriage and family had no place in her life.

"Look," Kurt said as they stepped out of the Bluebird after lunch and prepared to go in two different directions. "About what Danziger said before."

"Kurt—"

"I would never consider you a meal ticket, but you're good, Dani. You could go solo."

"Never. My place is with Firesong. Forever."

"Maybe not forever." He caught hold of her arm, sending a shiver up her back that made her whole body lock up. "Right now, you're lost without the guys. But that won't last forever. You're not ready to be known as Dani Paul and Firesong—"

"But that's the way it could be in the future?" She tried to laugh, but the sound caught in her throat. Dani yanked her arm free and took two steps back. "I would never do that to them, even if I could. And I can't. I'm nothing without them."

"You gotta grow up sometime, Dani."

"Grow up?"

"When are you going to let go of Andy and let him live his own life? That's what this is really about, you know. You're afraid of being alone, but you twist it all around and swear you'll never abandon him."

"You are so—you're crazy! Why are you trying to hurt me? You're not even interested in me."

"Then you aren't so smart after all."

"You said the woman you were interested in didn't even know you were alive." It took all her control to speak in a normal voice.

"Sometimes. I said sometimes *you* didn't know I was alive. Come on, Dani. Pull your head out of the sand. Are you so scared of being alone, you're bribing God to be nice? Is that all this devotion is about? You won't let yourself have a life because you're too busy keeping God happy?"

"I thought you understood!" She backed away from him, and she didn't care if her voice rose and people on the sidewalk and in the parking lot turned to look at them.

"I understand you're still a little kid who's scared of the dark and won't let go of your big brother's hand. That's your problem, and the sooner you let go of Andy and accept that bad things do happen to Christians and it's not a punishment, the better."

Kurt turned sharply on one heel and stomped away to his car at the curb. Dani stood frozen, staring at him. Part of her wished she could take the thick folio of papers and photos and art slicks and fling them at him, but the practical side of her wouldn't let her make the gesture.

How could he say such things? There was no way in the world he could be right.

Could he?

~~~~~

"The look on her face... I'll never be able to make it up to her," Kurt said, and buried his face in his hands.

"Why should you apologize for saying what needs saying?" Pastor Glenn asked.

"I could have said it better. Maybe I was right—no, I know I'm right—but I didn't have to be so cruel when I said it."

"I've heard that before." He chuckled when Kurt raised his head and stared, his mouth falling open.

The sound of a lawn mower filtered through the open office window, on a warm breeze sweet with the scent of the blackberries and raspberries growing behind the building, cultivated just for the pleasure of the children at the church.

Kurt had driven aimlessly for nearly an hour after leaving Dani at the Bluebird. He didn't want to go home and find Andy or Katie waiting to chew him out for being so harsh. He had turned his phone off during the lunch meeting, and now he was afraid to turn it back on, afraid of finding an angry message from Dani, or worse, another tearful message from Belinda.

Just before moving from Tabor Heights when he was a kid, a major fight with his parents drove him to go to the church. Kurt remembered sitting on the swings for hours, until the sun set, trying to reconcile his anger with his shame. He had wondered if he could do the same now, sitting until he got his head and heart on straight. Pastor Glenn saw him before he was halfway from the parking lot to the playground, and invited him in. The entire story spilled out almost without volition.

"I wish you had shown up earlier. Years earlier," Pastor Glenn continued. "That's a pretty accurate summation of how Dani handles her pain. She's a wonderful girl, so giving—but yes, I can see where all her dedication is a desperate attempt to ensure nothing bad ever happens to her again. She's a friend to everyone who will let her, but I think I can count on one hand the people she will let in close. She's afraid of being hurt. And love guarantees hurt and loss, sooner or later." He sat back in his chair, the cushion sighing a little as he adjusted his weight. "You're good for Dani. I think she couldn't find anyone better to spend the rest of her life with."

"She's not in the market. She won't even go near the store."

"There comes a point in fasting when you lose all sense of hunger." He smiled when Kurt frowned, lost by the sudden shift in the conversation. "You still need to eat, and desperately so as time goes on. But you're not aware of it. The same with Dani. She needs love, she needs a life partner, but she's gone so long without, there's a good chance she doesn't feel the hunger."
~~~~~

"And I kicked her in the teeth. Yeah, she knows I love her." Kurt wished he could stop his descending cycle of self-pity, but ironically, he enjoyed it too much. It didn't help to know Pastor Glenn agreed with him.

"You know... we had something of a crisis here, yesterday. You know my secretary, Jeanette Marshall?"

"Yeah. She was in Katie's wedding. She's been a great help with all the coordinating between the church and the crusade staff."

"She's a widow. Her husband's family drove her out of town after he died, forced her to take back her maiden name, and called her a liar when she said she was pregnant. Well, one of her brothers-in-law got transferred to Tabor Heights and met up with her and BJ. Yesterday, her mother-in-law showed up, trying to take custody of BJ. She claims Jeannette is a bad mother. She claims she loves BJ and he's better off with her, when she's never actually met the boy. Would you call that love?"

"How can anyone say Jeannette is a bad mother? I've seen her with BJ." Kurt shook his head. "What does that have to do with Dani and me?"

"There is a great deal of evil in this world that claims love as the motivation. Some hypocrites call it 'Christian love' to justify vicious attacks on others in the church. But they never suffer one twinge of guilt that they might have hurt someone with their so-called love. Their idea of loving someone in Christ is to remake them as they see fit, with no regard for what God actually wants from their lives. You..." Pastor Glenn shook his head and his smile widened. "You'd be happier, I think, if Dani had whacked you across the face with a hubcap, rather than you hurt her. That's love."

"It still hurts," he grumbled.

"It needed to be said. Better wounds from a friend than kisses from an enemy. That's in Proverbs."

"How can I show her that I love her? After what I said, even I can't believe it."

"If you love her, let go," Pastor Glenn said with that smile of understanding that soothed, even as it made Kurt writhe in renewed guilt. "Give her over to God and let Him bring her around."

"Easier said than done."

"But the only other option is making both of you miserable, until love turns to hate."

~~~~~

"He could be right. A little," Andy hurried to add. He wrapped an arm around Dani and rocked her gently, like he used to do when she was a lot smaller.

They sat in the barn, listening to the summer songs of crickets in the darkness outside. The barn had always been their talking place, the spot where they felt free to share their hearts. They had collaborated on songs
~~~~~

over the years and cried together during the first painful months without their parents. Andy had confessed his feelings for Katie to Dani right here in the barn and asked for her advice on the best way to propose—and had brought Katie here to do it.

Dani asked Andy to stay behind after rehearsal ended, so they could talk that night. With the problems Jeannette faced from her former in-laws, Dani felt both guilty and foolish for expending so much worry on her troubles with Kurt. Still, she needed to talk to someone, and Andy had always understood. She told him what had happened at the Bluebird Cafe that afternoon. In a way, after the day she had, Dani wasn't surprised that he partially agreed with Kurt.

"Gee, thanks," she said, fighting the thickness in her throat. "I thought I had figured out how to let go when you and Katie started getting serious."

"There're different kinds of letting go, I guess." He sighed and rested his chin on the top of her head. "We'll always be pals, Dani. Best buddies. But you need different friendships. Katie's your best friend, totally different from the way you and I are close. I really hope you find someone to be with, the way Katie and I are together. It's the greatest thing that'll ever happen to you."

"I don't want—"

"Maybe you're scared of letting Kurt close. Just like when you finally buckled down and started losing weight, remember?"

"What?" Dani sat back and gave him such a puzzled frown Andy laughed.

"Remember when you started dieting seriously? You wouldn't taste the goodies even when you were allowed, because you were afraid if you relaxed once you'd fall apart at the first temptation. Maybe it's the same way with Kurt. You made that silly vow of purity—"

"It's not silly," she muttered.

"Okay, not silly. But extreme. Smart, but extreme. Maybe you're afraid if you relax and get close to Kurt, you won't be able to resist temptation?"

"That's not it at all."

"Maybe you're afraid to open your heart beyond your little circle, because you don't want to get hurt anymore."

Dani opened her mouth to protest that theory too, but she wondered if he could be right. Off the top of her head, she could only think of a handful of new friends she had made and kept and allowed to get close to her heart, in the years since her parents died. Most of her friends were people she knew and trusted before she turned eleven. And as they grew up and graduated, moved away for school and jobs and marriage, that circle of total trust had dwindled. Someday, would it be empty? The idea frightened her.

"Everything is so complicated," she whispered, "how can we be sure of anything anymore?"

"That's what God is for." Andy shook her again. "The things you don't understand, you just wrap up and hand over to Him to handle and get on with the things you do understand."

"Easy for you to say." She regretted her flip words and tone the moment they left her lips, but it was too late.

Andy just nodded. "Yeah, it's always easier to talk a good fight, isn't it? That's why God has to keep us in training."

~~~~~

Kurt never appeared in the next two weeks. No more showing up at rehearsals unannounced or calls to update them on news from the packagers handling the CD. Dani missed him, and she didn't like admitting it. She didn't like reliving that moment in the Bluebird's parking lot, when Kurt told her she was the woman who ignored him. How could he say that?

With good cause, her conscience answered immediately. She had treated him like he was invisible. Those hungry looks that made her feel so weak, were real. The emotions hadn't been just her imagination. Kurt wanted to get closer to her, but she was always too busy.

Or afraid. She admitted that now. Andy was rarely wrong when he read her, and if he said she was afraid of letting Kurt near, then it had to be true. She feared tossing everything away to have him, and she hadn't even realized it.

She didn't want to think about Kurt's accusation that she was bribing God to be nice to her, to protect her from harm. How could he think that of her? She wasn't that shallow, that childish, was she?

It meant her love for God wasn't real. That she had been fooling herself all her life. Fooling others.

She hadn't fooled Kurt, though.

"No," Dani told herself, finally wound up to the point of speaking aloud. She could only be glad she had taken her struggles out to the apple orchard, where no one heard her argue with herself in the twilight. "It's not true. I'm real. I'm not playing games with anyone."

But her voice wobbled as she said it.

When Dani finally dared to ask Katie if she had heard from her cousin lately, worried he would miss the CD release party at McCready's Music, her best friend just laughed.

"He's going crazy with all the arrangements for the crusade. No matter how trained and reliable people are, something always goes wrong, and it turns into a domino effect. Kurt's job is to make sure that doesn't happen, and he's very good at what he does." Katie hugged her.
~~~~~

"He's just busy, that's all. And he won't miss the party. It's a big day for all of us."

"Yeah. A big day." Dani wondered how she was going to survive with Kurt only a few feet away all day long. She prayed the crowds at McCready's turned out to be as enormous as they hoped, so she would be too busy to face him.

"It's funny, though." Katie gave Dani a speculative look that made the hairs stand up on the back of her neck. "He can't seem to lose himself in it like he used to. Almost like he has something else on his mind."

Dani tried to find something else to bury herself in, so she wouldn't think about Kurt. There was plenty to do at the Mission.

Mrs. Evans had attacked Pastor Wally when he wouldn't give her BJ. The woman was forced to leave Tabor Heights and some of the pressure on Jeanette eased up, but Pastor Wally ended up in the hospital. He finally accepted the fact that he had to hand some of his duties over to someone else. Dani helped out at the Mission while everything and everyone was in turmoil, and constantly scolded herself to see things from the larger perspective. Her personal problems and ambitions were just too small to matter.

That didn't make them sting any less.

Wednesday, July 30

The big day came; the grand release day for Firesong's first professionally produced CD. McCready's Music in downtown Tabor Heights had offered to host the release party. They had premiered Firesong's homemade CDs, and loaned the band instruments during emergencies. They had been supportive since the days the boys had lip-synched in a church talent show.

At 9 a.m. Wednesday, the members of Firesong and their families showed up to help Mr. and Mrs. McCready hang the posters and the cover blow-ups, set up tables for autographing outside, and haul crates of CDs from the storage room. Kurt stayed out of Dani's way without visibly avoiding her. She wondered how he managed to do it.

It was probably just her imagination. He was so busy with the crusade, he wouldn't have noticed her presence unless she deliberately tripped him.

The irony of the situation didn't escape her.

Katie, Stephanie, Pastor Glenn and Rita stood with Aunt Betty and Uncle George at the front of the store by the windows, watching as fans started lining up nearly fifteen minutes before the store was to open at ten. Uncle George took pictures with half a dozen different cameras, so everyone had their own record of this special day. The McCreadys beamed brighter than anyone else. Every member of Firesong had worked at their music store during the last ten years. In a way, Dani reflected, this was a day of triumph for the McCreadys, too.

"Ready, gang?" Kurt asked, as the clock in the shape of Elvis's face inched toward the hour.

"Ready as we'll ever be." Tom bowed toward the door.

Mr. McCready grinned as proudly as a new father while leading the procession to the front door. He opened it with a flourish. The waiting fans standing on the grass and the sidewalk and even in the parking lane of Main, in front of the old house-turned-shop, let out cheers that could probably be heard past City Hall. Flashbulbs popped and someone at the edge of the crowd had a video camera.

Later, Dani estimated half of Tabor Heights had come for the release celebration, and a good number of people from surrounding towns as well. The day passed in vignettes, like snapshots of memories:

Kurt organizing the waiting fans into lines to buy their CD or poster at one table, then move to the next table where Firesong sat and signed autographs.

Aunt Betty and Uncle George, pushed back into the store by the sheer press of traffic, both wearing proud smiles.

Katie and Stephanie, wisely retreating into the shadowy shelter of the store, making faces at Dani. They had promised not to leave her alone with the guys.

Mr. McCready, making multiple trips in and out of the store, getting more change, getting more CDs and posters, grinning broadly despite his growing weariness.

Mrs. McCready, making change faster than the hucksters at Progressive Field selling pop and cotton candy and peanuts before the Guardians started playing.

Dani lost count early of how many fans stepped past her to get signatures from her brother and cousins. She knew she should feel slighted, but after two hours of signing autographs and trying to answer questions that couldn't be heard over the noise of the crowd, she was honestly relieved to be ignored. She decided she could safely retreat without anyone noticing her absence.

They weren't only *girls* who adored Firesong, were they?

Kurt followed her into the quiet shelter of McCready's store. Dani didn't look behind herself, sliding through the press of the crowd, and nearly shut the door in his face.

"Hey, I'm on your side!" Kurt yelped.

Dani grabbed his arm to pull him inside and shut the door with a bang. She stepped back and turned slowly, holding her arms out to fully enjoy the quiet and cool inside the store.

"Sorry. I didn't want anybody sneaking in after us. Although..." She paused to look outside. "I don't think anybody has noticed I've left."

"You sound relieved."

"I shouldn't be? It's crazy out there."

"You're just as much a part of Firesong as the guys."

"I don't appeal to the — the — "

"Teeny-boppers?" he offered with a grin.

Dani was glad to laugh with him. The laughter sounded so natural, as if he hadn't accused her and they hadn't yelled at each other and she hadn't allowed such strange, wistful, searching thoughts into her head. As if the two weeks of silence hadn't happened. Maybe Katie was more right than she knew.

They headed to the back room, where Stephanie worked on Sunday school papers and Katie read. They looked comfortable and cool, not half-deaf and sweaty and three-quarters crushed by the crowds.

"Shouldn't you be out there?" Stephanie asked.

"Nah." Dani settled down into the only other empty seat. "I have too much sense. A girl could get trampled."

"It's good for the group, though, right?" Katie asked with a wan smile.

"I don't think it's so good for you, though. Are you okay?"

"Fine. Just tired."

"She's been saying that for weeks now," Stephanie said. "Suddenly, I don't really believe you anymore."

"I'm fine," Katie said with a little more exuberance than Dani thought necessary.

The next moment, her eyes widened and she started to raise her hands to her head. She had been rubbing her temples too much lately. Her face blanched and she swayed forward. Dani leaped and caught her, just before she went limp.

Chapter Sixteen

Katie regained consciousness as Kurt helped them carry her out the back door to his car. She insisted they not tell Andy what had happened until the festivities were over. Dani seconded her, reasoning that they would get Katie to the doctor a lot faster if they didn't have to wait for Andy. He would insist on dropping everything once he knew she had collapsed again.

Stephanie fetched Uncle George and Aunt Betty, to have them call Katie's parents. Then they broke the speed limit getting down the side streets of Tabor Heights, out onto Sackley Road and down two miles to the hospital.

Andy stormed into Dr. Lucas' office more than an hour later, wearing a thundercloud. He nearly flew past Dani, Stephanie, Aunt Betty, Uncle George and Kurt, sitting in the waiting room.

"Where is she?" he demanded.

Dani hooked her thumb toward the closed door to the far left of the waiting room.

"Her folks have been with her the whole time," Aunt Betty offered.

The same moment, the door opened and Dr. Lucas peered out into the main room. He had been around since before Dani was born, and she couldn't imagine Tabor Heights without him. He always treated his patients as if they were family, scolding them and crying with them and cheering for them at sporting events and weddings and funerals and graduations.

"There you are, Andy," he said in that perpetually cheerful-yet-tired voice. "Thought I heard your voice. You want to come on back?"

Andy froze. He swallowed hard, glanced around the room, and nodded. Dani got up and hugged him, then gave him a nudge toward the door. All was silent until the door closed behind him.

"Well, folks," Uncle George said on a sigh, "if you haven't started yet, I think we ought to do a lot of praying."

~~~~~

That evening, after a too-quiet dinner no one tasted, Dani escaped outside to the barn. She doubted she would be able to practice or even touch the keyboard, but she needed to be there. It was her only sanctuary, the place where she felt closer to God than anywhere else; where music was like praying, even when she couldn't play or sing.
~~~~~

Somehow, she wasn't surprised to find Andy there, sitting at his keyboard but not playing.

Katie would stay in the hospital until Dr. Lucas was sure she had stabilized. She needed a quiet life from now on, no more traveling long distances and dancing around behind stage at concerts. Her trouble had finally been identified as a particularly insidious tumor, spreading thread-thin roots everywhere through her brain, causing pressure, choking off blood flow and denying nourishment to the tissues. Because of how it spread, it was impossible to operate and remove enough to make any kind of difference. It had now started to spread down her spine, to affect her entire nervous system. Her vision, balance, coordination and speech could all go without a moment's warning.

"They won't let me stay with her. They say she won't rest if I'm there," Andy said without looking up, though Dani was sure she hadn't made any noise when she came in. "She's not scared, though. I'm scared, but she's not." He caught a ragged breath. "Just before I left, she said it doesn't matter how much time we have. What matters is what we do with it."

"I keep praying Dr. Lucas is wrong."

"That's the wrong thing to do. We're wasting our time." Andy raised his head and favored her with a lopsided smile. His eyes had been cried red and swollen.

"But—why can't we pray God will take it away? Katie can't die. We all need her too much."

"I know. But if anybody deserves Heaven, it's her."

"Okay." Dani pressed her fists into her eyes, fighting the tears. She had fought them all through dinner as she thought and made her decision.

"Okay, what?"

"I'm quitting the group."

"What?" Andy stood up.

"I'm going to stay with Katie while you're on the road. So she won't be alone."

"No way." He shook his head, his smile growing a little more steady, a little wider.

"But—"

"Her folks will check on her when I'm not there. And when the time comes that she can't be alone, *I'll* quit."

"You can't quit. You started Firesong." She wanted to reach out and shake him for such a stupid idea, but the urge conflicted with the light sensation of relief soaring through her.

"Firesong can get a new keyboard player a whole lot faster than they can get a singer and songwriter and electrician and accountant, all rolled into one. Besides, maybe this is what God wants me to do."

"Oh, sure, He made Katie sick just so you'd quit the group," she said, ending on a snort.

"That's the stupidest thing you've said in years. Maybe God let her live longer than she should have, did you ever think of that? They think the tumor's been there for years. She could have died in high school. Maybe God let her stay so she could affect all of us, make us better people. It's time for her to go home, so... I don't know... maybe He's arranging all this to make *me* take a good look at my life. Maybe He has better things for me to do. Who knows?"

"But why Katie?" She blinked hard against a renewed, painful longing for tears.

"Why not her? Why not any of us? Heck, the way Jim drives, we could get creamed on the highway every time we go out—but we don't. The important thing is to do what God wants right now." He reached across the keyboard and drew her close to hug her. "Maybe God brought us this far just to sing at the crusade, did you ever think of that? Maybe that's all He wanted us to do. Maybe there's one person who won't be reached by anything but a song we wrote. That's reason enough to be grateful for the ride, for the journey, you know?"

"What are we going to do without you?"

Dani knew then, Kurt was right—she was afraid to let go of Andy. How could that be?

"You'll do what God wants you to do. What else is there?" Andy planted a kiss on her ear and released her.

Saturday, August 9

"What's with the munchkin?" Dani asked, joining Max and Bekka at the gazebo overlooking Poe Lake that morning.

She fought down a cold ripple that was pure jealousy, watching Tony and Shane Hopkins, Bekka's boyfriend, teaching BJ Marshall how to skip stones on the water. Dani bit her lip against complaining that their arrangements had been for the three girls to have a meeting about the fall Sunday school launch program. No mention of males of any age. She was honestly happy that Max and Tony had opened their eyes to how they really felt about each other, and even happier that Bekka, who had been her mentor for a few years, had found someone who seemed so perfect for her. Shane wore a cowboy hat, rode a motorcycle, and went to their church—what more could a girl ask for? Besides, he had proved how smart he was by chasing Bekka.

But did they have to flaunt their romantic successes?

"Jeannette's out of town," Max said, handing Dani a cheese Danish from a big box marked with the Rick's Bakery logo. "We're babysitting."

"Out of town for what?"

"Her mother-in-law had a stroke or something," Bekka said with a shrug. "The good brother-in-law asked Jeannette to come see her. Maybe there'll be a death-bed reconciliation or something."

"That's cliched and sappy, even in romances," Max said.

"You ought to know."

Max grimaced and flipped the lid closed on the bakery box. "Can we get to work?"

Dani settled down on the bench that let her look out over the lake. She rubbed her arms, suddenly cold from thinking about the vicious Mrs. Evans getting a taste of what she had inflicted on Pastor Wally. All right, so it wasn't very Christian of her, but she was glad. After all the trouble the Evans family had tried to cause for Jeannette, the false complaints made to the authorities to try to hurt the Mission and Tabor Christian for protecting Jeannette and BJ, Dani figured the woman deserved whatever suffering had fallen on her.

I'm a horrid person. Vindictive. Just like when we were kids and I loathed Sue-Anne. Dani picked up the bottle of pineapple-orange juice Max had brought for her and tried to force her attention onto what her two friends were discussing. That was why she had come out on this gorgeous Saturday morning, after all.

She was able to contribute to the meeting, but her thoughts kept gnawing on her vindictive feelings.

I'm not a nice person at all.

She immediately vowed she would think of something nice to do for George Evans and his family, to make up for her nasty thoughts. They weren't to blame for what his mother had tried to do to Jeannette, and Dani had heard that some people at church were ostracizing them because of it. She decided she would make up for her thoughts by sitting with them in church tomorrow, just like Jeannette had done a few weeks ago.

She choked on the last of her juice when she realized what she was doing. Trying to buy forgiveness. What had Kurt's words been when they argued earlier? Hadn't he said she was bribing God to be nice to her?

Yeah, and so what if I am? It hasn't done any good, has it? Sure, Katie is feeling better. We'd all like to believe the last spell was a false alarm, but... has anything I've done made any difference? Am I trying to blackmail God into keeping Katie from dying?

Maybe Kurt was right about a lot of other things he accused her of.

When the meeting ended, Dani was relieved to know she had been able to contribute and do her part in the planning. She stayed in the gazebo after the others went their different ways, and she thought a long time, about a lot of things.

How, exactly, was she supposed to let go and figure out how to live her own life, when she thought she had been doing that all along?

Monday, August 11

When Firesong arrived at the fairgrounds early Monday morning to get final instructions and set up for their part of the crusade, Dani felt as if they had walked into another world. She had gone to the fairgrounds for the Cuyahoga County Fair, for computer shows, to work the chili cook-off/golf scrambles in the winter, for horse shows and other events. It had never felt like this before. The sprawling fairgrounds had turned into an efficient, organized work camp and trailer city. The weather was predicted to be warm and dry, so the only tents set up were for counseling and the groups who would pray in teams all during the actual crusade meetings. Thousands of extra seats were added to the exhibition grounds bleachers, and carpenters worked at a steady, loud pace to erect the platform where Allen Michaels and his staff would preach, lead the audience in singing, and where Firesong and other artists would perform.

Dani looked at the platform as their group strolled through the organized chaos and a shiver raced up and down her spine and spread to her arms and legs. This was it. This was the moment they had risked their career to reach. She told herself not to worry about the outcome, because just the fact that they had come *here* was enough.

Curt Mehdlang, a reporter from the *Tabor Picayune* strolled around, snapping pictures of the workers, stopping to talk with people. Dani watched him out of the corner of her eye. She didn't know if she wanted him to leave them alone, or if she wanted her hometown newspaper to splash the news across the front page: Firesong would perform at the Allen Michaels crusade.

"Hey, gang!" Curt caught up with them from the right, when Dani thought she had seen him heading to the left a moment ago.

But that was his talent; getting in where he wasn't expected, seeing but not being seen. It let him do the work of three reporters and ensured him a permanent spot on the staff of the *Picayune*. Besides, she liked him.

"So, what's the scoop? When are you getting on stage? How do you feel about this? Big time, huh?" He winked at them, doing his impersonation of a "big city reporter" from a comedy show in the Butler-Williams summer theater program.

"Hey!" another voice called from behind them. "Wait up!"

Curt grimaced.

"Trouble?" Tom asked, turning to look toward the voice.

"Let's just say that this guy never heard of the Miranda rights." He hooked his thumb toward the end tent in a line of four. "That one is available for people to hide out in, if you guys want to make a run for it. I'll distract Mr. All the Dirt Nobody Needs to Hear, if you want."

"Oh, great. This must be the guy who's been calling for the last three weeks and never talks slow enough for me to get his number." Andy stepped out from the group. "I had to keep the phone on vibrate, because Katie couldn't get any sleep with him calling all the time." He clenched his fists.

"Don't ruin your hands," Dani said. "Where can we get another keyboard player this close to the crusade?"

Their cousins laughed. Unfortunately, their delay let the troublesome reporter catch up with them.

He looked like any other ordinary person; nice face, brown eyes, pale brown hair, average build—even a few freckles. Dani suspected that was the problem. People thought he was harmless, and then he started asking questions about things they didn't want uncovered. He had a camera around his neck, a recorder in his hand, and sneered briefly when he saw Curt. He nodded to the other reporter, then visibly dismissed him.

"So, you're Freesong?" he asked.

"Nope. Sorry. Let's go, gang," Jim said. He gave the reporter his most innocent smile and started walking away. A few snorts of laughter escaped Jason and Tom, and they followed him.

"But—hey—the guy at the gate said—" He scurried to keep up with them, leaving Andy and Dani and Curt in the rear, ignored.

That, Dani decided, was just how she wanted it. They followed, curious to see how the others would handle this unwanted addition to their group.

"We're Firesong. Freesong hasn't shown up." Jason turned to his brothers. "Have you guys ever heard of a Freesong?"

"There probably is one. You know how groups come and go so fast these days," Tom said. "Try the Medina County Fairgrounds instead."

"Oh, funny," the reporter grumbled. "I hear your manager is suing you for breach of contract."

"We ought to sue him. And that's *former* manager. The contract says he can't make any commitments without our approval. We told him we were doing the crusade and *then* he signed us up for the other jobs."

"How come you Christians can't ever get along when it comes to money?" he asked.

"What?" Tom gasped. They all stopped short. The reporter's friendly grin turned malicious just long enough for Dani to wish a swarm of bees would drive him away.

"It's more than money," Andy said, first to recover from the shock, "but that's all Mr. Danziger cares about. The important thing is what pleases God. If doing this crusade hurts our career, then we have to trust

God to take care of it."

"Uh huh. What if God tells you guys to get out of the music business entirely?"

"He hasn't said that yet," Dani couldn't help interjecting. She shivered a little, wondering if someone had told this man about all her prayers and doubts and worries lately.

"Well, you ought to know, huh?"

"What's that supposed to mean?" Jim asked.

"She's the preacher girl. Open line to God, right?"

"Hardly." Dani decided she had enough. She focused on the tent Curt had designated as a refuge and walked away.

"What if God tells you to quit the business?" the reporter persisted. Dani kept walking. She prayed her hands didn't shake.

"Then we quit and do whatever He wants us to do next," Andy said. A hollowness in his voice made Dani shiver.

"That easy, huh?"

"Who said anything about easy?"

~~~~~

Someone told Kurt about the encounter with the reporter and he came running. He assigned one of the security team to stay with Firesong.

"He shouldn't even be in here, yet," he said, raking his fingers through his hair. Dani thought he might just go bald by the end of the crusade, if he kept doing that. "I gave special dispensation to Curt from the *Picayune* because I know he'll be fair. Someone must have thought all reporters were allowed in. Did he give you too much grief?"

"Nothing we couldn't handle," Andy assured him.

"You guys let me know, understand?" Kurt shook his head again and consulted his increasingly ragged notebook. Several papers slid out to the canvas floor of the tent. He muttered about being late and made a hurried good-bye.

Dani snatched up the papers and followed him. She wanted to drag him back to the farm and make him sit down, give him some lemonade and Aunt Betty's fresh apple pie and protect him from all the stress of his job. The funny thing was, she knew Kurt thrived on this. He enjoyed doing this work. So why did it make her tense up inside in worry for him?

"Kurt." She scrambled to catch up. "Hey, where's the fire?" she called, when he didn't seem to hear her.

She almost laughed when he stumbled to a stop. His gaze landed on her. Kurt groaned and rolled his eyes and smiled. She was startled to realize how much she missed seeing him smile. She held out the papers in explanation.

"Thanks. I'd lose my head if it wasn't attached." He shoved the papers back into his notebook and tucked it under his arm. When she expected
~~~~~

him to run off, he took a deep breath and just looked at her.

"What?" she had to ask, when his mouth relaxed a little more. That smile almost touched his eyes.

"You know you can come to me for anything? No matter how stupid you think it is, let me know what I can do to help."

"Thanks." That warmth flowed through her when he gave her that "look" again. Dani cast about for something to say, anything, to break the hot, sinking, dizzy sensation that both frightened her and made her want to give in forever.

A handful of workmen stepped out from around the corner of the next building, saw Kurt and called his name. He glanced over his shoulder at them, then turned back to Dani.

"I've been meaning to apologize —"

"No. Don't." Her throat closed up when he took hold of her hand, but she didn't tug free. She liked the warm tingle from his touch. "I mean, you were right. Not about everything, but you were right." She managed a smile. Her hand shook so much in his grasp, she had to pull free or embarrass herself.

"Okay, where was I right?" He waved away the workmen who called his name again as they approached.

"Oh — ah — well, I know you're alive."

"Yeah?" That grin sent prickles up and down her back.

"And I know you have a lot of work to do, and if we keep standing here grinning at each other, both our reputations won't be worth dog doodies."

Kurt laughed, but he nodded. "You and me. Pizza at Mancuso's. A week from today. Deal?"

"Deal," she said, laughing too, and started backing away.

"Date," he corrected, and gestured for her to get going, then turned to face the approaching workmen. Dani ran, but not far enough or long enough to make her heart thunder the way it did for a long time afterwards.

Tuesday, August 12

Firesong was the first act to perform that night and they sizzled. Dani poured everything she had into every word, every movement, and trusted God to provide the energy when her own ran out. The rest of Firesong followed suit and she thought that if they never performed again after that night, she would be content, knowing tonight's ministry and performance could never be topped.

They had the audience on their feet within ten minutes, clapping and swaying and laughing and singing along with the more familiar songs. There was something about tonight that Dani knew would stay with her forever. She and Andy had never been better with their duet of *A Friend Like You*. She suspected there were tears mixed with the beads of sweat on her face and gluing her shirt to her back, and maybe the same for Andy.

Allen Michaels looked like Moses after facing the burning bush in *The Ten Commandments*, sans beard. Weathered, vibrant with energy, his gaze focused on a reality beyond the physical. He mesmerized the audience from the moment he strode onto the platform, and warmed them all with his friendly, caring smile. No one moved, no one spoke, no one even coughed from the moment he began to speak.

Firesong had seats to one side of the platform, where they had a good side angle view of the podium. Dani gripped the sides of her chair and held on, devouring every word he said. Beside her, Andy didn't even seem to breathe.

"Tonight," Michaels said as he wrapped up his sermon, "the Lord Jesus is saying directly to you — and you — and you, exactly what He said to the Rich Young Ruler. Are you willing to give up everything you value to follow Him? Are you willing to give up what you value most, give it all away to those in need, and set out on the road to follow wherever He leads?" He circled the podium, wearing a wireless microphone and facing all three sides of the audience in turn. "Are you willing to turn your back on what you *think* pleases God, to do what you *know* God wants you to do? You're thinking, right now, 'How can I know what God wants me to do?'"

Andy flinched. He and Dani glanced at each other for half a heartbeat. They grinned as their gazes locked, then turned back to focus on Michaels.

"What's a good test? Consider this: Can you do it under your own power? With your own connections? Does it fit into what you want to do with your life, without making any sacrifices or changes? If it does, then maybe it *will* please God, but I doubt it's that one big job God has chosen just for you to do. When God gives you that one, important, world-shaking, life-changing job to do, it's a God-sized job. There's no way a mortal man can do it in his own power. The only way he can do it is in God's power. Are you willing to give up everything you have, every resource, every connection, every bit of worldly wisdom and prestige — and rely solely on what God can provide?"

~~~~~

"Guys?" Kurt appeared from the back of the platform as seemingly half the audience streamed forward in response to the altar call. "Hey, some of our counselors didn't show up tonight. We're short-handed." He gestured at the people forming a spreading pond of humanity as far as the
~~~~~

eye could see. "Could you help out?"

"Us?" Tom spoke for all of them. He gestured at the milling, eager, sometimes tear-streaked crowd. "But—we're not trained. We didn't take any of the classes."

"You know what I've learned in the last few years?" Kurt smiled, meeting Dani's gaze a few seconds longer than anyone else's. "The Holy Spirit doesn't care about training. Are you willing to meet the need?"

For a moment, it seemed there was no one else in the entire stadium area except Kurt and Firesong, and the sense of a presence that pressed on them and filled the air with warmth and energy. Dani felt like she would lift off the ground in another moment.

"Hey, yeah, guys." Jim gave them all a crooked grin. "I mean, if God can talk through Balaam's donkey, He sure can use us too, right?"

"Exactly," Kurt said through their laughter.

"Lead the way." Andy gestured out at the people.

Chapter Seventeen

The night passed in snippets of impressions as Dani worked with three teens, Megan, Tammy and Beth. They had come to the crusade on a lark, thinking they would be bored but they would have something funny to talk about when school resumed. All three were in tears. Dani led them to a corner in the counseling tent and settled down on the canvas to talk about whatever they needed to say.

She saw Tom standing by the center pole of the tent with a grandfatherly gentleman, both of them very serious.

Jim and Jason stood just outside the door of the tent, surrounded by five baseball players still in their uniforms. Dani guessed they had come to the crusade directly from a game. Jason did most of the talking while Jim kept flipping through his Bible, finding verses and handing them off to Jason and then starting another search. Three of the five players kept gazing off in other directions, tapping their feet, giving the other two exasperated looks.

Andy sat on a bench with a filthy man whose brown hair, tanned face and dun-colored rags made Tabor Heights's resident street-dwelling eccentric, Maggie, look like a Technicolor monstrosity. Andy didn't say much, but he held his Bible open on his lap and leaned forward, visibly straining to hear the man. Dani flinched when she saw the man open up his coat and pull out a bottle and offer it to her brother. Andy hesitated, then took it and put it down on the ground. The man held out his hand and as Andy shook it, he wept. He seemed to crumple against her brother and Andy tentatively slid an arm around him. Her brother looked stunned.

Dani blinked the tears from her eyes and turned back to listening to her three teens. She wondered if anyone older than them ever listened to a word they said.

Most of the seekers and counselors had left by the time she finished with her three. All four had cried, but they smiled and Dani hugged each one as they emerged from the tent and departed. It was long past midnight and she had drained herself with the performance. Somehow, though, Dani felt like she could run all the way home, with energy to spare.

Andy, waiting in his truck, pulled up near the entrance of the counseling tent. He barely moved, just watching her as she waited until the girls crossed the shadowy parking lot to Beth's car.

"Thanks for waiting," she said with a sighing laugh as she climbed in. "Wasn't it great tonight? It's the most incredible thing that's ever happened in my life! I can't wait to get back to it tomorrow."

"It's already tomorrow." Andy managed a thin smile and turned the key in the ignition.

"Oops!"

"What was going on with those three? I mean, something must have been wrong with the redhead. I kept looking over and she was crying in your arms half the time."

"Megan. She's pregnant and she was high at the time, so she doesn't know who the father is. How's that for starters?" Dani could only feel hope for the girl. Was she simply too tired to think straight? She didn't think so.

"But?"

"But she's going to be all right. Tonight, I'm convinced there's nothing impossible when God is involved. Look how He took over and spoke through us."

"Yeah, just look."

"I could do this for the rest of my life. I thought the band was great, and God was using us to touch people — but this is a million miles beyond that."

"I know." He nodded and put the truck into gear and they rattled down the gravel road to the main gate.

Wednesday, August 13

Kurt and Ned took Firesong out for an early dinner before the crusade that night. It was unusual enough for Ned to show up during a crusade, since he preferred staying at headquarters. Kurt didn't know what to think when his mentor and supervisor suggested taking the band out to eat so he could get to know them.

Was there a problem? Kurt knew Ned would have said if Danziger's nasty tricks and smear campaign against Firesong had sent reverberations to crusade headquarters. So why all this unusual interest in a band that was still relatively new? Ned controlled the conversation during the meal, asking questions, drawing them out, learning about their education, their involvement in church, the basis for the songs they wrote, their dreams.

"Do I want to know what's up?" Kurt asked. They had left Firesong to prepare for the evening and retired to the main office trailer to talk.

"She's a special girl, that Dani." Ned sighed as he settled onto the sofa. "I can see why she has you tied into knots."

Kurt nearly swallowed his tongue. To his chagrin, his mentor laughed.

"You should be careful of that face. I can read it like a book. And no, Belinda didn't come whimpering and weeping about the vixen who stole your heart. I could tell just by watching you."

"And?" Kurt slid into the bench seat in front of the little dinette table.

"You're a lucky man if she's the one God chose for you. And I may be biased, but she's a lucky girl."

"Tell her that."

"That's the problem, isn't it? In situations like this, I think God is the only one who can get through. But... sometimes fallible humans do get to help out the Almighty."

"What?" Kurt didn't know if he liked that cat-in-the-cream smile Ned wore. "What's going on?"

"I can't tell you until tomorrow. Until I've seen them in action. But I guarantee, you'll like it."

~~~~~

That evening was a repeat of the first. Dani nearly got paper cuts, trying to follow all the Bible verses that Allen Michaels quoted, and the follow-up verses. She brought a notebook and wrote questions to herself, to God, even questions to ask Michaels if she ever got a chance to talk to him.

Tammy, Beth and Megan came back, bringing five friends. Dani had to take her growing crowd of students outside the main counseling tent. She glanced up from time to time to see her cousins hard at work, counseling, sometimes struggling to get through to someone visibly teetering on the edge of a decision. She nearly cried when a businessman-type Jim was talking with burst out laughing and walked away. She would have run to comfort her cousin, who looked as if a building had fallen on him, but Amber burst into tears, and she had to help her.

While her girls struggled through prayers, the first prayer some of them had ever made, Dani glanced up to check on the rest of Firesong. She saw Andy sitting not too far away, counseling a little white-haired lady who could have been anybody's favorite grandmother, with twinkling eyes and a giant knitting bag bursting with yarn.

Andy stood up, startling Dani. He beckoned, and two women counselors hurried over. They took over talking with the grandmother. Andy sat back and slumped in his chair, resting his face in his hands. Dani said a quick prayer for her brother and turned back to her group. Everyone had their nights of hitting the wall and not getting through. Somehow, it comforted her a little to know even Andy had moments of defeat.

Thursday, August 14
~~~~~

Thursday was Teen Day, with a series of small concerts throughout the day, a mini-Olympics and Bible studies. Firesong performed in the morning and was free until evening. Dani went to the counseling tent to see if anybody from her group had come. She didn't know whether to be proud or worried that all of the girls had returned. As before, she let the girls talk about anything, asking any questions they wanted. No one else had made a decision yet when they broke up to head to dinner, but she didn't let that worry her. The seeds had been planted, and she saw growth and interest. Tom and Andy waited for her when she left the tent.

"What's up, guys?" She felt like hugging everybody.

"Besides you?" Tom rolled his eyes in mock exasperation. He led the way over to the performers tent "You're going to head into orbit any day now. Be careful, Dani."

"Of what?" she asked with a chuckle.

"There's always a really deep valley after the mountaintop. This is great, but you're flying so high..."

"Let me enjoy it while I can, okay?"

"Some of us don't get any mountaintops," Andy said a little too quietly. He managed a smile, but he looked tired.

Dani remembered his moment of trouble the night before. "Is something wrong?" she asked after they stepped inside.

"Kurt and Mr. Vandewitt want to talk to us before we start setting up," Tom said as Jim and Jason came into the tent.

"I think we probably did something wrong last night," Jim said as they settled down in a loose circle of chairs. "Maybe some old fogies are complaining, and we have to pull back on the gymnastics."

"Gymnastics." Dani snorted.

"I have something to say before they get here," Andy said. "You guys are probably going to be... well, there's no easy way to say it." He took a deep breath. "I'm quitting Firesong."

"You're kidding." Tom grinned and looked around, as if he expected someone to jump in and shout "Gotcha!" Andy just looked at him. His grin faded. "Don't kid about something like that."

"I'm not kidding."

"But—why?" Dani silently congratulated herself on not breaking into tears. She felt frozen solid inside. "Katie's feeling better than ever. You said you wouldn't leave until she needed you to stay home."

"Basically, I've decided to go to seminary."

"Come on." Tom clamped a hand on his shoulder and shook him. "Something happened. What made you decide to bail?"

"I'm not bailing, if you really think about it. I'm just changing direction. Maybe finally going in the right direction."

"I know the crusade has been wearing all of us down," Jim said, "but—"

"Wearing us down?" Andy almost laughed. The sound caught in his throat. "Yeah, we're getting up early and staying up late and not eating right. But you guys are eating it up. Look at Dani—she can barely sit still, and she looks like she's going to collapse every night."

"I don't feel it," Dani said. "God gives the strength, I guess."

"Yeah, well He isn't giving me the strength. Or the words. Or any sense of peace. The words don't come when I'm trying to help people. Why? Because I need training. I've been thinking about seminary for years. Maybe God is giving me a good, hard nudge in the right direction. I'll start with Internet courses, so I can stay home with Katie. When we get to the place that I have to be in residence... well, we'll see where God leads."

"But you can't just leave. What would we do without you?"

"There's a handful of keyboardists just in our own church who are better than me. They'd jump at the chance to sign up. And people in the BWU conservatory. And what about Kurt? He'd love to take my place."

"Kurt works for the crusade team," she countered, her heart skipping some beats. Dani forgot to breathe for a few seconds at the mental image of Kurt traveling with Firesong. "He wouldn't leave," she added, more to convince herself than anyone else.

"Don't be too sure of that," Tom said without his usual teasing smile. "I bet he'd think about it if you asked him, Dani."

"You're crazy. Andy, what about the songs you write?"

"I can still write songs in seminary. I just have to get off the road and hit the books, that's all."

"Are you sure?" Tom continued. "We're finally making it, and now you want to leave? Miss out on all the rewards?"

"Maybe this is as far as I was meant to go. Help you get this far, and then step off the train and find another track."

"Wonderful!" Ned boomed as he hurried through the tent door with Kurt in his wake. "You're all here. Kids, you really add something this crusade team needs." He paused while the cousins responded with muttered comments on how glad they were to be involved. He beamed at them, like a favorite uncle about to bestow a wonderful surprise. "It's amazing how God has worked through you. I know you don't have the training, but you've handled every hurdle like seasoned crusade workers. The Board has been praying about this since we heard your first demo. We're impressed with the choices you made, the problems you've encountered because of your dedication, and your talent. It's unanimous. We want Firesong to join the Allen Michaels Evangelistic team."

"Like, full-time?" Tom blurted, his voice cracking. "Traveling with you? Doing all the PR trips and handling the music and all that?"

"We'll provide all the training you need, new equipment, trailers. This is our first year sending youth musical teams out on the road, and it's been such a success, we've decided we need a full-time musical tour. The timing can't be ignored. We're family here, and we believe God has prepared you to join us. I know this is short notice, but sometimes God speaks very clearly. What do you think?"

"I know I speak for all of us — I don't know what to say!"

"How soon do you need an answer?" Dani asked, watching Andy as she spoke.

"Within a month, if you can. If you decide to sign up, we'd like you to hit the road within two months."

"Wow," Jim whispered.

Ned looked around the group, studying their faces; a mix of stunned, delighted, and the shock of a kid finding himself locked into a toy store for the night. His smile dimmed a little as he looked at Andy, who sat staring at his fists clenched in his lap.

"Is something wrong, kids?" he asked, after glancing at Kurt and getting a shrug answer to his silent question.

"I just told them I was quitting," Andy said, finally raising his head.

"To go to seminary," Dani hurried to add.

"That's admirable. We'll pray for you. I know from personal experience how much you'll need it," Ned added with a chuckle. "You know, Andy, we're prepared to finance a full education for all of you, to equip you properly. You could travel and study, and you'd have a dozen pastors to be your teachers."

Andy visibly wavered. Dani knew the moment he thought of Katie, because the spark of desire in his eyes died. He was leaving the group for Katie, to be with her until he lost her. He was going to seminary to help him survive after she was gone.

Dani remembered Kurt's accusation that she threw herself into serving God to fill the emptiness where her parents used to be. Maybe he was more right than either of them guessed.

Andy tried to smile. He shook his head and bowed it again. The other four exchanged somewhat panicky glances.

"Thanks," Tom said, stepping into the silence. "We have to take some time to think before we talk it over. Right, gang?"

One by one the others nodded.

~~~~~

That night, Andy didn't leave the counseling tent until the very last straggler had gone home and the maintenance team came in to turn off the lights. He walked slowly through the shadows to his truck, sitting all by itself in the gravel lot. Sitting in the dark truck, Dani watched him come, aching for him, wondering what was going through his heart.
~~~~~

Through the years, he had talked about going to seminary. She wondered sometimes if he had given up on the idea to stay home with her. Their aunt and uncle had been perfectly happy to take full responsibility for Dani when she had been younger, but Andy wanted to watch out for her personally. The day they learned their parents had died they had promised to stick with each other forever.

Would Andy be a minister right now, if he hadn't been watching out for her? Would he never have fallen in love with Katie and married her? Would he have married her sooner, if he had a decent job, a pastorate to take her to? Would they have had more time together?

Andy reached the truck and opened the door. He rocked back on his heels when the light revealed Dani waiting for him.

"I thought you were going home with Aunt Betty."

"I had some people to talk to, first." She offered a tentative smile. Most of her talking had been praying.

"And you figured we'd have our heart-to-heart right away, huh?"

She could only shrug. Either way, he was stuck with giving her a ride back to the farm. Andy slid into the truck and they were both quiet for the first ten minutes, leaving the fairgrounds and getting out onto Sackley Road.

"It's not like I'm doing this on purpose," he finally said, after glancing at her a few times.

"Somebody's making you leave?" She tried to smile and make her words a joke, but her chest ached too much.

"You know what I mean. I didn't choose the timing. I've been struggling with this decision for a long time."

"I kind of guessed. Sorry I never noticed."

"Guess it looks like I'm running out on you, huh?"

"Running out on me?" she squeaked.

"We promised we'd always be there for each other, right?" He waited for her to nod. Had Andy been thinking exactly the same things she had tonight? "The band doesn't really need me. And you don't need me anymore, Dani."

"I'll always need you. You're my brother!"

"You know what I mean. Maybe the whole reason for me being in Firesong was to get you involved, get you hooked up with the crusade team. Now that you're here, God is telling me to move on. I kind of feel like John the Baptist, you know?"

"Yeah, but he got his head chopped off in the end."

"Well... some people say that about seminary, too."

"Who does?"

"Hey, I was trying to make a joke."

"Trying." She squirmed a little, hating the sick sensation twisting around inside her gut and her heart.

"Dani, if you can't go on without me, then I didn't do a very good job, you know? If you're still holding onto my hand, I cheated you. I promised Mom and Dad I'd take care of you, not turn you into a puppet. Understand?"

"I guess. It's just going to be hard without you."

"You think you're going to have it hard? Just think about me, ten years older than everybody in my class!"

It took a moment, but she was finally able to conjure the mental image. Andy crossed his eyes at her. They grinned at each other, tears in their eyes.

Saturday, August 16

Dani went back to the fairgrounds that morning just to wander around during the dismantling process and remember and assemble her memories into something with meaning. Ned and Kurt found her sitting in the grandstands, staring at the empty spot where the main platform had been.

"Tom just called with the group's decision," Ned said, holding out his hand. "Welcome to the team."

"Thanks." She shook his hand, concentrating on him because she was too aware of Kurt beyond him.

"Have you thought about who will replace Andy?"

"We're going to announce auditions when we finish up our run of commitments. Kind of take a breather."

"I'm auditioning," Kurt said, "so put my name at the top of the list."

"You play?" She blushed, remembering too late Tom had said Kurt was eager and able to join them.

"He's a virtuoso," Ned said with fatherly pride. He clamped a hand on Kurt's shoulder and shook him a little. "Whenever our local pianists bail out, Kurt fills in admirably."

"But what about all your work, setting up crusades and things?"

"That's the nice thing about our organization. We constantly train our own replacements, learning to do many different jobs. Kurt has been running around doing different jobs at the same time, leaving some of his duties for others to take over while he learns new roles. We've been planning to slide him over into the traveling music ministry division for a while now."

"Oh. Okay." She managed to shrug. "Guess I have a lot to learn, huh?"

"We learn by doing." He chuckled. "I believe Kirk said that to Saavik." His grin grew wider when Dani's jaw dropped. "What? Just because I'm an old preacher-man, I can't enjoy things like *Star Trek*?" Ned patted her on the shoulder. "I can see I've done enough damage to preconceived notions for the day. I'll leave you two to work out the details."

"Nobody can replace Andy," Kurt added, "but I'd like to help out."

"Sure. That'd be... great," she whispered. Dani barely heard Ned make his farewells, leaving her and Kurt alone.

"Any chance for some tips on the auditions?" Kurt asked after a few long moments of silence when she couldn't think of a thing to say. Why did he have to keep looking at her like that?

"Why? Don't you have enough to do?"

"Maybe I want to change my direction a little." He shrugged and settled down on the bleacher seat with only a foot of space between them.

Too close. The warmth of his leg soaked through the wood to her.

"We'll be able to see more of each other. Did you think of that?" he added, his smile softening, growing warmer.

"We'll be on the road all the time, Kurt. I don't date while I'm on the road. Remember? Or did you think that would change just because we're on the team now?"

"Oh, for—" He leaped to his feet and stomped away a few steps. Dani could only stare, shocked by the wordless fury bursting out of him. "You'll never give me a chance, will you? Did you think this might be *our* chance? You have no idea how much I've thought about this, wondering if you felt what I did, if you had any hope—"

"If I'm the reason you want to join Firesong, Kurt, then it's the wrong reason."

"You're punishing all of us for Andy leaving, aren't you?"

"Punishing?" She could barely breathe, as if he had physically punched her in the chest.

"When are you going to let go of your big brother? Why don't you grow up, Dani Paul, and figure out what really matters?"

"I'm trying!" she nearly shrieked, struggling to her feet. "I almost said no to joining. I was scared that I was joining because *you* would be here. I have to do what's right, not what I want."

"Why can't what *you want* be right?" he countered. "Why *can't* you want love and marriage and be in God's will? Why do you have to make things so hard? Oh, sure, your big fancy purity vow sounds so Christian, so good and true and noble. It's just an excuse for hiding from people."

"Hiding?" She wanted to punch him. She wanted to run away. Dani couldn't seem to move.

"I know what you're going through with Katie. I know when your parents died, Andy was all you had. But you're an adult, Dani! You have to let go. It's time to live your own life. Let go and trust in God for a change." Angry tears gleamed in his eyes.

"Trust God?" Her breath caught in her throat. "That's all I've been able to do. God is all I seem to have left anymore." A sob escaped her. "But what happens when God isn't enough?"

Silence wrapped around them, so thick and deep it muffled the thudding of her heart, the rasping of her breath as she fought not to break down in tears.

"God is always enough. He's more than enough. The only one limiting Him in our lives is *you* or *me*. You're afraid to be happy. You're afraid to want something just for yourself. Do you think you have to *buy* God's approval? If so, then you're not the girl who talked a pregnant girl out of an abortion. You're not the girl who drove Firesong into becoming a tool this crusade team needs and wants. You're not the girl who's going to be the main support for Andy when his wife dies. You're not the girl I want to marry." Kurt raised his hands, as if he would reach out and rest them on her shoulders.

Dani had a too-clear image of Kurt drawing her into his arms, holding her tight and close, and never letting go. She shivered, wanting it and terrified of it.

"I've always wanted to play piano and go a little crazy with praise music like you guys do." Kurt let out a long, loud breath. "I want you to stay with the crusade team, and I want you to stay in Firesong. That's a whole lot more important than anything else. Even us being together. If all we can have is friendship, then I'll have to be satisfied with that. Just do me a favor and think about the alternatives, the possibilities, okay?"

"Okay," she responded after a few seconds, in a very small voice.

Then Kurt simply turned and walked away.

Chapter Eighteen

"If there's one thing I've learned in the past few months," Andy said, "it's that if God sends love, don't walk away from it just because it doesn't fit your expectations."

"I'm not in love with Kurt," Dani muttered, studying her clenched fists in her lap.

She had come to dinner with Andy and Katie, first because they asked her and second because she needed to talk with someone about her fight with Kurt—or she might explode. Katie just sat safe in the curve of Andy's arm and listened with that warm, almost maternal smile on her face. As if she were a much older woman listening to the slightly silly, egotistical sorrows of an adolescent. Dani would have felt indignant if it were anyone but Katie.

"You're miserable enough, I'm guessing you want him pretty badly," her brother observed.

"Maybe," she admitted after a few seconds of thought.

"I know what you're thinking. How marriage doesn't fit with living on the road. Think about all the Christian musicians who are married and have kids."

"I have. That's why I won't do it." She finally raised her gaze to face them, her eyes red from repressed tears. "If I loved them, I wouldn't ask them to make sacrifices like that."

"Oh, sure, far more noble to make yourself miserable."

"Dani, if I thought like you do, I would have left Andy as soon as I found out I was sick," Katie said. She laughed, a tiny, hiccupping sound when Dani stared. "If I loved Andy, how could I marry him and make him suffer with me?"

"But—" She gave up searching for a response. There was no response that made sense. Dani simply knew in her gut that Andy and Katie belonged together, no matter what.

"It's more important to be together and enjoy what time we do have," Andy said. "However rough the journey gets, we'll be thankful to God that we had anything at all. We don't know when Katie will die, but we have to trust that God will take her home at the right time. Kurt loves you, and he'll take good care of you, and I bet if you ask him, you'll find out he's thought about the same things you have. But what you consider a roadblock, he just considers a challenge. He sure won't put up with this martyr act you've put together."

"Martyr act?" Dani felt anger flare for two seconds, before she recognized the teasing light in her brother's eyes.

"You'll make a great team," Katie said. "You have the drive and the imagination, and Kurt has the know-how and connections to get it done. God could do great things with you, if you'll let Him put you two together."

"I just don't know," she whispered.

Sunday, August 17

Stephanie was pregnant. She and Tom had kept it to themselves for a month, just for the fun of keeping a secret from everyone else. They made their big announcement with a conference phone call to all their various family members Saturday night.

The Gibson family celebrated after church the next day with a picnic at Lake Isaac, where there were picnic tables and grills and plenty of room between the waterfowl refuge and the jogging trail to play catch or just sit in the sun and relax. Uncle George presided over the grill, glowing and chuckling about finally being a grandfather.

The women gathered on a blanket in the shade of one of the ancient oaks that lined the park road and talked about baby clothes and layettes, equipment and decorations, whether Stephanie and Tom should find a bigger apartment or rent a house, and how they would handle the schedule and travel logistics when he joined the Allen Michaels team. Andy and Tom sat on the bumper of Tom's truck and talked quietly, while Jim and Jason played catch and delighted in addressing each other as "uncle." It was a perfect, sunny, warm afternoon with just the right amount of breeze to keep the bugs away.

They were all relaxed, happy, and even the shadow of Katie's illness had abated. She was energetic and feeling good that day and threatened to make Andy accompany her on a long walk down the jogging trail. It was a shock when the red Corvette screeched around the bend in the road the first time. Most of them jumped. Uncle George muttered under his breath about idiots needing to prove they were men by making lots of noise and ruining their tires.

"How are you doing?" Katie asked, when Stephanie and Aunt Betty got up to start putting out the food. From the aroma of the smoke, the hamburgers were nearly done.

"Fine. Why?" Dani leaned back, propped up on her elbows, and stretched her legs out. "Oh, this feels good. I could just stay here all day long." She winced as the sound of a straining engine grew louder for the second time. "What is wrong with that guy?"

The Corvette came back into sight, weaving from side to side, taking up the entire road as it took the sharp bend a little too fast. Dani caught her breath as the car skimmed the edge of the jogging path where it neared the road.

"Just what's wrong with everybody, I guess," Katie said with a chuckle. "Too much glorious sunshine and perfect weather. It's hard to believe it's nearly September. What happened to the summer? Where did it go?"

"Too fast, that's for sure," Dani murmured.

"You know, Andy still feels a little... I don't know. Guilty is too strong a word."

"He shouldn't. I understand." A tiny chuckle escaped her. "I really do. I wonder sometimes if I would have the guts to turn my back on everything I've been working for and start all over."

"You know what I think? I think it's more important to try to obey God than to have accomplished something. This is one instance where the journey *is* more important than the goal."

"Yeah, Andy keeps saying that," she mused.

"It's funny. Andy has more peace now, with an uncertain future, than he's had for the last six months when it looked like Firesong was turning into a full-time job."

"It all depends on your perspective, I guess." She grinned at a new thought. "Maybe Andy needs to let go of me, too."

"Oh, now wouldn't that idea knock him for a loop?"

They laughed together. Then Dani yelped when Katie got up on her knees and called for Andy to come over and join them.

"What are you doing? The last thing he needs—" Dani choked and her face warmed when Andy sauntered over.

"Dani thinks you're having a hard time letting go of her," Katie reported.

"Really?" Andy reached down and lifted his wife to her feet. He wrapped his arm around her, taking most of her weight on himself. "Gee, all this time, I thought Dani was the problem."

"You're a lunatic," his sister said with a solemn nod as if pronouncing judgment.

"Thank you so much. The compliment is returned. How about we make a deal, Dani? You let go of me, and I let go of you, and we stop feeling guilty about each other, okay?" Andy held out his hand.

"Deal." She scrambled to her feet and shook hands with him. Dani tried to smile, but there were tears in her eyes—and then Andy yanked her into a one-armed embrace. She forced herself to laugh. "Hey, I thought you were letting go."

"I am." He released her. "And I am taking my wife for a romantic walk before lunch. If you'll excuse me." Andy turned himself and Katie around and headed down the jogging trail.

Chuckling, yet wiping a few stubborn tears from her eyes, Dani settled down on the blanket and reached for her notebook. An idea for a song just came to her.

Saturday, September 6

Firesong was two songs into their portion of the school year kick-off rally at the Gilley Stadium at Butler-Williams University. Dani stepped to the back of the stage, letting Jason and Jim be the focus as they sang their duet. She scanned the crowd in the bleachers and wondered if the rally would have to be rearranged next year, to use both sides of the field. Maybe put chairs on the field itself. Her satisfaction in the high attendance numbers dropped for a moment, when she remembered that Firesong most likely wouldn't be involved in the rally that all the churches in Tabor Heights and surrounding communities sponsored every year. Next fall, Firesong would be on the road for Allen Michaels.

Change is good, she told herself for probably the hundredth time that week.

Fighting not to look at Andy, who only had four more concerts with Firesong, she turned to study the crowd. Familiar faces in the front row on the far left of the stage made her smile. She waved at the knot of girls she had counseled multiple times during the crusade. Megan, Beth, Theresa, and several other girls who had only come once. Dani was pleased to see them.

The brothers finished their duet and she moved up to join them as Andy changed keys and played the bridge to the next song. She almost turned to glare at her brother when she realized he had changed the order of songs. Not just changed, either—he had slipped in a song Firesong hadn't sung in three years. A song she had hoped never to have to sing again.

There was nothing wrong with the Michael W. Smith song, *Friends,* but Dani had always secretly hated it. There was something painful about it. She suspected Andy knew how much she disliked the song, and was making her sing it, just as a final jab of on-stage teasing.

I'll get you for this, she mouthed, turning to Andy. Her brother fluttered his eyelashes at her and gave her his cheesiest grin. It was all she could do not to burst out laughing, just two beats before she had to sing.

Two songs later, their part of the opening of the rally was finished. Firesong was free to do what they wanted for the next two hours, while the various speakers and the drama team from a church in Padua took their turns. Firesong was slated to come back on stage and close it with two more songs.

"Dani?" Megan and another girl pushed through to the path to the backstage area, neatly slipping around one of the security team in their bright orange t-shirts. "Can we talk to you?"

"It's okay," Dani said, seeing the tears streaking the other girl's face — what was her name again? Amber? — just as she saw the bypassed guard reach for Megan's arm. "What's wrong?" She signaled the guard that it was all right, lifted the gate latch to swing it open and let them in. A few moments later, she led the two girls off to a seating area behind the stage, where they were hidden from the crowds filling that half of the stadium.

"Dani?" Andy ran up to her, holding out his phone. "Rearrange the closing songs, would you? Katie's — " He swallowed hard. "Mom Green just called. She's having seizures. They're taking her to the hospital. If I don't get back in time — "

"Don't come back at all. Katie needs you." She hugged her brother hard and gave him a shove in the general direction of the parking lot.

"What's going on?" Amber asked, watching Andy run.

"His wife has brain tumors." Dani rubbed at her eyes, refusing to burst into tears.

"That's rough."

"God gives the strength." She managed a shrug. "Okay, you look like something's bothering you. What can I do?"

Half an hour later, Dani's hands were still shaking as she closed her phone and walked back over to the sheltered corner where Megan and Amber shared a bench and held hands. She took a few deep breaths, fighting down the mixture of nausea and fury that kept trying to break through.

Amber had made a commitment to turn her life over to God at the crusade. Her boyfriend hadn't cared one way or another, until she refused to continue having sex with him. In just the few weeks since the crusade, he had gone from verbally abusive to physically abusive and wouldn't let go when she broke up with him. Dani had thought that was bad enough, until Amber revealed that just before the crusade, her boyfriend forced her to have sex with several men twice her age, to pay off his debts for drugs and gambling. He had promised her to someone last night and tried to take her off the street yesterday when she was walking home from school. Amber had hidden at Megan's house until they decided to come to the rally today to find Dani. Both girls were afraid the boyfriend would kill Amber if she didn't cooperate.

Dani was afraid they were right. She had called Nikki James, knowing the Arc Foundation sponsored shelters for abused women and children. If anybody had connections and could get Amber away to safety, it was Nikki. Dani knew she could depend on several men from her church who were in the Tabor Heights Police Department, starting with Chief Cooper, but she also knew they had to abide by rules and follow procedure. The Arc Foundation would take Amber away to safety immediately, while the police would have to investigate. The delay might leave Amber in danger.

"My friends are on their way," Dani said, rejoining the girls. "You'll be safe back here until they arrive."

"What are they going to do?" Megan asked.

"Get you away to safety, first of all. That's all I care about."

"Yeah," Amber whispered, wiping tears off her cheeks with her palm. "Me, too."

Dani sat with them, filling them in on the details. Nikki was in Akron at Quarry Hall, the headquarters of the Arc Foundation, when she got hold of her. It would be more than an hour until someone arrived at the stadium to take Amber away. Vincent, head of security for the foundation, had gotten on the phone with Dani and made her repeat everything the girls had told her. He suggested that Megan might want to go into hiding for a while, too. Just in case. After all, the boyfriend had to know Amber would go to her for help, especially if he knew they had gone to the crusade together. Dani decided to wait until she got both of them out of the stadium before broaching that idea.

She was relieved when both girls seemed to be listening to the speaker currently on stage, and they grew calmer. When she thought they were feeling better, she excused herself to go to the refreshment table set up for the performers on the other side of the backstage area. The hot dogs were starting to scorch in the big electric roaster pan and the buns were drying out, but she thought neither one of her guests would mind. She filled a plate with hot dogs, chips, and cookies, and cradled cans of cola in one arm. Dani wished they were indoors, instead of at an outdoor venue. She could have put the girls in a safe room where no one could see them. All it would take for Amber's furious boyfriend to find her would be to walk around the perimeter of the stadium seating until he could see them sitting behind the stage.

Dani's phone buzzed against her hip ten minutes into the drama sketch. She nearly yelped, and hurried to pull it out. She grinned and nodded to the girls when she saw Nikki's name on the display. Ten minutes later, the three of them slipped out the maintenance entrance of the stadium. Gray Brother, Nikki's big Akita bodyguard, ran down the sidewalk to meet them, and led them back around the side of the stadium, down a side street, where Nikki and Vincent waited in a van. Dani had never met Vincent, and she was duly impressed with the sleek head of security, from his shaved head to his sturdy black boots. Nikki had confided in Dani once that she wasn't sure what Vincent's background was, but she knew it was dangerous, and Joan had hinted he had been on the wrong side of the law for a time. Both Megan and Amber hesitated for a moment to get into the van with him, but Vincent radiated a strength and calm that changed their minds in just a few heartbeats, with no need for words from him. Nikki amazed Dani, suddenly seeming so much older, stronger and wiser than the girl she had known most of her life. She explained the simple plan to the girls and left it up to them to get in the van with her and Vincent.

After she promised to keep in contact with both girls and the van drove away, Dani found the maintenance entrance door was locked. She laughed, sighed, and started the long hike around the tall, poured cement walls of the stadium, to get to the front entrance gates again.

"What'd they do," Andy called, pulling up in front of the stadium in his truck, just as Dani was about to turn the corner and walk up the slope to the entrance gates. "Throw you out?"

"What are you doing back here? False alarm?" Dani's smile froze when she got a good look at her brother's face. "Andy?" She stepped up to the open passenger door window.

"She's..." He inhaled shakily. "She's had five seizures since they got her to the hospital. They're going to induce a coma, to try to... I'm going home to get some things so I can stay with her."

"Then go. What are you stopping here for?"

"Will you come with me?" His eyes glistened with sudden tears. "Dani, I can't do this alone."

"Let me get my purse and tell the guys. I'll be right back." She reached into the truck, nearly falling inside, to grab his hand and squeeze it. Then she ran.

Just before the gates, she ran right into Officer Mike Nicholls, who was off-duty and had volunteered to head up security for the rally.

"Just what do you think you're doing, young lady?" he said, laughing, and guided her through the gate.

"Andy needs me — the hospital — Katie — " She choked, not wanting to say the words that would make the situation more real.

"Go." He patted her arm and reached for his walkie talkie. Dani guessed he was passing the word to the security people backstage, so no one would stop her. She headed down the stairs to the field level.

There were too many benefits to name, she suddenly realized, from living in a small town and going to a church where people really did consider themselves family.

"You," a man growled.

A big hand grabbed Dani by her upper arm, stopping her. But her feet kept moving for a few steps and the momentum nearly pulled her shoulder out of the socket. She let out a yelp, cut off half a heartbeat later when the mate to that big hand grabbed her other arm and slammed her up against the concrete wall of the stairs.

The man was big, rough-hewn, handsome in an action hero way, with wavy golden hair, blue eyes, and a dimple in his chin. But his eyes were filled with ice and he snarled at Dani as she gasped for breath.

"Where is she?" His hands squeezed tighter, as if he would pierce her sleeves and draw blood in another moment.

"She who?"

"Don't play stupid. Amber. I saw you take her behind stage." His snarl changed to a sneer when Dani's eyes widened and she realized this had to be the nasty boyfriend. Funny, but if Amber had said his name, Dani couldn't remember. "Where is she?"

"On her way out of the state by now."

She flinched instinctively when he let go of one arm, but never saw him raise his hand or swing down. Her head slammed back against the wall and she saw stars for a few seconds. Everything spun around her, and when she could see again, he was dragging her up the stairs again, toward the gates.

"You know who has her, so you can just get on the phone and call and make them bring her back," he said, his words spat out like hailstones, punctuated by his stomping steps.

"Hold on there," Mike called, stepping into their path, holding out a hand as if he would grab hold of Amber's boyfriend.

The next moment, he stepped back, raising his hands. Dani staggered when she saw the gun now in her captor's hand. She went to her knees. He let go of her arm to grab her by her hair. Despite the pain in her scalp, she couldn't stand up. She stumbled onward, half-falling, as he dragged her through the gates and out of the stadium.

Please, God, please... the words stuttered through her brain, running in the same circle.

"Dani?"

That was Andy's voice. She blinked back the tears and realized they were heading down the slope to the street.

"Let go of my sister!" he shouted, running toward them, while everyone else was running away.

The gunshot deafened her. She convulsed, tearing her hair free, and went to her knees, staring through tear-filled eyes as Andy jerked and leaped and hit Amber's boyfriend, taking him down.

Then Mike was there, and half a dozen other security workers, piling on top of the gunman. All Dani saw was the blood. She scrambled on trembling arms and legs to Andy's side and helped him stagger away. His blood soaked into her clothes and he went limp, taking both of them down to the sidewalk. She screamed for Mike and tore at Andy's clothes, not sure what she should do, only knowing she had to find the wound and stop the bleeding.

Mike ripped open Andy's jeans and swore. Dani flinched, stunned silent. She didn't think he even knew how to swear.

"Gimme your hand." He grabbed hold of her hand and pressed it against what felt like a hot, sticky waterfall pulsing out of Andy's thigh. "Press. Hard."

Andy groaned and shuddered and she almost let up, but the grimness in Mike's expression made her press harder instead.

"What happened?" she asked, teeth chattering.

"The bullet hit a major artery." Mike whipped off his belt and slid it between Andy's legs, wrapping it around the bleeding leg. He yanked hard, tightening it. "Press hard. Gotta stop the bleeding."

All Dani could pray was *Please, no, please, God, no...* until the EMTs arrived and pushed her aside and stuck needles into Andy's arms, pumping in fluid, slapping on bandages that soaked up blood with blinding speed. She stayed kneeling, focusing on Andy's face, willing all her strength to him. It took everything she had to stagger to her feet when they loaded him onto a gurney. She stumbled down the sidewalk to the EMT truck. Mike helped her climb up into the back, and she held Andy's hand while the EMTs worked over him on his other side.

They were still working on him, pumping in fluids, when the truck arrived at the hospital, only a few miles down the road from the stadium. A nurse had to pry Dani's hand loose from Andy's and hold her back, while they wheeled him into the ER.

Aunt Betty, Uncle George, and Pastor Glenn were still on their way, so Mike was the only one with her, his arm around her shoulders, when the ER doctor came to her with the verdict.

Andy had lost consciousness from blood loss before they even loaded him on the gurney. Despite everything they did, it wasn't enough.

"He shouldn't have come back," Dani said, her throat thick and stiff, so the words didn't want to come out. "I told him to stay with Katie." She looked up at Mike, and her eyes were dry. "Why did he come back?" She swallowed down the scream that threatened to rip her throat open.

Andy had come back to get her. If she hadn't helped Amber... she couldn't seem to focus on how different everything would be right that moment. All she could see was Andy's white face, and all that blood.

Sunday September 7

Dani insisted on staying at the hospital with the Greens. She knew Andy would want her to be there for Katie. She wandered down the hall, away from the waiting room where it seemed half the church had come to camp, just like when the Randolphs were hurt. She needed to be alone.

She found a waiting room that was blessedly empty, and sank down on a couch. It took her a few seconds to realize the TV hanging in the corner by the ceiling was still on. She debated ignoring it, like a fly buzzing and banging against the window.

A woman said "Firesong," and jerked her into double alert awareness. Dani stared at the TV screen. The TV anchor looked familiar, but she couldn't remember what local station she was with.

Then the image shifted to the big, wooden, white arch of the secondary gate into the Cuyahoga County Fairgrounds. That irritating reporter who had invaded before the crusade stood there, talking about the crusade and how Firesong had been a driving force during the week-long event.

"Yeah, shows just how much attention you paid to what was going on," Dani muttered. She wrapped her arms around herself, shuddering from a cold that came from deep inside.

" — their former manager, Troy Danziger, who was shocked at the sad news," the reporter said.

A photo of Danziger, about ten years out of date, appeared on the screen, and his staticky voice buzzed through the speaker.

"I'm just heartbroken. They were all good kids, but Andy, he was the heart and soul, the driving force of Firesong. It made me so proud when the kids turned their backs on a skyrocketing career to dedicate themselves to working with Allen Michaels and his fine organization," Danziger said. "Without Andy, I don't know how they can go on."

"We'll go on, you lying slimebag," Dani ground out between gritted teeth. Somehow she was on her feet, standing directly under the TV, staring up at the screen. "You couldn't stop us, and Andy wouldn't want us to give up." Her breath caught in her chest like a hard, cold fist.

She staggered back to the couch, shaking, a burning sensation at the backs of her eyes. It took all her energy to breathe. She couldn't cry.

Not even when Kurt found her and wrapped his arms around her. Even when his warmth drove away the cold that made her shudder until she ached, she couldn't cry.

Chapter Nineteen

Monday, September 8

Kurt supported his aunt and uncle when they made the heart-wrenching decision to turn off Katie's life-support. There was no use in prolonging the agony. The doctors verified late on Sunday that the seizures had been brought on by a rapid growth spurt in the tumor. It literally squeezed the life out of her. Katie had slipped into a coma on Saturday afternoon before the doctors could induce one. Sunday night, there was no brain activity. By Monday morning, her vital signs had deteriorated to the point that the machines were all that kept her alive.

Kurt believed that Katie had died with Andy. He knew better than to voice that thought to anyone. Especially Dani.

She was there in the hospital room, at the end, holding Katie's hand, dry-eyed, saying nothing. How much she heard, he wasn't sure. She didn't react when he held her other hand or put an arm around her shoulders. When he spoke to her, she looked him in the eyes, but he suspected Dani wasn't quite there.

Thursday, September 11

At the double funeral, everyone cried, but Dani. Kurt sat in the front pew with his Aunt Kathy and Uncle Ben, the Gibsons beyond them, and watched Dani. Her voice wavered a little as she and her cousins sang Rich Mullins' *Elijah*, but for the rest of the service, she moved as if in a dream. Or made of ice.

She didn't talk, didn't seem to hear anything until someone spoke directly to her. He had watched during visitation at the funeral home, and then at church before the service, and she couldn't take her gaze off the caskets. When the families got in the limousines to drive to the cemetery, she followed the hearse with her gaze as if it would vanish if she looked away. She held herself straight and tall and moved as if she were totally alone, even in a crowd.

Kurt called himself a thousand names for coward, aching for her and hesitating to approach because he had no idea what to say. How could he offer any comfort when those harsh words from their last conversation were still between them, and he ached so badly with loss himself?

When the reception moved to the Gibsons' farm, he stayed on the sidelines, listening to people talk. Tom brought the stereo outside where the tables were set up for the luncheon and played all Firesong's CDs, old and new.

Dani flinched every time Andy sang a solo part. She turned white and ran for the barn when her duet with Andy came up. Kurt remembered how they had clowned during the song at the crusade, their love for each other bright in their eyes. Something cracked and shattered inside him and he ran after her.

She stood alone, shuddering, her hands resting flat on Andy's keyboard. Still no tears.

"Dani?"

Her head jerked up and he saw the aching little girl he remembered from so long ago. Terrified and so tight with tension, he thought she would break all her bones. Her eyes gleamed, but not with tears.

"Please, I want—"

"No. I'm not leaving you alone, Dani. Not ever." Kurt reached across the keyboard and grabbed hold of her arms. "You're not alone, Dani. You hear me? You're not alone."

The tears came. With waterfall force, nearly tearing her from his grasp. Kurt twisted sideways, to get around the keyboard without letting go of her. He knew Dani would fall if he didn't hold her up. She crumpled as he drew her tight into his arms and a quiet part of his mind marveled at how light she was. Like a bird, so full of energy but no substance.

As if her silent grief had eaten her hollow.

"I love you, Dani," he whispered as she dug her fingers into his arms and buried her face in his shoulder. "I'll always be here. Forever. I'll never leave you alone."

If she heard him, he had no idea. Dani shivered and soaked his shirt and sobbed quietly but with wrenching depth that made him afraid for her. And when it went on too long, he carried her back outside to look for help.

Aunt Betty and Max and Bekka took Dani inside and put her to bed. They appeared relieved more than concerned when they came back out. Kurt could only accept that Dani had needed to break down like that, but it still tore at him inside as the afternoon wore on. The wide damp patch on his shirt stayed wet, despite the heat of the day.

"You should really go," Aunt Betty said, when all the friends had left, the last table and chair had been put away, and Tom and Stephanie were preparing to leave.

"Dani—"

"I'm thinking of Dani." She glanced back at the house. "She made plans to go to Kelly's Island after the funeral—she says she needs to be alone to think—and right now I think it would hurt too much to see anyone when she comes out. Especially you. Especially after what happened."

"She shouldn't be alone." He bit his tongue against telling her he had promised Dani she would never be alone again.

"No, I think she needs it. Maybe that's been the problem. We wouldn't leave her alone." Aunt Betty wiped a few tears away and managed a reasonable smile. "I'm sure she'll be ready for company by Sunday or Monday. Give her time."

Kurt wanted to go up to Dani's bedroom, pick her up while she still slept, and carry her home with him, so he could take care of her. He knew Aunt Betty was right, though.

It felt like he tore out part of his chest, to get in his car and drive away. He watched in his rearview mirror, hoping for one last glimpse of Dani, praying as he went.

Friday, September 12

Dani slept late the next morning. Her aunt was the only person at home when she came downstairs after a long, hot shower, with a few changes of clothes, her Bible, and a notebook in her backpack. They said very little to each other, and it hurt when Aunt Betty hugged her and put the insulated picnic bag in her hand. The thought of eating anything made Dani feel nauseous, but she took the food anyway.

Uncle George had put the carry rack and her bike on the car, and tears prickled her eyes when she saw it waiting for her. He wasn't anywhere around, and she was grateful. She was afraid to try to say good-bye.

It was early afternoon by the time Dani got to Kelly's Island and biked down the road to the bed & breakfast where she had made her reservations. She welcomed the sense of solitude and the golden island light. The floating, empty sensation that wrapped around her wouldn't let her think when other people were around.

Saturday, September 13

Some time during the second day of solitude, riding her bike around the island and stopping at secluded coves to look out over the lake, a few thoughts came clear and settled in her mind and heart. Fragments from the funeral service finally made sense, as if she had recorded the words to think about later.

Dani discovered she was angry with God, and the very idea terrified her. Who was she to be angry at what God had ordained? And yet, as she struggled through it, she realized she wasn't being rebellious, just expressing her hurt. How many of the Psalms had bothered her during the years, because they were so full of anger and pain and pleading for God's justice and vengeance? It had taken a speaker during summer camp when she was fourteen, who pointed out that the Psalms were honest conversations between hurting, wounded humans and the God they loved and trusted, before the Psalms made sense. It was impossible to express hurt and anger in full honesty, except with someone who was utterly trusted.

Had she lost her trust in God? Dani didn't think so. She hadn't lost her faith in God when her parents died. Katie didn't have to wake up and learn Andy had been killed. In a way, that was the greatest mercy God could have granted her. Andy didn't have to watch Katie fade away and suffer, she didn't have to see his sorrow for her, and she didn't even know Andy was gone.

They had died with a future still ahead of them and plans for what time they had left. They had been happy. They had been together. They had stayed dedicated to God despite what He had allowed to happen to them.

What right did Dani Paul have to be angry, when in the final analysis, God was being merciful?

"I have to let go," she whispered to the gulls that swooped around the rocky shores and took the bits of crackers she tossed to them. "Keeping a strangle hold will only crush everything I love, and I won't be able to accept anything else in my life. I have to let go." She choked on tears, knowing it would be hard.

Echoes of years before filtered through her mind, as if Andy were right next to her, speaking words of comfort through his own pain and confusion.

"Why did God make them die?" Dani whispered, hearing her child's voice inside her own.

I don't know, Andy whispered on the wind.

"We need them. Right here."

Hey, idiot—you're talking about God, remember? Since when do we tell Him what He can do? Andy's memory seemed to laugh at her. *No matter what happens, God knows best. Just because we don't understand, doesn't mean there isn't a good reason.*

Do you really believe that? the child she had been asked.

I know it's the truth. It's just going to take a little while to get down to my heart, the wind whispered.

Perched on the damp rock where she could look out across the water toward Sandusky, Dani whispered, "It's just going to take a little while to get down to my heart."

It was time to think about Kurt. Had she been afraid to trust him? Even afraid to trust God? Suppose she opened up her heart to Kurt and they got married? And had children?

"Stop it," she scolded herself, much later. Laughter instead of tears choked her. "If Kurt can set up crusades in three different cities and get CDs recorded and ride herd on bands, and a thousand other things, he can handle a couple of babies on the road, can't he?"

Dani felt dizzy as she realized what she had just done. Not only had she considered marriage with Kurt, she had considered children. How had that happened?

One thing she did know, when she finally conceded defeat to the twilight and cycled back to her bed & breakfast. It was time to go home and face the world again. She had found as much peace and balance here as she could. She had a career and a life waiting for her, and a chance at love that might not wait very long.

Sunday, September 14

When the first ferry of the day coming from Sandusky pulled up to the dock, Kurt disembarked.

Dani stood at the side of the dock with her backpack on her back, holding up her bicycle, staring at the sight of him walking at the back of the straggling group of passengers. Kurt smiled at her, as if there hadn't been any trouble between them the last time they had a real conversation. As if she hadn't fallen to pieces in his arms.

"Hi," she managed to say without squeaking.

"Hi, yourself. You heading back?" Kurt rolled his eyes and grinned when she nodded, then turned around and walked back onto the ferry with her and the boarding passengers. "I came to give you the first ream of paperwork, for joining AME."

"It could have waited until I got home, couldn't it?" Maybe not the best response she could come up with, but she couldn't just play mute all the way back to Tabor Heights.

"Yeah. I guess." He shrugged and gazed out across the water, back to Sandusky, instead of looking at her. "Maybe I just wanted an excuse to check up on you."

"Uh huh." She grinned, feeling giddy. "Should I prepare to be stalked?"

"I won't go away, but I'll give you space." Kurt gripped the side of the ferry, still looking away. He swallowed hard. "So, how far away do I have to stay?"

"No. Not away." She waited until he finally turned to her. That warmth and hunger flickered at the back of his eyes, as if he fought not to let it return. "Closer."

"Yeah?" He grinned, prompting a breathy chuckle from her.

The ferry launched, the first lurch making them wobble. Kurt took a step closer to her and Dani welcomed that. It felt good, natural, to stand in silence for at least the first third of the voyage and just enjoy being together.

She was glad Kurt was someone she could be comfortable with in silence. As C.S. Lewis had said through Screwtape, silence and music were the languages of Heaven. She suspected there would be many more pleasant things she would discover about Kurt.

"So," she began, when they had stolen more than enough smiling looks at each other, "looking for a girlfriend?"

"Nope. Already got one."

"Oh." She felt her heart drop, and then remembered the last time she thought he was talking about another woman.

"What I'm looking for right now is the other half of me," Kurt murmured, and raised one hand from the rail to cup her cheek.

"Oh... and how long will that take?" she said, her voice fading away as he drew closer, so close he shielded her from the lake wind, and the warmth of him wrapped around her.

"Not long."

THE END

THANK YOU!

Thank you for reading this book from Mt. Zion Ridge Press.

If you enjoyed the experience, learned something, gained a new perspective, or made new friends through story, could you do us a favor and write a review on Goodreads or wherever you bought the book?

Thanks! We and our authors appreciate it.

We invite you to visit our website, MtZionRidgePress.com, and explore other titles in fiction and non-fiction. We always have something coming up that's new and off the beaten path.

And please check out our podcast, **Books on the Ridge,** where we chat with our authors and give them a chance to share what was in their hearts while they wrote their book, as well as fun anecdotes and glimpses into their lives and experiences and the writing process. And we always discuss a very important topic: *Tea!*

You can listen to the podcast on our website or find it at most of the usual places where podcasts are available online. Please subscribe so you don't miss a single episode!

Thanks for reading. We hope you come back soon!

About the Author

On the road to publication, Michelle fell into fandom in college and has 40+ stories in various SF and fantasy universes. She has a bunch of useless degrees in theater, English, film/communication, and writing. Even worse, she has over 100 books and novellas with multiple small presses, in science fiction and fantasy, YA, suspense, women's fiction, and sub-genres of romance.

Her official launch into publishing came with winning first place in the Writers of the Future contest in 1990. She was a finalist in the EPIC Awards competition multiple times, winning with *Lorien* in 2006 and *The Meruk Episodes, I-V*, in 2010, and was a finalist in the Realm Awards competition, in conjunction with the Realm Makers convention.

Her training includes the Institute for Children's Literature; proofreading at an advertising agency; and working at a community newspaper. She is a tea snob and freelance edits for a living (MichelleLevigne@gmail.com for info/rates), but only enough to give her time to write. Her newest crime against the literary world is to be co-managing editor at Mt. Zion Ridge Press and launching the publishing co-op, Ye Olde Dragon Books. Be afraid … be very afraid.

And please check out her newest venture: Ye Olde Dragon's Library, the storytelling podcast. Interspersed between the chapters will be interviews with authors of fantastical fiction. Listen to the podcast on your favorite podcast app or listen on the website: www.YeOldeDragonBooks.com, and click on the Ye Olde Dragon's Library link.

www.Mlevigne.com
www.MichelleLevigne.blogspot.com
www.YeOldeDragonBooks.com
www.MtZionRidgePress.com

NEWSLETTER:
Want to learn about upcoming books, book launch parties, inside

information, and cover reveals?
Go to Michelle's website or blog to sign up.

Thanks for reading!
If you enjoyed this book, would you help Michelle by posting a review on Goodreads?

Are you a member of Book Bub? If so, please follow Michelle on Book Bub, and you'll get alerts when new books are coming out.

As a way of saying thanks, Michelle invites you to the Goodies page on her website. It will change regularly, offering you a free short story, a sample audiobook chapter, sneak peeks at new cover art, inside information on discounts and new release dates, etc.

Please go to: Mlevigne.com/good-stuff.html

Also by Michelle L. Levigne

Guardians of the Time Stream: 4-book Steampunk series
The Match Girls: Humorous inspirational romance series starting with **A Match (Not) Made in Heaven**
Sarai's Journey: A 2-book biblical fiction series
Tabor Heights: 18-book inspirational small town romance series.
Quarry Hall: 11-book women's fiction/suspense series
For Sale: Wedding Dress. Never Used: inspirational romance
Crooked Creek: Fun Fables About Critters and Kids: Children's short stories.
Do Yourself a Favor: Tips and Quips on the Writing Life. A book of writing advice.
To Eternity (and beyond): *Writing Spec Fic Good for Your Soul.* A book defending speculative fiction.
Killing His Alter-Ego: contemporary romance/suspense, taking place in fandom.
The Commonwealth Universe: SF series, 25 books and growing
The Hunt: 5-book YA fantasy series
Faxinor: Fantasy series, 4 books and growing
Wildvine: Fantasy series, 14 books when all released
Neighborlee: Humorous fantasy series
Zygradon: 5-book Arthurian fantasy series
AFV Defender: SF adventure series
Young Defenders: Middle Grade SF series, spin-off of *AFV Defender*

Magic to Spare: Fantasy series
Book & Mug Mysteries: cozy mystery series
Quest for the Crescent Moon: fantasy series
Steward's World: fantasy series reboot and expansion
The Enchanted Castle Archives: fantasy series